I0613920

Saldringal
The Keys to the Kingdom

J. Douglas Adams

WALDENHOUSE PUBLISHERS, INC.

WALDEN, TENNESSEE

Saldringal:The Keys to the Kingdom

Copyright ©2022 Jonathan Douglas Adams 1970. All rights reserved under the International and Pan-American Copyright Conventions. No part of this book may be reproduced or transmitted in any form or by any means, electronic or mechanical, including photocopying and recording, or by any information storage and retrieval system, without express written permission from the publisher.

This is a work of fiction. Names, places, characters and incidents are either the product of the author's imagination or are used fictitiously, and any resemblance to any actual persons, living or dead, organizations, events or locales is entirely coincidental.

Warning: the unauthorized reproduction or distribution of this copyrighted work is illegal. Criminal copyright infringement, including infringement without monetary gain, is investigated by the FBL and is punishable by up to five years in prison and a fine of $250,000.

Cover art is used under license from Shutterstock.

Published by Waldenhouse Publishers, Inc.
100 Clegg Street, Signal Mountain, Tennessee 37377 USA
423-886-2721 www.waldenhouse.com
Type and Design by Karen Paul Stone
Printed in the United States of America
ISBN: 978-1-947589-53-7
Library of Congress Control Number: 2022944108
    Tells the fantasy story of a teenage boy, Jaxson King, who is transported to the magical realm of Saldringal. After learning that he is the true king, Jaxson and his new friends must collect the weapons and allies needed to overthrow an evil sorcerer and his puppet king.
    - provided by Publisher
FIC009000   FICTION / Fantasy / General
FIC009100   FICTION / Fantasy / Action & Adventure
FIC009120   FICTION / Fantasy / Dragons & Mythical Creatures

Dedication

This book is dedicated to my Mom and Dad
who always encouraged my creativity and
taught me to value both education and the written word.

Acknowledgments

Thank you to my wonderful wife, Andrea, for reading my first draft and giving me feedback for improving my characters. Thanks also to my sister-in-law, Julie, for the grammar and proofreading help. I appreciate your time spent picking through my prose. Lastly, I want to acknowledge all of my former teachers who helped to shape my writing, especially: Joseph Brewer, Ellis "Butch" Couch, Bette Chesser, and Sheryl King. I never could have written this without your instruction.

Table of Contents

Map of the Realm

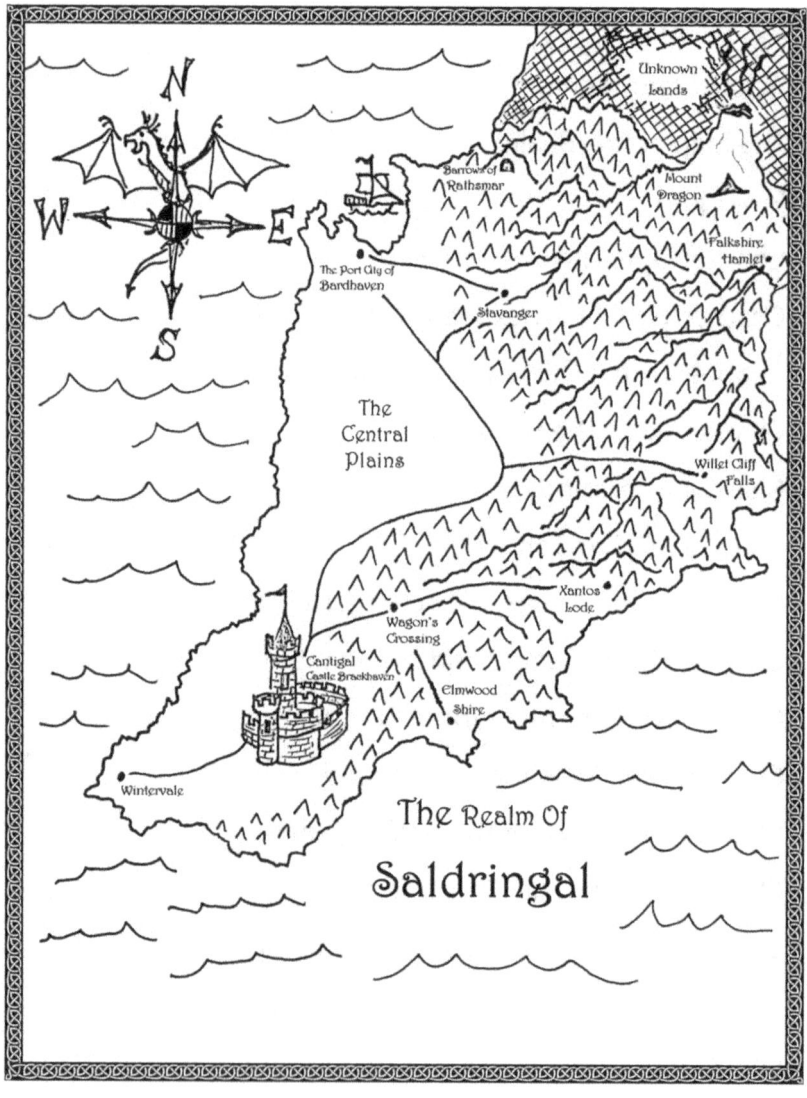

The Realm Of

Saldringal

Prologue

The mountain was tall and craggy. Steam and smoke rose from various cracks and vents across the mountainside, and especially from the peak. It was an active volcano; black, sharp-edged, and ragged, but it wasn't prone to eruption. In fact, for as long as anyone can remember, it was like an old retired man on a porch with a pipe; it just sat there and smoked a lot. Trees had encroached up the flanks of the mountain until the soil petered out and the sharp black rocks of the peak took over.

It was called "Mount Dragon" by the locals, which is a trite and silly name, but what else would you call a mountain that is the home to dragons? Twelve dragons lived here in the volcanic peak. Well at least, there had been twelve; now no one was really sure, as the number seemed to have diminished over the last few decades.

Up a narrow trail worn into the rough terrain trudged two halflings. It is really unfair to call these people "halflings" because they were about three fourths the height of an average male human, but that was the term attached to them by those who did not know any better.

The leader, young Bringle, carried a small leather bag, which was thrown over his shoulder like a backpack. His companion, Jaster, used a walking stick which was sharpened on one end into a makeshift spear. It was really only a weapon in his imagination, but these were younger halflings, and they still liked to dream and pretend in their spare time. They were tired from climbing, and not a little winded, but they had the energy of youth and were used to walking and climbing the mountainside trails.

Below them, the trail wound around and down to their village, called Falkshire Hamlet. It was a small collection of a few odd shops, a town hall, a tavern and a mill, surrounded by farm homes and the peasant dwellings of the people of their own kind, who were known through the realm as Falkans. They weren't rich in this village, but they were happy, and very proud of their heritage.

The people of Falkshire were the long-fabled "dragon healers," which of course was a misnomer. No one can actually heal a dragon. When a dragon body begins to fail, the dragon draws its essence into its heartstone, casts off its earthly shell, and is re-hatched into a new body. Unfortunately for the dragons, it takes a little assistance to accomplish the re-hatching, and so the Falkans had accepted the solemn task of helping the dragons centuries ago. In Falkan culture, it is the greatest of all honors to be selected as a re-hatching assistant and gain the title "Dragon Healer." Like nobility, the role is passed from parent to child, and being a dragon healer guarantees a great chance of success in Falkan politics.

Bringlebear the Great, Bringle's father, was the mayor of Falkshire Hamlet, and he hoped to pass that title along to his son, as he had already passed on the dragon healer role. Bringle secretly hoped to someday add "the Great" to his name like his father did, but first he would have to do something pretty great or his friends would mock him unmercifully.

As Bringle and his friend, Jaster, reached the pass where the treeline ended, they paused to sit and rest. Both Falkans collapsed in the shade of the great trees on patches of sparse grass. Jaster unslung a leather waterskin from his side and took a long drink before passing it to Bringle.

"Are you scared, Bring?" he asked. "What do you think the mountain fire will be like?"

Bringle finished his drink and laughed, "I would suspect that the fire is hot! Just like the fires at home." Jaster laughed as Bringle continued, "Dad told me all about what to do. I just take the tongs, shove in the stone, then sit back and watch. When the dragon is hatched, he will thank me and send me on my way. Nothing to it."

"Well, it would scare me," Jaster moaned. "Dragons aren't exactly warm and cuddly. They look like they would rather eat us than thank us for our help, and they have the fire up there to cook us first!" He paused for a moment and then continued, changing the subject, "It was something else watching that dragon just burst into fire and fall to ashes in the town square. I'd heard about it since I was a kid, but I'd never actually seen it before. He just burned up, whoosh, and was gone." Jaster looked wistful. "I wish I could watch him hatch too."

"Now Jas, you know the rules. The dragons themselves told us how to do this." Bringle stiffened up and affected a proper, haughty voice, "Only one may enter our lair to do the task at hand. One will be thanked and blessed. Two will be shamed and destroyed. Our lair is sacred and precious to us. We welcome your help, but not your disrespect." Bringle went back to his regular voice. "Do you want to be the Falkan to bring the wrath of the dragons down on our village?" He glared a little. "Keep your wishes to just that – wishes – or we may all suffer."

Jaster looked contrite. Trying to change the subject again, he asked, "What do you think your blessing will be?"

Bringle beamed. "I don't know. Probably a few gems, or maybe a magic weapon of some kind," he started. "Dad got a hunting knife that never needs sharpening and two little gold coins his first time." Jaster noticed that Bringle's eyes shone with delight thinking about it. He had guessed this might be his friend's new favorite subject.

"In fact," Bringle said as he jumped up, "c'mon, let's go get this done, and we can find out."

Together the two Falkan youths turned towards the peak and the short climb up the path to the door of the dragons' lair. The door was like a cave opening, only with a threshold of gold around it that was carved with magical runes. There was not a door proper, just an opening; large enough for a massive dragon to enter or exit, but small enough to keep out the weather – not that it mattered. Some sort of magic kept the wind and weather out, and the knowledge of dragons living here kept everything else out. Only dragon healers, and the dragons themselves, were allowed to leave again if they ventured into the lair. Anything else that wandered in was considered "food."

As they reached the broad flat ledge leading to the door, Bringle looked at Jaster. "Wait out here for me," he began, "I don't know how long it will take, so rest and eat something." Bringle began to walk away, then turned around. "And for Aeric's sake, stay away from the door."

Dejectedly, Jaster turned and began to look for a comfortable spot as Bringle passed through the magical doorway into the dragons' lair. Jaster was jealous, and mumbled to himself, "He better pray to Aeric that the dragon doesn't eat him." This was the first of Jaster's prophecies, and probably the most prescient of his own, although it did not turn out to be entirely true.

Inside the door was a long and dark passage. Bringle had a magic, fire-lighting device that was passed to him by his grandfather, who had once received it as a blessing from a newly-hatched dragon. He took out a torch from his sack and lit it using the device. With the new light, he could see that the walls were expertly crafted. The stonework was exact and beautifully done. It was much better than the Falkan stonemasons could do.

Inspired by the magic fire-lighter, Bringle began to think about the dragons. There were twelve of them; eight males and four females. There had always been twelve, and they were always the same twelve. Re-birthing did not change the dragons' appearance or personality. They even retained the wisdom of their age when they re-hatched. Only their bodies were replaced, not their essence. Bringle knew that dragons did not reproduce as most animals did, but together the four mating pairs created the eggs that were used for re-hatching. His father had told him that they kept a surplus of eggs, but there were only twelve heartstones, so always twelve dragons. The eggs were useless without the heartstones.

The fact of there "always being twelve dragons" was what the young future dragon healers were taught, but Bringle knew that the elders in the village were keeping a secret. There had been no sighting of nine of the twelve dragons in a very long time. The elders worried that for some reason the dragons were angry with the Falkans, and maybe they had found someone else to help them with re-hatching. Of course that was crazy. There weren't any other settlements anywhere near Mount Dragon. The only place within a thousand lengths was the abandoned Royal Barrows of Rathsmar, and nothing alive lived there. The Woodland Rangers were a little farther south of there, but he had never seen a ranger in person, and he doubted that they were coming in to help the dragons without being seen.

In fact, as far as the Falkans knew, it had been years since any dragon needed to be re-hatched. Bringle, at twenty four years of age, was one of the oldest dragon healers in memory to be taking his first visit to the dragon lair. His father had taken his first trip at sixteen. So when the black dragon, Ishthmar, counselor to the dragon king, flew into town and immolated on the dragon shrine in the town square, Bringle was elated to finally have his chance. He happened to be in the tavern that evening, with Jaster of course, and they ran out to see it. To Bringle, Ishthmar looked damaged; wounded, though he had heard no one else mention it. The dragon landed, the fire in his eyes winked out, his heartstone glowed, and then the whole body burst into flames, consumed to ashes and collapsed, leaving the heartstone on the altar. Bringlebear himself collected the stone and secured it in the bag that now, two days later, his son carried.

Bringle saw a dim glow at the end of the passage. It grew brighter until he entered a large chamber. A wave of heat hit him as he passed the chamber threshold. The passage was warm, but this room was hot. Bringle slipped off his traveling cloak and hung it on the wall peg just inside the door. This was an accommodation for the dragon healers. Dragons themselves had no use for clothes or clothing hooks.

Great columns of polished black volcanic rock surrounded the chamber and supported the vent cone far above. He thought that perhaps a dragon could fly out through the cone, but he wasn't sure. The opening did not appear to be as large as one might think, and the immense heat from the volcano might make it uncomfortable, or might even be deadly. Maybe. He knew that dragons liked heat and fire, after all they did live in a volcano, but he really didn't know to what extent they could be exposed to fire. He knew their bodies burned up when they were preparing to re-hatch. Maybe that's why they used the tunnel to enter and exit their lair.

At the far end of the large chamber on a raised dais were the dragons' pallets for resting in their home. The pallets were arranged in a circle and the dais also was circular with evenly-spaced columns surrounding it. The pallets were all empty. This struck Bringle as unusual; he had expected several dragons to be here. He wondered how many dragons it took to hunt for food at one time.

Behind the raised dais with the pallets was another chamber. Bringle couldn't see into it, but he suspected it was a treasure room. Dragons had an innate need to possess treasure. Gold and gems called to them. That is why it was such a privilege to be a dragon healer. To be gifted treasure on purpose by a dragon was an immense honor.

He could not imagine anyone being brave enough to try and take treasure from the dragons. First of all, the dragons would probably end the thief's life right then as punishment, but most of all, the entire realm of Saldringal depended on the dragons. The northern mountain range where Mount Dragon sat separated Saldringal from the wilds beyond, which were populated by war-like tribes. Without the dragons to drive back the hordes, Saldringal would be overrun by all kinds of monsters, sentient and not. It was not wise to anger the dragons, if they chose to move their lair to another realm, it would not go well for Saldringal.

Across the great room and to the right was a pool of lava that produced the great heat that filled the room. The lava was held in place by a low wall of black stone. The wall was as expertly crafted as the tunnel had been, with each stone carved and fitted perfectly in place. Each stone also had a rune carved into it. Bringle rightly suspected that the runes magically held back the lava, protecting the chamber, even from sudden rises in the lava pool.

Just beside the stone wall, near the lava, were twelve, beautifully-jeweled eggs. The eggs were very large, about eight feet tall, and five feet in diameter. They were spaced very far apart; about fifteen feet from each other, but all were very near to the lava retaining wall. The outer egg shells were somewhat transparent, as if they were made of gemstone themselves. They weren't smooth or polished looking, but more knobbly as if many large gems had been melted together to create them. The eggs glowed with an internal fire, like they were soaking up and storing the heat from the lava just behind them. They were uniform in color, with a rich blue sapphire cast to them. Each egg had a single flaw:

a small round opening in the side. It was here that the heart-stone must be placed.

Bringle supposed that if a dragon wanted to break tradition, it could manipulate a heartstone into the crevice with its great clawed fingers, but it would be difficult. Dragons normally were about thirty feet long, and their clawed fingers were more than a foot long each, with nailed claws extending beyond. The heartstones were only about six inches long and were two and a half inches across the widest point, but they were shaped roughly like an elongated teardrop becoming narrower all the way to a sharp, pointed tip. It would be awkward for a dragon's long claws to handle them, hence the need for dragon healers.

Bringle spied the tongs hanging where they were supposed to be. It was when he went to get them that he first sensed that something wasn't right. As he walked across the room towards the tongs, he thought he saw something on the floor around the corner from the column that held them. Curiosity got the best of him, and when he peeked around to see what it was, he discovered what appeared to be the remains of two dragons. There were two heartstones lying on the floor with ash piles around them.

One stone was blue, and the other was gold. The blue was either Styvestant or Comptelion. Bringle couldn't tell for sure because both members of the breeding pairs shared the same colors. He knew from his training that Styvestant was a close companion of the dragon king, so maybe it was his stone because of the gold one. The gold one had to be Ragnussen, Leader of the Dragons. He was the only golden dragon of the group.

Bringle was suddenly afraid. He quickly looked around, scanning the corners of the room. The dragon lair now felt eerie to him and he longed to finish the job and get out. Something terrible had to have caused this. The dragons always flew to Falkshire to molt their earthly bodies. Something had to have killed these two outright before they could fly down to the village. But what could kill a dragon?

Bringle decided that he would complete his task and then tell the newly re-hatched Ishthmar about the discovery. Maybe he would know what to do. Ishthmar was the most powerful magic user of the dragons; some even called him a dragon wizard. Maybe he could use a scrying glass and see what had happened.

Using the tongs to hold the black heartstone from his bag, Bringle tentatively approached the closest egg. The heat of the lava was intense, but the tongs seemed to have some magical cooling property. He felt the heat was there, but it didn't hurt him. Carefully, he placed the tip of the heartstone into the gap in the egg's shell. Once it was in, it stuck in place and protruded slightly. Following his training, Bringle released the stone from the tongs, then closed them and pushed on the end of the stone. The stone clicked into the socket perfectly, and with just the slightest pause, the egg sucked the stone inside and the shell closed around the gap until it disappeared.

Bringle backed away as the egg's glow increased in intensity. The shell lightened in color until it ceased to be blue at all and became diamond-like. Mesmerized, he continued to watch as the interior of the egg began to writhe and roil. A snakelike figure emerged and darkened to deep black in the deepest center of the egg. The creature coiled and rolled about, developing, growing. Wings and limbs burst into existence before his eyes as the new dragon body formed. The black figure became his size, then passed him to be larger than a human. It kept expanding until it was pressed against the very shell itself. With a crack, the shell split in several places as the fledgling dragon continued to grow. The pieces of shell fell away and Ishthmar emerged. Wobbly at first, he took a couple of steps towards Bringle. His head swept up as his shoulders widened, his neck lengthened, and his body continued to grow. A few minutes later, Ishthmar was back. As dragons go, he wasn't the largest; probably twenty-five feet long, but any dragon is intimidating in person, especially when you are a halfling and you are alone.

Ishthmar looked at Bringle and spoke. "Halfling, thank you for your service. It is good to be back in a whole, unbroken body again."

"You are welcome, oh great Ishthmar, vizier of the dragons," answered Bringle. He spoke, as had the dragon, in the common tongue that all beings of Saldringal spoke. The dragons had a language of their own, but other races were unable to produce the sounds in that tongue with their non-dragon mouths. Bringle continued, "Oh great Ishthmar, I regret to tell you that there has been a terrible tragedy. Just before I placed your heartstone, I found the remains of two dragons in the alcove over there." Bringle pointed to where he had found the stones.

"What?" the dragon cried, "Please retrieve their heartstones for me." Bringle did as he was asked. He gently picked up the stones and brought them to Ishthmar.

"Shall I place them in eggs for you, Great One?" Bringle asked.

"No, thank you. I would like them here, please," the dragon answered. Bringle carefully laid them at his feet.

The dragon smirked at him. "Oh young Falkan, you have been most helpful, though you have made one great mistake. I am not the dragon vizier anymore." He paused. "Now I am the dragon king! I have slain my brothers and sisters and taken what should have been mine!"

Bringle was overcome with sudden dread, but he managed to sputter out, "but the other dragons will stop you!"

The dragon laughed at him. "What dragons?" he sneered. "One by one, I have taken their heartstones. These two complete my silent coup." He raised his voice in a mocking tone. "Everyone was so worried, 'Oh, where have all the dragons gone?'" His voice dropped to normal. "Ha! I have taken them! I have all eleven stones now, and I will use them to ensure my power."

Bringle was becoming desperately afraid. He now wished he had never come here. He thought, "Why would Ishthmar tell me all this? He must know that I will reveal his plan," and then it hit him: Ishthmar knew he would never repeat the plan because he would never leave this place alive. Panic set in, and the young halfling began to look about, preparing to flee.

The dragon continued. "I am ruler of the dragons now, and what's more, I will soon rule all of Saldringal. From the port of Bardhaven, to the castle at Cantigal, to your pitiful little village, I will rule it all! And as my blessing to you for your service, I will let you help me."

Bringle turned to run, but the dragon was too fast. His clawed hand shot out and snatched Bringle around the waist. Flipping him over, he pulled the halfling in close. Bringle watched in horror as the dragon raised the newly-collected blue heartstone and drove it straight into his chest…

Chapter One:
The Day Arrives

Amber traffic control lights flashing, the school bus ground to a stop at Jaxson King's driveway. At just shy of eighteen, he was a little embarrassed to still have to ride the bus, but he was one of the oldest and biggest kids on his route, so at least the other kids mostly left him alone.

Jax got off the bus and started down the half-mile, dirt driveway to his house. It was a fall day, and the weather was perfect. It was warm without being hot, so you could go without a jacket, but long sleeves weren't too much.

Jaxson wasn't the tallest in his class, but far from short. He wasn't quite six feet tall yet, but very close, and he still hoped to grow a bit. He was lithe and muscular, and decently strong from his daily workouts. His hair was shaggy, but could not really be called long, and was sort of a nondescript color that he had heard called "dishwater blonde." He wasn't fond of that term, as he found it a little insulting, so he usually said his hair was light brown. Others may have said dark blonde, especially since his blue eyes went along with blonde hair more regularly than with brown.

"Nondescript" covered Jaxson in a lot of ways. His clothing was typically a drab color, and he just sort of blended in at school. He wasn't the best student, but far from the worst, and he got along with everyone pretty well. He was never part of the petty drama at school, and he talked with everyone, but he also wasn't especially close to anyone.

Jaxson lived with his Aunt Allissandria, who had been his guardian his entire life. It was she who bought Jax his drab, boring clothes, but he had long assumed it was her style and he didn't want to hurt her feelings by asking for something more interesting. As a child, he impulsively had asked for a bright yellow t-shirt once when they were shopping together. She quickly refused, and it seemed to upset her, so he didn't ask again, and just accepted the bland styles that she selected.

He had never met his parents, that he could remember anyway, and other than "Aunt Allie," as he called her, he had never known any other family than her and his weird old Uncle Marlin. In fact, Jaxson knew very little at all about his parents. Aunt Allie rarely talked about the past, even when he asked. All he knew was that his father had been a fine man with an important job who had died in an unfortunate accident, and that his mother was a beautiful but sad young woman, who was a dear friend of Allie's, but had also died very young. He didn't really know any more than that. It seemed that every time he asked Allie about his parents, somehow the subject was changed and he never really learned more.

He wasn't totally sure that Allie was even related to him. He couldn't remember anyone else in his life, but he secretly wondered if Allie had maybe abducted him when he was a baby, like you sometimes saw in the movies. Maybe he had another family out there in the world somewhere, missing him and wondering what happened to their child.

Jaxson thought Uncle Marlin was about a hundred years old, and he was pretty sure he was senile. Every year or so, Marlin popped by unexpectedly and brought Jax strange gifts; mostly lavishly bound fantasy books, unusual clothes, and every once and a while a new sword. Well, fencing foil, usually. Once Marlin brought a fabulous saber that was razor sharp and built to the highest quality that Jaxson had ever seen. Jaxson suspected that it was incredibly valuable and he searched online to try to find one like it for sale so he could see what it was worth. He hadn't been able to find anything like it on any website. He was disappointed because he had hoped that Aunt Allie would let him sell the saber to buy a used car when he was old enough to drive.

Jax studied fencing, like, all the time. He had studied epee, foil and saber and was skilled with all three weapons. He took lessons at least three days a week, and he worked out and practiced daily. He also competed in tournaments as much as he could, when Allie would take him. According to his teacher, he was a natural, and he won most of the time. His bedroom was full of trophies from his various tournament victories, but in his experience, being good at fencing was not as high up the "coolness scale" as being good at football or basketball.

Jax often wished that fencing was a school sport, so he could get a varsity jacket. Maybe that would help him find a girlfriend. Even the marching band kids had varsity jackets. As accomplished as he was in his sport, he didn't qualify for a letter, and he was jealous. Besides a car, the only other thing Jax really wanted was a girlfriend, and he thought a jacket would help.

Jax had had several school "girlfriends" when he was younger, but they were just at-school friends, and the brief schoolboy crushes never blossomed into anything real. He had liked the girls, and had had the courage to sneak a kiss now and then, but he wanted a real girlfriend. A go-out-on-dates-and-make-out-in-the-car girlfriend, and so far that wasn't happening. Not that he had a car anyway.

He took a girl out on a date once, but it was disappointing. Aunt Alissandra had gone along to drive them to dinner and a movie. She had stayed with them the entire time, and she had asked the poor girl so many questions that the girl felt awkward, and Jax was completely embarrassed. She avoided him after that, and Jax never asked anyone else out. He decided to just wait until he had his own transportation so he could lose the chaperone.

Jaxson had been fencing for so long that he didn't really remember how he got started doing it. Marlin probably made it happen. He had that way about him. When he wanted something, it usually happened. Not that Marlin was pushy or controlling, he just had an infectious excitement about him that somehow convinced you that his idea was fabulous, and that you really wanted whatever it was to happen, too. After years of practice, Jax just took fencing for granted, and it helped fill his time.

Secretly, Jaxson thought that Uncle Marlin might be crazy. When he was fifteen, Marlin took him for a walk in the woods on their property and told him that he needed to share a big secret.

"You are not what you think," he had said. "King is not just your last name. You are truly a king. Your father was the King of Saldringal, which is a realm in a different reality from this one. Your throne was stolen by someone who is pretending to be your uncle. I am not sure who that is yet, but I am working on it. Someday, I will know all I need to know, and you will leave this world and return to reclaim your throne, but we have to wait until you are old enough, and until I have the knowledge and preparations in place for you to succeed in getting back your throne."

Marlin had paused after this revelation, and Jaxson had just stared at him and said, "Ohhhkaaay, Uncle Marlin. Umm, do you want to sit down a little while? Maybe you need a rest..." but Marlin had cut him off.

"I know you think I'm crazy, but this is the truth," he said, "I want you to be ready to go at any time. Keep a bag packed with the clothes that I have brought you. I know you think they are odd, but they are normal clothes in Saldringal."

"Great," thought Jaxson, "I'm king of a world with terrible fashion sense."

Marlin went on. "Keep your saber with your bag. You know how to use it, and it's too sharp for sparring, so just keep it ready to go in case you need to protect yourself."

Jax was happy that he hadn't sold the saber now, it would have been hard to explain that to his uncle.

Marlin was still talking. "When it is time, you will have to move quickly. You must be ready, and then move without hesitation."

They were walking as they talked, and they were approaching a clearing as Marlin finished this thought.

"Someday, maybe in a few days, maybe a few years, you will see something unusual in the woods. When you do, I want you to come here to this clearing." They entered the clearing, and as they did, Jaxson saw that there was a stone slab in the center about two feet tall. It looked like a piece of old foundation, but none of it was concrete, it was all one piece of cut stone about four feet across and square. The sides were smooth but not perfectly straight and they showed signs of old tool marks.

"This isn't like some weird Abraham and Isaac thing, is it?" Jaxson joked.

"No." Marlin stared at him. "And I am not crazy, nor am I senile." He continued to stare deep into Jaxson's eyes. "I speak the truth, Jaxson. You. Are. A. King. Your people are counting on you to someday lead them out of tyranny. The kingdom is struggling, and has struggled for the past eighty years. Their defenses are ruined. Raiders have begun encroaching. The people are afraid, and they are taxed unmercifully. Something has to change. The rightful rule must be restored. So be ready, and wait for the sign," Marlin ended.

"How will I know the sign?" Jaxson asked.

"Ohh, you will know," Marlin replied.

"Crazy old coot," Jaxson thought to himself as they walked back to the house. Still, Marlin was always kind to him, and he didn't want Allie to put Marlin in an old folks' home, so he kept the story to himself. "He isn't dangerous or anything," Jax told himself. "He probably thinks his story is true." Jaxson privately sniggered at the old man.

Jax wasn't really thinking about Marlin today as he walked down his driveway. This was a walk he had taken every school day for the past thirteen years, so he was beyond marveling at the beauty of nature along the way. Mostly he just stared at the dirt of the road and wished that he had a car. He had been old enough for a license now for over a year and a half. Two and a half if you counted the year that he could have had a learner's license, but here he was, trudging along on foot and hating every unfair step.

Aunt Allie had been kind to him his whole life, and she always treated him well. "Firm but fair," she always said, and she really had been, but when it came to the car discussion, she always put her foot down and cut him off. He even tried talking with Uncle Marlin about it once, but Marlin laughed it off and somehow convinced him that it was best to wait.

His lack of a car wasn't a money problem. Actually, although their life was far from extravagant, Jaxson couldn't remember Aunt Allie ever being low on money. She bought simple foods, simple clothes, and really, simple everything, but she never said they couldn't afford something. She always paid the bills on time, and she never denied any reasonable expense that he requested. Sometimes he had to compromise on brands, but he got everything he truly needed, and many things he wanted.

Jax wondered what the problem with a car was. "Maybe my parents really died in a car crash, and she's afraid bad driving runs in the family," he mused.

As Jaxson trudged along, he noticed something odd. In the woods, just off the drive ahead of him, half of a tree was gone. It was the oddest thing he could remember; especially because it was the bottom half of the tree that was missing. Jax stopped and looked behind him. The driveway curved, so the road was no longer in sight. Looking the other way, the house was also out of sight around the next bend from here.

Jax left the road and stepped into the trees. The top half of the great pine was there, but it started about ten feet off the ground, the trunk just came down and stopped. It was as if something had sliced the trunk and left the top hanging, except there wasn't anything to hold the top off the ground. It was perfectly suspended in the air. He walked over and saw that there was a stump where the tree used to connect to the ground, and on the stump was a brass clockwork owl. Jax looked around and saw no one. He gingerly picked up the owl and noticed there was an old-fashioned-type key sticking out of the back. He gave the key three careful turns, listening to the clicking of the gears as the spring wound. When he released the key, the owl spoke.

"Jaxson, It's time," was all the owl said. The key continued to turn for a few moments, but the message had ended.

Jax turned back and noticed that the tree was whole again. "I guess it just needed me to find the owl," he whispered. Carrying the clockwork messenger, he hurried home.

• • •

Jax burst through the back door of the house and called for Aunt Allie as he crossed through the mudroom. He found her almost immediately, just inside the door. She was holding his backpack and his saber in its scabbard and belt.

"It's time, isn't it?" she asked. He noticed tears in the edges of her eyes.

Jax was shocked by her emotion. He softly replied, "Marlin isn't crazy, is he?" She shook her head no.

"You knew about this?" he asked, incredulous. "Why didn't you tell me about it?"

"Oh, Jaxson," she cried, "you don't understand. We have been hiding you all these years. We didn't want to frighten you, or cause nightmares, but you have enemies who would do anything to prevent you from returning to Saldringal any way they could." She continued, "Marlin and I didn't want to keep secrets, but the less we talked about it, the safer you were. We *think* that we are the only ones who know how to cross from Saldringal to this world, but we don't know that, and you are the best hope for our realm. If they found you here, Saldringal may not have survived."

"Wait. You are from Saldringal?" Jaxson almost shouted.

"Yes. Like you, actually with you. I crossed over when you did. I was your governess in the castle, and you trusted me. Marlin helped us escape and set up a life here in his birth world after the death of your mother. Now he lives in Saldringal and has been plotting and planning for your return for the last ninety years."

"Ninety years?" Jaxson stammered.

"Yes, ninety," she began. "Time moves differently in Saldringal than it does here. Mostly, people age according to where they are, except for Marlin of course. He has cheated his aging with magic." She continued, "You have lived here for almost sixteen years. You were barely two when I helped steal you away from there." Then almost as an aside she mumbled, "It was after the attempt on your life, just after your mother died." She caught herself and returned to full voice. "In Saldringal, ninety years have passed. Marlin has been preparing for you. Now he needs you to come. Please go and help our people."

"So how old is Marlin?" Jaxson queried.

"I don't know if anyone knows," she replied, "but you can ask him yourself." She shooed him with her hands. "Now off with you. Marlin is waiting to answer your questions and fill you in on all you need to know. Off to the stone door to meet him."

Jaxson was overwhelmed with loss as he suddenly realized that he may never see Allie again. "What about you? Aren't you coming too?" he asked.

"No Jaxson, my world is here now," she said. "In their world, I too left Saldringal over ninety years ago. Everyone I knew, my family, friends, co-workers, are all long dead by now." She paused to wipe her eyes. "Understand, I was only nineteen when I left Saldringal, and I was barely a step above a peasant. I only say I was *above* because I worked in the castle for the royal family, but I had no real possessions, and what I had was given away long ago. There is nothing there for me to return to." She took a deep breath and continued, fighting back tears. "Here, I am thirty-four. I have a long life ahead of me. Longer than I would live in Saldringal."

She looked at Jax, shifted to a more matter-of-fact tone and said, "Their technology isn't even close to ours, and neither is their health care. Don't tell Marlin, but I have hidden a first aid kit in your backpack. You won't find Band-aids or antibiotics in Saldringal."

She paused, and then went back to her story. "Anyway, thanks to Marlin, I have enough gold to live here comfortably for many years to come, but now that I don't have to guard you and live in hiding, I think I am going to go to college." She smiled at him. "I have always wanted to learn a career. Now is my chance."

Jaxson grabbed her in a huge hug. "I never knew what you gave up for me," he said. "I love you, Aunt Allie."

He began to cry a little too, and he clung to her for a moment.

"I love you too, Jax," she whispered. "It was worth it," she said. Then she added, "my king." Trying to pull away, she whispered, "You had better go. Every minute here is several minutes there, and Marlin may be running out of time."

He released his hug and wiped his eyes. He shouldered the pack, belted the saber around his waist and slowly headed out. As he walked away, he turned and looked back one more time. Aunt Allie smiled and waved from the steps.

• • •

The "stone door" as Allie had called it, was a short walk through the woods. It was late afternoon and the shadows were beginning to get long. The temperature was falling, too. As he had left the house, Jax had shrugged into a hoodie he had found hanging in the mud room. He now had one arm through his backpack, and the other rested on the hilt of his saber so it wouldn't swing around as he walked.

It occurred to him that this may be the last time he ever wore a hoodie and jeans. The clothes Marlin had brought him didn't even have zippers. They resembled apparel from the middle ages in his world, and he dreaded wearing them.

As Jaxson approached the clearing, he realized that it wasn't empty. There was a figure standing near the stone. Jaxson silently slid the saber from its scabbard, and began creeping forward cautiously. As he got closer, he saw that though the figure looked like a man, it was not. It was roughly man sized, but shorter, and it had a scaly, reptilian look to it, with a short snout where it's nose should be, and a long tail coming out through its clothes behind. It reminded Jax of the Spiderman villain called, surprisingly enough, "the Lizard." Now that Jax thought about it, that name was kind of spot-on and a little too obvious.

The center of the stone he had visited with Marlin now held a pulsing portal. There was a frame of white light with a shimmering glossy mist suspended inside of it. It looked to Jax how you would expect a magic portal between worlds to look. In fact, he wondered if Marlin had modeled this on a video game portal so he would recognize it, or if maybe some game designer had actually crossed over before and knew how portals should look.

The lizardman appeared to be guarding the stone and was rhythmically pacing and turning his head to keep a constant watch in all directions. It held a short spear with a wicked-looking point on one end and a heavy, iron knob on the other. The spear looked as though it could be used as a quarterstaff or a piercing weapon, depending on its wielder's mood.

The being was several inches shorter than Jax. It wore a dark gray, hooded cloak that might have once been black, a filthy light-colored tunic with ragged holes and a couple of prominent stains. It had a leather belt around the tunic with a pouch hanging at its side. Its brown pants were a little baggy, but also ragged and torn as well, and they ended in shreds just below its knees. Scaly legs and feet protruded from the pant legs, and it did not wear shoes. It kind of looked to him like a raptor from Jurassic Park would look if you took it, smashed its face almost flat, gave it human shaped hands, and dressed it up in old rags.

"Are you looking for me?" Jax called out, assuming the lizard was there to help him through to Saldringal. The lizard turned to look at him, and Jax saw that its eyes looked milky and dead on the outside with what looked like literal fire burning bright behind them. The creature let out a howl of recognition and, dropping its spear point, it charged him.

"Oh, crap!" Jax swore as he raised his saber and shook off his backpack, dropping it to the ground. He caught the spear tip with his saber and turned it aside as the lizard passed him, then countered with a backswing that narrowly missed removing the lizard's head. The lizard was faster than he expected. It ducked his whistling blade, and circled to bring its spear back to a defensive position.

They were facing each other, and the lizard was preparing for its next attack when suddenly a bolo weapon whipped around the lizard's body, pinning its arms to its side. A green-clad girl crashed into the clearing right behind the bolo and knocked the lizard to the ground. She quickly bound its legs together and added a rope around the bolo to help keep the arms pinioned.

She stood and turned to face him. She was shorter than him, probably about five foot six, and just a little curvy. Like the lizardman, she was also wearing a cloak, tunic and pants, but her clothes were in great shape. They were not new, but well kept, and she wore knee-high, soft leather boots. Some sort of emblem was on her cloak depicting a tree with arrows crossed behind it. All of her clothes were shades of green and brown. Almost like camouflage, Jaxson thought to himself.

Her hood had fallen back in the scuffle, and her head was ringed with dark brown curly hair that fell to her shoulders. It was full of highlights, but Jax thought they were truly from the sun, not from a bottle.

Her face was plain, but pretty, with soft green eyes that caught the afternoon light. She wore no make-up, and Jaxson actually thought that made her more attractive. He liked that she didn't try too hard to be pretty. He thought she was about his age, or maybe a little older. He wasn't great at knowing that sort of thing. She smiled at him, then turned to her captive.

The lizardman writhed and twisted, trying to get away, but to no avail. It snarled and hissed ugly reptilian sounds as it fought its bonds. After making sure the lizardman was secure, she quickly searched the leather pouch hanging from its belt. She removed a small glass bottle that looked hand-made. The girl looked satisfied with her find. She stood and smashed the bottle against a tree, and it burst in a small explosion, which made Jax jump.

The girl looked at Jaxson again and said something, but the words made no sense at all, and his head spun a little in confusion. He couldn't even identify what language she was speaking, let alone make sense of it. Realizing he didn't understand, she pointed to his backpack, then at the portal. He nodded and grabbed the bag. She said something that sounded like "plo" to get his attention, and then she pointed at the lizardman and then back to the portal again. Jaxson thought she wanted him to help her move the lizardman through the portal. He nodded to her, but then, just to make sure he was correct, he waited until she grabbed the kicking and squirming captive before he did too, and then together they dragged the lizardman to the stone and up through the portal itself.

Jaxson wasn't sure what he expected when he passed through, but whatever it was, it wasn't what he found. As they dragged their captive through behind them, he realized that they were stuck in a closet. It was a larder with cheeses and other food items on one side, and cooking pots on the other. An old-fashioned rush broom leaned in the corner by the door, which was opposite the portal itself. It was quite cramped and the three of them barely fit.

Jaxson was the closest to the door, so he turned the handle, and it swung open to reveal a rustic cottage. In front of him, against the right wall, was a bed. Marlin stood next to the bed, looking healthy and younger than Jax had seen him in years. Another Marlin lay in the bed in a pitiful state. The bed ridden Marlin looked to be at death's door. Beside the healthier Marlin stood a young man who looked to be a little older than Jaxson. For some reason, the young man looked very fearful about something.

The healthier Marlin saw Jaxson enter, and with a broad smile he said, "Ahh, you have arrived!"

Chapter Two:

An Unexpected Visitor

William sat on the hillside watching the sun rise. It had been a very long night, and his eyes drooped from fatigue. He hadn't slept, afraid that if he did, the fever that gripped Thallon would overwhelm the old man and kill him. William had no idea what he would do without Thallon. The old man was his master and was teaching him the trade of blacksmithing, but the learning wasn't complete and William wondered how he would survive, seeing as he was an expert horseshoe maker who couldn't really forge anything else. Now that Thallon was sick, he desperately wished that he had paid more attention to his master and learned more of his trade while he could.

When William was apprenticed to Thallon at ten years old, he had had a lot of doubts. Thallon looked to be way too old to even swing a hammer, let alone spend a whole day working a forge, but the man's appearance belied a wiry strength that never failed him. They spent day after day together with Wiliam stoking the forge and Thallon creating the most amazing iron pieces. He was a master of both function and artistry. Their customers loved that their products both looked beautiful and worked beautifully.

Thallon was also a good master to serve. He treated William kindly, like a son, and he never hit him in anger or beat him for his mistakes. William knew that it was not the common practice to treat apprentices in this way, so he was grateful, and quickly grew to love the old man like a grandfather.

At first, William only ran errands, took care of the livestock, and learned lessons in smithing at night as they sat around the fireplace after dinner. When he was twelve, he tended the fire in the forge, while Thallon explained everything he was doing. Eventually, Thallon let him try the hammer himself, and he developed a good feel for working the metal. By the time he was fifteen, he became the shop's horseshoe maker, which was by far their most requested product, and Thallon began taking turns at keeping the fire, or simply staying out of the way and letting him work. Swinging the hammer day after day made William strong. He could produce horseshoes with the best of them, and they were well stocked.

Now at twenty, William had thick, strong muscles and was taller than most people he knew. His shoulders were well-muscled and he could lift great weights from the daily, upper-body workouts in the forge. He knew from competitions with the other local young people that he wasn't much of a runner, but when it came to feats of strength, he was always the best or at least a close second. His muscles turned the eye of many of the local young ladies, as did his dark, almost black hair, lopsided smile, and piercing black eyes, but he was a little shy and unsure of himself, so nothing really ever came of their flirtations. He kept a close-cropped bit of beard, but only because he thought it made him look older.

Now that he was more established at smithing, William was just starting to branch out into various pieces other than horseshoes. Thallon would sometimes disappear for a couple days at a time and leave William to work the forge by himself. As long as the customer didn't want anything intricate or hinged, then William would attempt it. Of course, even his small pieces weren't as beautiful as Thallon's, and several customers had decided to "just come back in a couple of days when Thallon returns." William was disappointed when that happened, but he didn't blame them. Thallon was truly the master.

Of course, if William had had more confidence in himself, he would have realized that he knew enough to operate the forge on his own. He could do more than he gave himself credit for, and even working alone, he would continue to learn through trial and error. His work would improve with practice over time, and he would be fine. But William was a humble soul, and he lacked self-worth and self-confidence, so here he sat, worrying and lacking confidence in his future.

Thallon had been sick now for several days. William, in his twenty years, had never seen anything like it. The old man was weakened by the fever. He couldn't leave the bed without help, and at times, his temperature would spike very high. He seemed to be getting worse, and William, who had little experience treating the sick, didn't really know what to do.

All through the previous night, William had used cold, wet compresses to constantly fight the fever down. William was sure that his fatigued eyes were playing tricks, but at one point, he could swear that Thallon actually became blurry and slightly transparent. He blinked hard, and the illusion went away, so he knew it must have been a dream. Finally, an hour or so before dawn, the fever broke and Thallon fell into restful sleep.

William was exhausted, and he lay down on his thick pallet to try to sleep himself, but his worries kept him awake. Finally, at the crack of dawn, he decided to step out for fresh air and a bit of breakfast. He cut the end off a loaf of bread, smeared it with homemade butter, and he walked up the little rise above their cottage to welcome the day.

He knew that he needed to go take care of the morning chores. The few animals they kept in the small barn behind the cottage must be fed, and the forge fire must be stoked no matter how sleepy he was. He popped the last crust of the bread into his mouth, and groaning out loud, he climbed to his feet.

As William descended the hill, he noticed that smoke was rising from their chimney. This seemed odd, as he had not yet built a fire, and he was pretty sure that Thallon was too weak to do it. He picked up his pace and hurried back to the cabin and burst through the door.

Their cottage was made of logs with a stone foundation. The inside walls were covered with what had once been white plaster, but time and smoke had darkened it into a dingy yellowy beige. The log-framed bed was against the left wall, with a thick pallet stored under it for William to pull out and use, and the right side of the room had a round table with four chairs nearer the door and a large stone hearth and fireplace near the back end of the great room. Four comfortable chairs circled the fireplace. It was here that Thallon and William spent most of their evening times and entertained their few guests, like their friend, Bergen, the tavern owner from the nearby village, who popped by occasionally to gossip and eat with them.

The only other features of the cabin were a small corner cabinet in the back right corner of the room, and three doors across the back wall of the cabin. The left one led outside to their small barn. The center was a pantry where they stored their food, and the right was a storage closet with all sorts of unusual items as well as the more mundane: extra clothing and travel supplies.

Thallon was in his bed, but his body was gray and even more feeble than before. William gasped at seeing how he had deteriorated, and feared the old man had passed, he started toward the bed, then noticed the ever-so-slight rise and fall of breath. Thallon was still alive. It was at this moment that he noticed the other Thallon in the room.

"Don't be afraid, William," said the figure by the fireplace.

"Sorcerer! Get back!" yelled Will, grabbing the first item he saw that could be used as a weapon and trying to look as menacing as possible. Unfortunately, the item was a fork, and the other Thallon only laughed.

"William, dear boy, please don't attempt to fork me to death. We have a lot to discuss and a very limited time." He chuckled lightly and continued, "My body is dying, William, and there is a lot you need to know before I am gone."

William lowered the fork and asked, "How is this done? You are in two places at once."

"You see only my shade before you," he answered. "I am truly only here once, and the body that speaks to you is neither solid, nor, as you might guess from my pitiful fire, capable of lifting more than a few light pieces of kindling."

William warily scuttled to the fireplace, keeping his distance from the Thallon shade and being careful not to turn his back to it. He stoked the weak fire, fanned it a little and added a few more pieces of kindling with a couple of larger chunks of wood on top.

"As you impulsively guessed, I am a sorcerer," the shade said. "I have always been a sorcerer. In fact, my blacksmithing work has all been sorcery. I was never trained as a smith, and my body was not truly strong enough to work all day without the support of magic." Smiling, he added, "So now, you know the truth."

William glowered, "Why would you take me as an apprentice then? I know nothing of sorcery." William's upbringing guaranteed he would be afraid in this situation. As a child, all the fables and folk stories he had heard taught him that sorcery was scary, evil, and wrong. The idea that his mentor, friend, and almost-father was a sorcerer clashed with his worldview, and he didn't know how to take it. Anger was the simplest approach.

"Why don't we sit?" said the shade, trying to diffuse Will's rising anger. They took their traditional chairs. William wondered if shades could get tired, or even sit. Maybe it was just floating right over the chair. He casually tried to look under the shade.

"William," said the Thallon shade. "I took you as an apprentice because I wanted to prepare you for your true calling." He paused, then continued. "Your great-great grandfather was the Captain of the Guard for the late King Pallindor, the Second. Before him, your family members were in the king's guard for centuries, often serving as captains or other leaders. I was in the court as well, as a magician and sage advisor to the king."

Looking more serious and slightly sad, he said, "Your grandfather was betrayed and killed by the current king, who is a pretender and has stolen the crown." He smiled again. "Your family swore allegiance and fealty to the king of Saldringal for all time, but the current king threw that away. Your ancestors loved this realm and vowed to defend it." Looking William in the eye, he continued. "Now it is time for you to avenge your bloodline, keep your family's oath, and help the true king regain his throne."

At this point William was truly worried. Speaking out against the king was considered treason, and he knew several examples of good men being arrested or assassinated for less than the shade had just said. The shade could probably get away with it since he could just disappear before he was caught, but Will thought he probably could be charged with treason just for listening, and so his anxiety grew, even though he was curious about the shade's revelations.

"Who is the true king, then?" He asked. Will mostly asked this to stall and give himself time to think. He wasn't sure about this story, but he knew the part about his grandfather was true. His father, Garrulon, had told him one night, after a couple flagons of mead, how the king had executed his grandfather after falsely accusing him of the theft of a golden trinket that had been in their family for generations. Garrulon, in his drunken state, had cursed the king that night. By the next night, William's father had disappeared.

"Well," answered the Thallon shade, "he should be here soon, and you can meet him. If he doesn't show up, then all is lost."

William looked lost in thought for a moment. "How do you know that the king is an imposter?" he asked.

The shade studied him. "How long has he been king?" he asked.

"Hmmm." William thought for a while and said, "Since long before I was born. I really have no idea."

"Ninety-two years to be exact," said the shade. "And he was eighteen years old when he took the throne, which puts him at one hundred and ten years old."

"Wow. He doesn't even look like an old man!" William replied. "He must use magic, then."

"Yes," the shade replied. "But who cast the youthfulness spell?" Continuing he said, "I knew Arkendor well when he was a boy. He had no magic about him, and I was the only magic user in the court." He went on. "Understand, we magic users can feel when magic is being used around us. If someone in court were casting spells, I would have known! And lasting spells have to be held in a vessel. I could feel it if a spell vessel were around me. Arkendor did not use magic."

William looked doubtful at the shade, but it continued. "I have been hiding here in this little hamlet for decades trying to unearth who could be behind this. I have traveled all over Saldringal searching for clues, and I have a good idea of who it might be." The shade paused, and then continued.

"Remember how I said that spells must be contained in a vessel?" William nodded. "Well, have you heard of the Arkenstone?"

The shade waited, and William shook his head and said, "No."

"Well," he went on, "early in the reign of King Arkendor, some of the nobles began to grumble that he wasn't the true heir, and that maybe they should hold a council and decide if he should stay on the throne." The shade continued. "Arkendor brought out an obelisk of soft stone and had it installed in the courtyard of the castle on a pedestal. He announced that this was the Arkenstone, and that it was the seat of power for his family, and that it represented his right to serve as king. He said that anyone could attempt to destroy the Arkenstone if they wished, and any individual who broke it could replace him as king. However, he warned that anyone who failed, would be charged with treason." The shade muttered a low chuckle. "It looked soft, like soapstone; like a child could break it."

William nodded. He was enjoying this story. It was vaguely familiar to him. Maybe he had heard it as a child. "Go on," he said.

The shade continued, "So three nobles attempted to break the stone." He leaned toward William for effect, "These were big, powerful knights, mind you. Each of them smote the stone with powerful blows. One used a broadsword, another a mace, and the last a heavy war hammer."

"And?" asked William.

"Nothing," said the shade. "Not a scratch of damage to it. All three knights were dragged to the dungeon and were never seen again. After that, no one would try." He looked grim. "Shortly after that, the Saldrant wraiths showed up."

William shivered. He had heard scary stories about the lizardmen who couldn't be killed. They slunk around quietly killing anyone who publicly questioned the king. Though he couldn't prove it, he suspected that a wraith had taken his father. They were why no one really thought about the king's age. It was best to keep that subject, and anything else about the king, out of your mind and off of your tongue.

The shade continued. "The wraiths have been looking for me for close to eighty years. They get close, but so far, I have eluded them by hiding here in plain sight." He laughed. "And, of course, using strong magic to protect us!"

It was easy to forget that the shade wasn't really Thallon. He had all of Thallon's personality and charisma.

"I have to confess something to you," the shade said. "I recently traveled to Cantigal and entered Castle Brackhaven myself." The shade looked almost guilty as he went on. "The Arkenstone is still there, and it absolutely reeks of magic. It must contain a very powerful spell, or maybe even multiple spells." He looked very serious as he said, "I fear I have underestimated our adversary, and that is why I am now dying." The shade hung his head. "I used a concealment spell to enter the court. I now believe the imposter king's magician felt it, and hit me with a weakening curse." He sighed. "I am leaking the mana that makes my magic possible, and when the level gets too low, not only will I die, but all my protection spells will cease."

The shade looked at the bed. "Understand, my magic is all that's keeping my body alive. I am very, very old and not only am I still alive because of my magic, but this home is protected by it as well, as are you, and also the true king. All of our protections end when I do. We need to get you both out of here and on your way before I expire and the protections fall. I can survive for a few more hours; long enough to tell you both as much as I can and get you safely on your journey."

There was a sudden commotion in the pantry closet. "Excellent," the shade said while standing up. "They are here."

William stood too, and they moved back across the room by the bed. The pantry door swung open and a boy came in wearing weird clothes. To William's shock, their neighbor's daughter, Talisia, was with the boy. Together the two of them dragged a kicking, hissing, angry Saldrant wraith into the room behind them. William noticed the wraith was bound hand and foot, and that it did not like it one bit.

Thallon the shade spoke some odd language as they entered the room. William wondered if it was a sorcerer's spell language. He began glancing around the room for a better weapon than a fork.

Chapter Three:
The Keys to the Kingdom

Talisia spoke first. Addressing Thallon, she said, "One of them got through. I think I closed his portal though. He was carrying a vessel, and I destroyed it." Of course, all of this was gibberish to Jaxson, who only spoke English, not Saldrani. Thallon raised his hand to acknowledge her.

"Great work!" he replied. "I had a feeling that they were trying to open a tear between the worlds. My protections are failing, and their scrying glasses must be starting to work. That's the only way they could have found out where he was. Thank goodness we are moving now. You should be gone before they figure out where we are."

Turning to Jaxson, he said in English, "Welcome to Saldringal, Jax. Let's get you speaking the language, shall we?" The shade pointed to a small cupboard in the corner. "Please open the top doors and find the small rack of bottles."

Jaxson walked to the corner and followed Marlin's directions, turning around with the rack in his hands. "Hand me the square bottle with the black liquid in it." The boy held it out to the shade of Marlin, who cupped it carefully in both hands, and struggled under its weight. He carefully passed it to Talisia, then turned back to Jax.

"Do you see the small purple one on the end? " He asked. "I have been saving it for you. Please drink every drop of it."

Jaxson wasn't sure about this, but Marlin had always been kind to him, and it seemed unlikely that Marlin would go to the great trouble of bringing him to another world just to immediately poison him, so he pulled the stopper and drank down the contained liquid that was obviously a potion.

As he swallowed, his brain exploded in a flash of not quite pain, but a rushing cacophony of sound, language, and incredible knowledge. The sensation overwhelmed him, and he collapsed in a heap on the floor.

"Oh, dear." Marlin said.

Talisia walked over and pulled Jaxson back to his feet. He was a little groggy, and she helped him to a chair. She looked into his eyes and asked, "Are you okay?" Jaxson realized that he understood her now. He turned to look at Marlin, who smiled.

"Yes," the shade said. "You now speak the basic language of Saldringal. I know it was a lot to take in at once, but we didn't have time to teach you the regular way."

Looking to Talisia, Marlin said, "Please pour that potion on the wraith. If you can get some in its mouth, it works better. She did as he asked and the wraith immediately calmed, quit struggling, and fell fast asleep. Talisia cut the strap of the wraith's side pouch. It was the same one she had searched before they crossed the portal. She emptied the pouch on the nearest table. There were a couple dried up husks of rotten food, a small collection of odd coins, and an interesting silver device. Jaxson thought it looked like a fantastically well-built cigarette lighter.

"It's a fire starter," said the shade. "Why don't you take it? You may find it useful, and I don't think wraiths care about fire."

Turning back to Jaxson, Marlin said, "Jaxson, this is Talisia. She is in training as a Woodland Ranger, but more importantly, she is a neighbor and a friend." He gestured to the girl. "And this," he said, gesturing to the young man, "is my apprentice William, who is an old friend of your family."

"How can there be two of you?" stammered Jaxson in his new language.

The younger Marlin turned to look at him. "The real me is in the bed, this is a shade of my personality. I am using magic to project it and talk with you because my body is too weak to do so."

"Ohh, so you're my Obi-Wan Kenobi!" laughed Jax.

"What's an 'obee wand can-oh-bee?'" William asked, fearing that this young man was a sorcerer, too.

Ignoring him, the shade replied to Jax. "Not really. I am more like Luke in *The Last Jedi*. Except that when I am gone, I am really gone. I won't be able to return to you in times of need with advice as the Jedi do."

Turning to William he said, "This young man is your king, but he grew up in a very different world from you. He knows nothing of Saldringal and will need your help learning how to act and think as we Saldrings do. He has knowledge of all sorts of things that you do not, and he can share those with you if he wishes, but more importantly, your job is to teach him how to live here. He must not stick out and make a spectacle of himself, or he will be captured and your family will always stay shamed. As the future king, he also mustn't be allowed to look foolish in public, or later, when he takes the throne, his subjects will not respect him."

The shade raised his voice so that all could hear. Although he was still primarily talking to William, he wanted all to know. "Before you arrived, I had a long talk with William about my reasoning behind why all of this is necessary. William, I will need you to share everything you can remember of what we discussed earlier. I don't have time to go over it again."

The shade harrumphed a little and took on a more commanding voice. "Now everyone, please sit down and listen. I have a lot to say. Just let me talk, and hold your questions until I am done. I will tell you the story as I believe it has happened and then we can discuss at the end.

"For the sake of clarity," the shade began, "I will refer to Saldringal as 'my' world and where you lived, Jaxson, as 'your' world. This isn't quite accurate, but it makes the most sense based on where we have lived most of our lives.

"Jaxson, your real name is Barrindor, son of Pallindor." he continued. "I changed it because I didn't think there would be very many Barrindors in your kindergarten class, and we didn't want you sticking out, therefore I picked one of those silly, 'modern', made-up names, so you could blend right in with the others." He smiled, then went on. "We were hiding you, and as your world says 'when in Rome…'" The shade chuckled. "I chose 'King' as your last name because, well, you were one. Ha! And I didn't think anyone would put that together." He suddenly looked more serious. "I will no longer burden you with that name. 'Barrindor' is a much more kingly name, and 'Jaxson' is not a Saldrant name at all, so you need to go back to your birth name."

Addressing all of them, he continued, "You should all know that my real name is Thallinius the Wise. I am a wizard, and I once served the Kings of Saldringal." He looked at Jaxson. "I served your ancestors, Barrindor, for several generations." Again he addressed Jaxson directly. "I chose to be 'Marlin' in your world because it humored me that it was close to Merlin of the famous stories, and my life has paralleled his pretty well." He turned back to address them all. "In this world I was hiding my identity, so I simplified to Thallon, hoping that no one would realize that the old blacksmith was truly a sorcerer in hiding who had once served the king, and was now hiding from him."

This time the shade turned to William. "Will, you know your family name already, but I would keep that a secret if I were you. The pretender king has tarnished your good name, and using it may bring unwanted attention. Stay the anonymous 'William Ironsmith' until you can restore your family's honor."

Next he turned his attention to the Ranger. "Talisia, you are the only one who doesn't have a false name or a deep secret. I am blessed to have a Woodland Ranger living so close to here, and I appreciate your help in this matter. Your father has been a good friend to me, and I regret I won't be able to say 'goodbye' to him. Please share my regards when I am gone, and I thank you for your continued help."

The old man in the bed coughed and turned a little, restlessly. The shade flickered, and then resumed his speech. This time he went on for quite some time without stopping.

• • •

"Barrin, I was born into your world one hundred and fourteen of your years ago. I grew up like most anyone else, and as a young single man I studied the most modern sciences of that time. I was known as Thomas Byrne back then, though no one has called me that name for almost five hundred of our years.

"One day, due to a careless error, I stumbled across an accidental tear between worlds. I went through and found myself here in this land, which is called Saldringal. There is really a lot more to this story, but I don't have the time, so, in short, I stayed here. I found that this world knew very little about science, and some of the science tricks I knew came across to the people of this world as magic.

"Well, I was apprenticed to a magician, and guess what? I did have a propensity for magic! You have to be born with it, and I was; I was supremely gifted. Perhaps my being from another world enhanced my ability; who knows? I learned everything that my master knew, and then I traveled the other realms across the sea, learning as much as I could of the ways of magic anywhere I could find a teacher.

A century passed, and later, when I returned to Saldringal, the king – your ancestor – wanted me to serve as his advisor, so I did, and I continued to serve for many, many years; generations really. Your great-grandfather added "the Wise" to my name. That wasn't my bragging, you see. When one king died, I served his son, and then after his death, the next king, and on and on until I served your father. I used my magical abilities to lengthen my life considerably, and here I am still, when by all rights I should be long dead.

About a hundred years ago, the northern border dragons began disappearing. No one in Cantigal was aware of this because the dragon healers didn't want to cause a panic, and they kept this information secret. I think there was a certain amount of shame involved in this decision. They seemed to think that somehow they had failed in their service to the dragons. I didn't even know about the missing dragons myself until a few years ago. The secret was well kept, and thank goodness it was! If word got out that the dragons were gone, Saldringal would be overrun by the hordes from across the mountains. Even now, a few horrors have encroached and are running amok in the northlands. Great wolves and monsters are reappearing after centuries without them.

Ninety years ago your father, King Pallindor, was killed when his horse fell and rolled over him while he was out riding with his younger brother Arkendor. I was away when it happened, and when I returned, I was not granted entrance to the castle. I was told that Arkendor was now king, and that my services were no longer required.

This seemed suspicious to me, because Arkendor and I were great friends. I was one of the only members of the court who spent time with the boy. I had taught his lessons when he was young, and we were close. Even with my suspicions, there was nothing I could do. The king's command is the king's command.

I came to believe that the Arkendor on the throne was not the true Arkendor. I thought that it was likely that someone, or something, had killed both Pallindor and Arkendor and replaced the younger.

As the younger brother of the king who was not in line for the throne, I am sad to say that Arkendor was largely ignored in the court. Except for myself, no one would notice if he acted differently, especially because he had never been king before. No one knew how King Arkendor should behave. Everyone knew Pallindor. It would be difficult to replace him and not get caught, but the brother was easy.

When Pallindor passed, the queen, Aravis of Narinia, was pregnant with you, Barrindor. You were born mere days after your father's death. A very short time later, it was announced that Arkendor would marry the former queen. This too struck me as very odd. Aravis was about ten years older than Arkendor, and she had always regarded him as a child. Arkendor then announced that with their marriage, the child, Barrindor, would be adopted and become his heir. This also struck me as an odd play. Why wouldn't he want his own offspring of his new marriage to have access to the throne? I suspected that the adoption was the Queen's condition of marriage.

When Queen Aravis died only a year and a half later, shortly after conceiving, I feared that you, as the child of the old king, were now expendable. I contacted the young governess and we began planning to smuggle the child – you, of course, Barrin – out of Saldringal and out of the reach of Arkendor. Two nights later, a royal guard stumbled on a creature attempting to kill the child. We did not know what the creature was at the time, but we now know them as Saldrant wraiths. They are suspected to be assassins for the king. Although the guard died, he did raise the alarm, and the wraith fled. That next day, Allessandria, the governess, smuggled you out of the castle, and I spirited you both away to your world, out of the reach of the Saldrant wraiths and your treacherous false uncle.

"I began to travel this realm searching for clues to who could have replaced the king. I accounted for every known magic user in the realm, and it wasn't any of them, so I was stymied. I found this little hamlet and made a place to hide out and bide my time.

"For many years now I have become aware that someone was concerned about me. Someone was searching very hard to find Thallinius the Wise, and I feared that they suspected what I was up to. They may also have suspected that I had aided in the removal and hiding of the heir, and maybe knew that I knew where he was hidden. I am not sure, but I took more and more precautions as time passed.

"Years went by, and I made little progress. Friends grew old and passed on, but I kept tottering around."

• • •

The shade paused, and looked at William. "A little more than twelve years ago, I found your family, William, and arranged to have you as an apprentice. Your father had disappeared, and your mother was desperate to have one less mouth to feed." He smiled at his apprentice. "You should know that she has been on a remarkable string of good luck. Ever since you came here, she keeps finding gold coins lying about, and has for years. She finds them in the wash, in the dust of the road, all over, really. She thinks it's the damnedest thing. It's enough to live on comfortably and care for your siblings, too, especially as a supplement to what she grows and earns on her own." He chuckled. "Just recently, she discovered a chest of gold in the garden while weeding the pole beans. Interesting that she didn't find it when she plowed or planted, but then, such is luck." The shade shrugged his shoulders with a grin and went back to his narrative.

• • •

"Now, just before William moved here twelve years ago, I traveled to the far north of Saldringal to a village called Falkshire Hamlet. Here I met a very old Falkan halfling called Jaster. He was bedridden and feeble, but his mind seemed sharp. The locals treated him as an outcast, and he fancied himself as a seer or shaman. He was one of the last to see a dragon in person, and he swore to me that the black dragon, Ishthmar, killed his friend and flew away with his body. Jaster was on the mountain when this happened, and after he saw the dragon fly away, he entered the dragons' lair. He said that all the dragons were gone. He saw no heartstones, and no treasure left. Only empty eggs and a few drops of fresh blood. He also found his friend's cloak.

"The few remaining Dragon Healers told me that according to their teachings, Ishthmar, the black dragon and vizier to the dragon king, was a powerful magic user. This knowledge was not known to the humans of Saldringal, and so I had not accounted for the dragon in my investigation of magic users. I have searched for the last twelve years to no avail. The dragon cannot be found. I believe that he is the magician behind the imposter king. This Ishthmar may have also led to the disappearance of the other dragons."

• • •

The shade stopped for a moment. "This is a good place for questions. What do you want to know more about?"

"The queen," Barrindor began. "Was she from Narnia? Like, *the* Narnia?"

"No, she was from Narinia, which is across the sea. However, I have long wondered if C.S. Lewis visited Narinia before he wrote his books. There are several parallels between the world in his books and Narinia. Our time does move somewhat like in his stories, too. No talking god-lion though. I am afraid he made that part up. Maybe he met a Neferkali."

"What about my Mum?" asked William. "Will she be safe if I help with this plan?"

The shade looked empathetic. "I have taken every precaution to see that you are never tied to your family. Keep your name secret, and she should be perfectly fine. And, by the way, the chest should help her for several years. By the time she is in need again, hopefully you can be safely reunited and help support her needs. "

There was a slight pause as the shade waited for the next question.

"Why couldn't I have a car?" asked Barrindor. Talisia and William looked confused at this because they had no idea what a car was.

The shade paused. He looked directly at the teenager and said, "The minds of young people never seem to disappoint." He almost laughed, but he contained it and answered. "Several reasons come to mind, but I suspect that none of them will satisfy you." He raised his hand and counted on his fingers with the other. "The main reason was that young people with cars are more independent and always on the go. It's hard to know where they are at all times, and therefore it is more difficult to provide defenses for them. Secondly, young people are more likely to drive poorly and be killed or injured in a collision. We couldn't risk that. The last is that I hoped you would return here, and the car was something you could not bring with you and that you would greatly miss when you left that world."

Barrindor, who still felt very much like Jaxson, rolled his eyes. He understood what the shade was saying, but he had really wanted to drive, and he suspected now that he never would.

The shade continued, "Barrin, when I lived in your world it was a different time. Cars were new and rare. I may have underestimated their modern importance. I apologize for not understanding."

The others had no idea what they were talking about, and they were ready to move on.

"If the dragon is providing the magic, then who is being the king?" asked William.

"I don't know." the shade replied. "It could be anyone. Probably a vagrant whom he bribed to help."

"So if what you believe is true, then what are we going to do about it?" asked Talisia.

The shade smiled. "Well. Let me tell you about that. Again, hold your questions until I am finished." He shared this history with them.

• • •

"Barrin, I found this history recorded in the scrolls of the Academie Magica in the port city of Bardhaven. Long before I came to Saldringal, one of your ancestors was the first king of Saldringal. His name was Mortingas, and he was a tremendous warrior and leader of a great army. He was the de facto leader of Saldringal, but at that point the realm was overrun with monsters, wild creatures, and primitive tribes of raiders. There were no settlements of any size, and no organized government above the tribe level. He was more of a war chief. His people were nomadic, and they were one of the largest bands in the realm.

"Mortingas took a group of his finest warriors, and they sailed to the Outer Worlds. He was the first Saldrant person known to do so. He made treaties in those worlds and then later, when he returned, he created the port at Bardhaven to trade with the peoples of the Outer Worlds.

"Somewhere in his travels, Mortingas found a land of dragons, and he managed to convince twelve dragons to move back to Saldringal with him. With the dragons' help, Mortingas drove the monsters and barbarian hordes out of Saldringal. He never lost a battle, and he struck fear in the primitive men and monsters as he pushed them over the mountains and out of our realm. The dragons took up residence in the mountains on the border to prevent the evils from returning.

"In addition to our port, King Mortingas built the town of Cantigal, and Castle Brackhaven. He took the throne as Saldringal's first king, and then spent the rest of his reign in peace. He believed that he had created a perfect realm that would never see war again.

"Mortingas as a warrior always fought with two blades. He called them the 'Keys to the Kingdom'. They were known to be magical, but not much specifically is recorded about them.

"He so firmly believed in the kingdom being at peace, that he had the keys buried with him at his death. Like I said, not much is known about these swords, but I suspect that they are your only chance to reclaim the throne. Maybe the keys can destroy the Arkenstone and win the throne back for you."

• • •

Seeing the confusion in their eyes, the shade looked at William. "You can tell them about the Arkenstone, correct?"

"Yes sir," stammered William.

"Good," said the shade. "Time is fleeting."

"Where do we find Mortingas's grave?" asked Barrindor. The shade and Talisia looked darkly at each other.

"He is in the Royal Barrows of Rathsmar," murmured Talisia.

"Ohhhhh," moaned William.

Barrin looked bewildered.

"Don't worry," said the shade. "Barrindor is family. The ghosts of Rathsmar will be happy to see him." He went on. "Besides, I think I have the key to the door for you."

The shade walked to the bed where the real Thallinius lay. "One of you, take the chain from around my neck."

William jumped up and carefully removed the chain. He felt possessive of the old man, and didn't want the others to handle Thallon's body. His familial feelings for Thallon still ran strong.

"Take my ring off as well, William." William looked at the shade with a pained expression. He quietly slid the ring from the old man's withered finger.

"The ring is for you, son. It will give you all the knowledge you need to be a master blacksmith. Anything you want to make, just think of it, picture it in your head, and you will have the skill to produce it. The better you can imagine, the better you can make." He continued. "You may never work as a smith again, but who knows." William slid the ring onto his finger. It adjusted size magically to fit him perfectly. This startled him, and the shade chuckled.

William had noticed that Thallon wore the necklace, but he had never seen it up close before. The chain itself was exquisitely made, with links of heavy silver. A pendant in the shape of a dagger hung on it. The dagger was only about three inches long, with a heavy hilt and crossguard on one end, and a slightly rounded point on the other. Near the crossguard at the thickest part of the tapering blade were notches cut in an odd pattern. It looked very expensive, and William was pretty sure it had not been made recently, maybe not even by humans. It struck him as too perfect for human work.

"Go to the hearth with it William," the shade commanded. "From the right, count up eight stones from the floor, then over five to the left."

Counting carefully, William found the designated stone. He turned to look at the shade.

"Brush your fingers across the upper part of the stone, going from left to right," directed the shade.

William complied, and as he brushed it as directed, a slight notch appeared in the stone. It deepened and became a keyhole.

The shade continued. "Insert the key, notches side down, and turn it to the right."

William did as the shade said and turned the key. There was a slight click and all the mortar around the stone instantly dissolved. William pulled the stone toward him, and it slid free. Behind it was a large golden ring, three small leather drawstring pouches, and a small clay pot.

"Give the ring to Barrindor," the shade commanded. "It was his father's signet ring that he used to seal royal decrees." He continued. "Also give him the necklace. I used it as a key, but I didn't create it. It is an artifact of Mortingas's time that I 'borrowed' from the Academie. I think it may help you get into the Barrows. The ring may help too, since it proves a connection to the King."

Speaking to all, the shade said, "The bags are coins for you to use in your travels. They don't contain a fortune, but plenty to see you through your mission. Guard them well."

Then he gestured to Talisia. "Talisia, could you hold onto the pot for me? I will tell you more about it later." She took the pot from William.

Once the items were distributed, the shade moved to the closet door where William knew Thallon stored his traveling gear. Gesturing to the door, he advised the three to take what they would need, and quickly pack a few essentials, mostly food and warm traveling cloaks.

The shade pointed out two well-balanced war hammers for William to carry. He gingerly swung them around to get a feel for them, and happily stowed them in his belt. His experience swinging hammers in the forge made these a perfect choice of weapon.

"I would arrange for you to have a shield, William, but looking too much like a soldier would arouse suspicion." He went on. "You two need to look like simple travelers. Talisia can carry more weapons since she is recognizable as a ranger, and it makes sense for rangers to be armed."

Barrin glanced at Talisia. She had a short bow slung over her shoulder, and two long daggers in sheaths, one on each hip. He admired the curve of her hips for a second, and then felt self-conscious and blushed. Looking up, he saw that she had caught him looking. Embarrassed, he quickly turned away and took his turn in the storage room.

Barrin picked up a walking staff, and a heavy cloak for himself. He waited, and after everyone was done gathering what they needed, he used the walk-in storage closet to change into Saldrant clothes. When he was changed, he sadly tossed his last hoodie, his jeans, and all his old clothes into the fire and watched them consume. The last item from his world to go in the fire was his iPhone. He almost tried to hide it, but he knew that there would be no way to explain such a thing if it were found, and besides, the battery was almost dead, and he was sure he would not find an outlet and charger in the rustic cottage, or even in all of Saldringal.

Barrin's backpack had been a Christmas gift from Marlin a few years ago, and though he did not know it then, it was Saldrant in design. As he repacked it after changing clothes, he found the clockwork owl. He showed it to the shade and set it on the mantle. It was really cool and he wanted to keep it, but like the phone, it would be hard to explain, and it had served its purpose.

When the preparations were complete, Thallinius the shade looked closely at each of them one at a time. "I know that you have a lot to discuss with each other. You haven't even had time to formally meet yet." He paused, and emotion filled his voice. "Once you are away from this house, Talisia, I want you to smash the pot from the fireplace. It holds the spell of protection over this cottage. Without it, the portal I opened to Barrin's world will close, this building will be destroyed, and hopefully along with it will go any clues the King's wraiths could use to trace you."

"What about you?" asked William.

"Will. You know I'm dying." The shade made eye contact with the young man. "Be happy that we had this time together. I have lived a very long, mostly good, life. I die with the knowledge that I have done my best for the land I love, and for all of you." He paused, and the shade seemed to flicker a bit. "You had better leave, and go quickly. If I die before you are away, the wraiths will catch you." They all looked at the sleeping wraith.

"What about him?" asked Talisia, gesturing toward their captive.

"Leave him," the shade replied. "When the protections go down, he will be destroyed with this place. Perhaps he can finally be at peace."

As they left, William and Barrindor both paused to kiss the forehead of the old man in the bed. Talisia led them out the door. She was followed by William and then lastly, Barrin. When he reached the doorway, Barrin paused. He turned back to the shade and said, "Thank you, Uncle Marlin." The shade smiled as Barrindor followed the others out the back door.

Chapter Four:
The Road North

The three new companions left the cabin and walked out to the small barn. There, following the shade's last parting directions, William opened all the stalls and freed the few animals that were kept inside. The only animal they took with them was a pony. He was a shaggy chestnut with a long blonde mane and a forelock that fell over his eyes. Barrin silently laughed to himself when he saw the pony. "He looks like a California surfer," he thought.

William informed them that the pony was named Toby. Together they loaded a pack saddle on Toby's back and attached their small supply of rations. William added a halter with a lead, and leading Toby along behind them, they all followed the slight path toward Talisia's home.

Talisia's father, Bergen, ran the local tavern, which was only a short walk away. "Shorter than my old driveway," thought Barrin as the tavern came into view. In front of the tavern was an open area that served as a town square. A cobblestone road passed through the town, and the "square" was really just a wide place in the road. There was a pedestal in the middle of the wide spot that had once held a statue, but over time everyone forgot who the guy was that the statue resembled, and eventually, he was replaced with a signpost. The poor demoted statue now stood behind the tavern, his upraised sword proudly pointing the way to the privies.

Barrin looked at the signpost as they neared the tavern. It pointed the way to Cantigal, Bardhaven, and a couple of other names that Barrin had never heard of. He assumed they were smaller communities, but he knew better than to ask in a public place where it might draw attention. Across from the tavern, Barrin noticed a small bakery, and next to that was what looked to him to be a general store. Sloping stone walls lined the road, creating entry and exit routes to the town square, and there were pots of flowers in prominent places around every building and the central signpost. The people here were proud of their little town.

It was very quiet. The noises of an assembled crowd leaked out of the tavern, but other than that there were no signs of life.

"What do you call this town?" Barrin whispered quietly.

"Wagon's Crossing," Will hissed back.

There were six horses picketed in the grass on the opposite side of the tavern when they approached. Talisia pointed subtly to the horses. "King's men," she whispered. Turning aside, she led them around to the back of the tavern where they quietly entered her family's residence, which was attached to the back.

Inside, they could hear the raucous tavern crowd, eating, talking, and enjoying themselves. It was lunchtime and pretty much everyone from Wagon's Crossing had joined together for the meal.

Talisia gestured to the others to be quiet, and then gave a sign for them to stay. She slipped through a curtained doorway into the tavern proper. Barrin looked at William who shrugged to show he didn't know what she was doing. A few minutes later, the ranger slipped back through the curtain and rejoined them. She had a cloth bag in one hand, and in the other a rolled blanket. She had two more blankets; one under each arm.

"Help me," she quietly hissed. "Take these out and wait with Toby." She handed off all she carried and she ascended the stairs to the upper private rooms as the two perplexed young men slipped back outside to the waiting pony.

By the time Talisia returned, they had loaded the three blanket rolls and the bag, which turned out to be more food, onto Toby. Talisia carried a satchel, and when she reached Toby, she knelt and rummaged in it. She stood up and handed each of them a water skin. She also took one out for herself. Grabbing Toby's lead, she led them all to a small well behind the tavern, where they worked together to fill the bottles, then they each slung one over their shoulder. Now if anyone should get separated, at least they would have water. After filling the small bags, she brought out a larger one, filled it and hung it from Toby's pack saddle.

When this was done, Talisia pointed to a gap in the hedge that circled the backyard of the tavern. She handed the lead to William, and she strode out toward the gap.

"Hey," called Barrin quietly, causing her to stop and turn back to him. "Why don't we steal the horses from around the front? We can make a lot faster time."

Talisia shook her head and gave a quick, "No." Then she turned back on her original path. Barrin was a little angry, and a lot annoyed. He felt like she didn't even consider his idea. "Aren't I the king? I should be the boss," he thought to himself. He knew that he should trust his new companions' judgment in this world, but in his opinion, riding would beat walking any day.

Just after they had all passed through the hedge, Talisia took out the small pot and smashed it against a stone. There was a loud pop and bright flash as the spell was destroyed. They walked away, but within minutes they heard calls of "Fire! Fire!" from the direction of the town. They looked back and saw that thick black smoke billowed up from where the cottage had been. The fire raged so strongly, that even from the distance they had reached, they could see tongues of bright flames licking up to the sky.

• • •

They walked in silence for what seemed to Barrin like an hour or so. Without his cell phone, he had no way to tell time. He knew it was afternoon by the position of the sun, but his body felt very confused. He had left his world before dinner, and arrived after breakfast, so he hadn't eaten in hours, and on top of that, his body thought it should be bedtime right now, even though in Saldringal it was only about two in the afternoon. "Man, I am majorly jet-lagged," he thought. Reconsidering, he laughed to himself, "I guess it's portal-lag."

Just as Barrin thought he couldn't go on another step, Talisia slowed to a stop and turned around. "We should be safe to stop and eat here," she said. "Barrin, you look like you could drop. Maybe we can let you sleep a bit too."

When they had left the tavern, they had skirted the edge of a large plowed field, then crossed a small wood, and crossed another farmer's land, before re-entering a thicker forest.

The woods here were old-growth forest. Large trees spread irregularly with a sweeping, broad canopy above. It appeared to be all hardwoods – at least in this area – and there was little undergrowth. It wasn't hard to walk through, but you had to pick your way around deadfalls and the occasional clumps of shrubs or brambles. Although there wasn't an actual trail, Talisia often found game trails headed in the general direction of their destination so they could move more easily through the undergrowth.

Where they stopped, there was a small clearing with some lush grass and clover. They picketed the pony and let him crop the grass while they distributed apples, a bit of bread, and pieces of dried meat evenly, and then they lay down to eat and rest.

Right before they ate, Talisia looked to Barrin and said, "Taking the horses was a good idea, but you must understand that horses are very rare here." She continued, "Most every farmer keeps a couple of ponies for plowing and pulling carts, but only soldiers have horses. If we took them, we would stick out and everyone would notice us." She went on, "Also, the King would be furious that someone stole his horses. His men would never rest until they chased us down, and even if they didn't recognize you, they would hang us from the nearest tree as punishment for the theft. So, anyway, I wanted you to know why I didn't agree to your idea. I'd rather ride too."

Barrin smiled at her and thanked her for telling him. He promised himself that next time he would trust her judgment more.

As they ate, the three talked between bites about their pasts, and got to know each other better. William knew Talisia by sight, but he had not spoken to her since they were children together in the village many years ago. She was apprenticed to the Rangers when she was ten years old and moved to the north to train with her master. She had not been home since.

She shared that she was now eighteen, and that she was almost ready to pass the trials and become a full-fledged ranger, but her master had disappeared a couple of months before, and she couldn't qualify for the trials without his word to the Guild Council that she was ready. Talisia had searched everywhere she could think of for him, and then she had notified the Guild of his disappearance and returned home to wait for him to contact her, or for the Guild to assign her a new master.

William shared as much as he could remember from the morning's talk with Thallon. He still couldn't bring himself to call the old wizard Thallinius. He made sure to give all the details about the Arkenstone as Thallon had requested.

As they talked, Barrin began to yawn more and more frequently. William also had missed sleeping the night before, so both young men were fairly exhausted, and soon both were nodding. Finally, the conversation dragged, and Talisia suggested that they nap while she surveyed the area and kept guard. Within minutes, both were sound asleep.

• • •

Talisia shook them awake in a few hours. Both the young men were still groggy with sleep, but she said that they needed to move right away. As they resumed their trek, she quietly told them that as they slept she had seen two foot patrols of the king's soldiers off in the distance. She did not know if they were pursued, or if it was just a coincidence, but she thought that they had better keep moving for a while. This announcement raised the tension level of the group, and they fell into silence as they followed the ranger through the woods.

After what felt like an hour or more, they stopped for a brief rest. They sipped their water, and sat for a few minutes.

"Guys, I, uh, need to go to the bathroom," Barrin sheepishly admitted.

"We don't have time for a bath," Talisia matter of factly replied. "And we don't have a tub."

"No." Barrin tried again. "I need to relieve myself. You know. Uh. Poop?"

"Ohh," The girl laughed. "Well go ahead. We'll wait."

"Umm. Where?" Barrin asked.

"Anywhere in the woods, just not here," she said. "And try to go downwind. It's polite."

"Okay," Barrin said, thinking to himself, "This should be interesting." Then out loud he asked, "What do you use for, you know, cleaning after?"

"At home we have corn cobs," said Will.

"Out here, leaves will do," replied Talisia. "Collect some leaves before you go, or you won't have any. Avoid three pronged leaves. They are an irritant, and you will regret using them."

Will wandered a short distance into the woods and figured out how to take care of the problem. It was a somewhat humiliating process, but he managed, and when he returned to the others, they went on along their way.

When they stopped again, it was dusk and the woods were beginning to look very dark around them. Talisia found a small clearing with a sparse patch of grass. They picketed Toby in the middle of it, and then rolled out their blankets around the edge of the clearing where he was unlikely to step on them.

As he rolled out his bedroll, Barrin said, "I'm glad you had these waiting for us. They look more comfortable than just sleeping on the ground."

"Dad keeps several of these in the tavern," she replied. "Some people drink too much to go home, others will pay a coin or two to sleep on the floor instead of outside." She continued, "Our town doesn't have an inn, so he likes to help out the few travelers looking for a place, and of course to make a little extra for the till."

"Why aren't we using the road?" Will asked. "Wouldn't it be faster?"

"Well, yes, we would make better time," Talisia replied. "But the soldiers always use the roads, and bandits sometimes wait along the roads, too. I know all the woods around here, and a lot of the northern wood as well, so I can get us where we are going and avoid those particular dangers."

"Are there wild animals to watch out for in the forest here?" asked Barrin. It was now almost fully dark. They had decided to forego a campfire since they didn't need to cook, and they did not want to advertise their presence.

"There is nothing particularly dangerous here in the southern part of Saldringal," she replied. "And I think we are far enough off the beaten path that we won't even need a guard, so we can all sleep tonight."

Barrin's feet hurt. He wasn't used to the leather boots that Marlin, er, Thallinius had given him. "Apparently Saldringal has not yet discovered the wonders of arch support," he thought to himself. He desperately wished for a pair of good hiking boots, or even his old Nikes. He also missed his cotton Fruit of the Loom boxer briefs. The linen ones he wore now bunched up and fit awkwardly. This reminded him of a Big Bang Theory episode, and he laughed to himself remembering how Sheldon had "borrowed" Leonard's pillowcase to make underwear for a Renaissance Fair.

They all lay down on their pallets and as they became quiet, the woods around them came alive with small noises. Rodents skittered, night birds called, and the trees swayed and creaked in the gentle evening breeze.

Barrin lay still, wondering about this strange new place. Was he on Earth? Was this place in the past of his world, or maybe a post-apocalyptic future? Maybe he was in a totally different plane of existence. Nothing here fit exactly with any of the time periods he had studied in World History class. Saldringal was somewhat medieval, but not exactly so. Maybe Earth didn't even exist in this world. He assumed that he was on some planet, but travel seemed difficult here, and from what Thallinius had told them, this realm seemed to keep pretty much to itself. What was out there in other parts of this planet, whatever it was? No matter. He would have to remember to take everything here on its own merit. Assumptions based on his world may get him in trouble, as nothing was quite the same.

His mind wandered to other things, and then settled in on frustration. Barrin missed technology. Now that he had a little down time, he was bored. He wanted to watch a few YouTube videos, stream a show, or scroll some social media sites. He missed his phone.

Studying the middle ages in school, it had never really occurred to him how boring and uncomfortable daily life really was. He didn't even want to think about the bathroom situation. He didn't mind peeing in the woods, but… he tried not to think about their lack of toilet paper as he drifted off to sleep.

• • •

They woke early as the sun came up. For breakfast they had some bread and cheese and drank from their water skins. As they ate, Talisia told them that they would reach the central plains of Saldringal later that day. She warned them that they would have to cross the road there, and that the plains presented a specific challenge, as they would be visible for a very long distance. Crossing was by far the fastest way, and so she thought it was worth the risk, especially since she did not think the King knew what they were up to yet. She was still considering their options for how and where to cross, and she would tell them more when they reached the edge of the wood later.

When they got up to walk, Barrin lifted Talisia's pack for her to put on. She smiled and thanked him. He was very attracted to her, and he wanted to do as many nice things for her as he could.

They walked quietly for hours, pausing for the occasional drink of water, or brief rest. Barrin's feet really hurt, but he tried not to complain. He started to develop a blister on the edge of his left big toe, so at a stop, he dug out the first aid kit that Aunt Allie had packed, and found some moleskin to put on it. "God bless her," he thought. He covered the hotspot, and then carefully hid the first aid kit deep in its pack where it was unlikely to be noticed by a stranger.

Shortly after midday they stopped for lunch and Barrin told them about his world. He wasn't sure they understood, or even believed his tales about automobiles, airplanes, computers, cellphones and the like, but they politely showed surprise and were a good audience. Suddenly he understood how Marlin felt telling him about Saldringal when he was younger, and he felt ashamed for how he had dismissed the old man as crazy.

Their chatting eventually led to sharing folk tales of the two worlds. It surprised Barrin how similar their stories were. One commonality was the "Big Bad Wolf" character that was a villain in stories from both worlds. However, unlike in Barrin's world, Talisia warned Barrin that Saldringal actually had big, bad, wolves.

"Regular wolves are okay," she began. "They are predators, and they serve a need in controlling the population of the herd animals. That's what Rangers do too; you see, we try to keep the balance for the good of all the creatures of Saldringal." She continued. "Now the 'big bad' wolves – we call them 'night wolves' because they are always black – are alpha-predators. They are incredibly dangerous, but at least they don't normally run in packs. One night wolf can take out a herd of cattle in just a few days. They are about the size of a horse, eat voraciously, and truly serve no purpose other than killing. They are the only beast I know that kills for sport. My master had gone to investigate a night wolf sighting when he disappeared. I worry that the wolf got him." She paused, then continued. "I searched the area looking for signs of him. I found nothing, not even evidence of a wolf in the area."

They went back to walking, and later that afternoon, Barrin noticed a brightening between the trees up ahead. He could tell that the forest was ending, and they had reached the plains. The companions continued forward, stopping a few feet shy of the forest's edge, where they could survey the open land and see if danger was about. The northern road was on their side of the plain, only about fifteen yards from the forest. It was a road only in the sense that people traveled on it. It was dirt and mostly just consisted of two ruts at the approximate width of a wagon's axle. Barrin hadn't expected pavement or concrete like the roads in his old world, but he thought it would be cobblestone because of the town square they had seen.

Beyond the road was grassland, undisturbed and blowing in the light spring breeze. The tall grass was still brown and dead from winter, but new green grass was sprouting all through the field at the foot of the older weeds, and the overall effect was beautiful and verdant.

Off to their right, the road followed the curving treeline. Then where the forest ended, it broke to its left and cut northwest across the open grassland towards Bardhaven and the sea, which were both several days' journey out of sight. Barrin noticed that a small dilapidated cabin sat near them in the curve of the road, and he gestured to it.

"Should we use that place as a rest stop?" he asked.

Talisia considered it and answered, "We are much safer in the trees. Besides, the weather is nice, and it isn't cold. We don't need a shelter."

Barrin appreciated her giving a reason beyond "no." He agreed with her logic, but he was tired and really did want an extended period of rest. Talisia spoke to Barrin and Will, "I am going to scout ahead. Why don't you two take Toby back where he won't try to get out to the grassland. There was an opening just over there," she pointed, "where he could graze out of sight. I'll scout around and will come back to you in a couple hours and we can make a plan of how to go on. Bandits are very common in this area, and we've heard reports of a rogue orgrum band that crossed the mountains and has been causing a lot of trouble. Let me scout for tracks and see which way looks safest. If for some reason I don't come back, you need to keep traveling north. Rathsmar is at the western end of the Dragon Mountains. If something happens, we can try to meet up there."

The two young men agreed to her plan, and they took Toby to where she had suggested. They lounged about, resting after the long walk. Neither of them was accustomed to long walks like Talisia was. William's job was mostly stationary, and other than the walk to and from the bus, Barrin wasn't much of a hiker.

Talisia slipped off to scout. She found Barrin interesting. He was like a child in some ways; like how he didn't know anything about living in their world, but she thought he was handsome, and he made her laugh. She looked forward to getting to know him better.

After a few minutes resting, Barrin grew restless. He was fighting a light headache, probably from a lack of caffeine, and he was fidgety, mostly because he missed his cellphone. He picked up his staff and as quietly as he could, he worked his way back near the edge of the forest. He enjoyed watching the grass wave with the breeze and the way the ripples ran through it almost like water. He had been watching for a few minutes when all of a sudden he realized two things almost at once. First, there was smoke rising from the chimney of the cabin, and second, someone was out in the grass walking steadily toward the cabin.

Barrin retreated back to the clearing and motioned for Will to join him. Together the two of them made their way back to the forest edge. They carefully stayed out of sight and watched as the figure in the grasslands approached the cabin. Barrin thought it looked familiar.

"Hey," he whispered. "That's one of those lizard guys."

"They're called wraiths," replied Will. "And they are dangerous. Everyone I know says they are the king's assassins."

As they watched, the wraith unslung a bow and nocked an arrow. Holding the bow to its side, it whispered to the tip of the arrow, which sputtered and burst into flame. Drawing the bow, it let the arrow fly in a long arc unto the roof of the cabin. When the arrow hit, flames exploded out of it, quickly catching the roof ablaze. The wraith repeated the process and prepared another arrow.

Just as he released his second flaming shaft, the door to the cabin burst open and a cloaked figure flew through the door and headed for the woods. She ran a zig-zagging pattern, roughly toward the trees and the two hidden watchers. The wraith reacted with anger as it realized the poor timing of the second arrow, it quickly strung a third arrow and, without fire this time, he let it fly into the running creature's back. She staggered with the hit, but kept running, trying to increase the distance between them.

The wraith nocked another arrow, but realizing the distance she had achieved, it did not draw its bow. Instead, it began pursuing its prey at a fast pace; not a run, but faster than a walk, steady and unrelenting. It held the bow ready as it followed her, trying to get in range.

"Oh, crap," whispered Barrin. "They are headed right this way." In fact, the wounded figure was quickly approaching them as she fled to the trees. Her outfit was light colored, and they could see blood running down the front of her tunic from where the arrow protruded through her right shoulder. "Let's hide behind the trees and jump the wraith right when he enters," Barrin said. "We can bind him up the way that Talisia did with the other one."

Will didn't look too convinced, but they didn't have much choice as both figures were rapidly approaching. Will drew a hammer out of his belt, and they spread out a little and hid behind the trees where it seemed the wraith was most likely to come between them. Just after they got in place, the wounded one stumbled by them. She was struggling to keep going. "Probably from the blood loss," thought Barrin. She ran by them frantically, but quickly slowed to a trot, continued for about twenty yards, and then collapsed face first into the underbrush. She struggled to rise a couple times, and then fell over and quit moving.

Both the young men hoped she wasn't dead, but they were in no position to help her right at this moment. The wraith was not far behind. They waited, listening closely. They heard the creature's footsteps crossing the road. It seemed to be slowing, sensing a possible trap. Barrin pictured the scaly legs and clawed feet of the last wraith he had seen. Suddenly it was between them. Barrin drove the end of his staff into the wraith's stomach with all his might. He was peripherally aware of Will's hammer crashing into its forehead at the same time, and then he was charging after the beast slamming it again and again with his staff.

Their blows staggered the creature, throwing it onto its back. Its bow flew out of its clawed hands, and the arrow fell away as the bow bounced from the stunned creature. The wraith's skull was broken from the hammer blow, but it didn't seem to mind. It immediately began struggling to rise and tried to pull its long knife from the sheath at its side. Barrin yelled as he dove on top of the creature, wrestling with its arm to prevent it pulling the new weapon. Will was right behind him trying to contain its other arm and keep its claws off of Barrin's back and his own back and face.

The wraith was incredibly strong, and both began to question their choice. Talisia had made this look easy, but it was not. One thing that struck Barrin as they fought was how much bigger this wraith was than the one Talisia had captured. That one was several inches shorter than him. This one was a good bit taller. It also was much more heavily muscled. Barrin cursed his luck.

Under its cloak, the wraith wore a leather breastplate strapped around its chest. Barrin found the edge and was holding on to the armor piece with one hand, and had the creature's left arm in his other as they wrestled. This grip allowed him leverage to keep the creature from throwing him off.

The wraith seemed to simultaneously want to get away, but also to attack them with its claws and even teeth. They had to be careful of its sharp toed feet as well as the arms they had pinioned down.

As they continued to struggle, the straps holding the wraith's breastplate tore, and for a second Barrin wasn't able to hold tight. The wraith redoubled its efforts and almost got its arm free, but Barrin threw the torn armor away, and looking for a handhold, his hand closed on a hard round object on the wraith's chest. Looking down, he realized it was a large gem. With a slight twist he wrenched the gem free and pulled.

The wraith screamed in pain and terror and then its head fell back and it was immediately still. Barrin rolled to his knees and staggered to his feet. He noticed that the fire had gone out of the wraith's eyes. He held the gem up and looked closely at it. Will also got up, carefully keeping an eye on the still form of the wraith. They were both breathing heavily from the exertion of the battle.

The gem in Barrin's hand was about two and a half inches across its widest part. It tapered to a sharp point, with an overall length of about five or six inches. The entire piece was one stone, and although it was currently dripping black blood and ichor, Barrin could see that underneath it was bright emerald green in color.

"What is that thing?" asked Will, huffing and puffing.

"I have no idea," Barrin replied. "I was just trying to find something to hold onto so he wouldn't get away. I didnt even mean to pull it out. It just kinda happened."

"Let's go check on the one it was chasing and see if she knows," Will said.

They decided to hide the wraith's body first, in case anyone came down the road, but just as they went to move it into the trees, with a sudden flash, the body burst into flames. The scaly reptile's remains flashed with intense fire for a moment, and then the flames puffed out and a thin layer of ash fell off the body revealing the form of a normal human man. There was still a gaping hole in his chest, and his forehead was still smashed in, but the reptilian features were gone. The fire had been intense, but short lived. The ragged remains of his clothing smoldered a bit, but had not fully ignited.

The man was muscular and seemed to Barrin to be middle aged, probably around forty. His head, and in fact his whole body was completely bald, perhaps because of the immolation of the lizard body that had covered him. His eyes appeared to have been blue, but they were hazed over now in death. Barrin remembered the fire that had burned there just a few minutes ago.

They tentatively touched the corpse's hands, and after confirming they were cool enough to handle, they dragged the body into the woods and away from the road. They also collected the bow and unstrung it, returning the arrow to the quiver they had removed from the body. With that task done, they went to check the wraith's victim.

They approached her stealthily. Barrin was pleased to see her back moving with rhythmic breathing. She was still alive, though apparently unconscious. Neither of them had gotten a good look at her when she was running, as they had been so focused on the wraith and preparing for battle; a battle they nearly lost. Her cloak was very light gray, so much so that it was almost white. She had matching knee-high leather boots with dark maroon breeches tucked into them. Blood stained the back of the cloak where the back of the arrow was plainly visible. The hood of the cloak covered her head.

The arrow was through her right shoulder. Barrin was pretty sure that it was high enough to have missed her lung. They carefully rolled her onto her side with the shoulder the arrow was in on the upward side.

As they moved her, Barrin and Will were startled to realize that she was covered in fur. In the cloak, she resembled a normal human in shape and size, and she was obviously female. They had noticed her feminine outline as she ran. Her hands were slightly large for her size, and pawlike, but with a genuine opposable thumb like a human. Her hood fell back, and they saw that her face resembled a large cat. Barrin thought she most looked like a young white tiger, but with fewer, actually almost no, stripes. A few light gray stripes came out of her hairline and across the side of her face ending at her cheeks. Her nose was feline in shape and slightly pink. Her teeth, especially her canines, were slightly larger than a humans, and her large eyes were outlined with long black lashes. Under her cloak, a long white tail ran out of her breeches. It had been covered by her cloak. Her eyes were closed, and her breathing was strong, but a little ragged.

Barrin got Will to hold her still while he cautiously snapped off the back half of the arrow to get rid of the fletching. He then grabbed the iron-tipped front part of the shaft and pulled it through and out of her shoulder. She flinched, and made whimpering and groaning noises in her sleep every time he touched the arrow.

Will suggested that they move her to where Toby was still tethered. Together they carefully lifted her and carried her to the clearing. As they raised her from the ground, her cloak fell back further exposing a shock of white shoulder length hair. It resembled any woman's hair, except that most of it was rooted between her ears, which were set higher than a human's and were cat-like in shape. The high-placed hair reminded Barrin a little of a Mohawk, but mostly because it was bound behind her head in an up hairstyle. Her short tunic was a dark golden yellow, but like her cloak, it was also bloodstained.

When they reached the clearing, they removed her outer garment, and folded it with the blood on the inside. They gently laid her on it, with a bedroll underneath for added thickness. They did this for her comfort, but also so her already ruined cloak would help prevent blood from also ruining their blankets.

While Will helped get her situated and comfortable, Barrin dug his first aid kit out of his pack. "At the rate I am using this," he thought, "it will be gone soon." Using the medical scissors from the kit, Barrin cut away the shoulder piece of her tunic. He assumed that when she became conscious, she would rather have a totally ruined tunic than find herself topless with two strange men. Besides, the tunic had holes and blood stains on it anyway.

Using the ruined piece of tunic as a rag, he poured water on her wounds and bathed both sides of her shoulder as well as he could. He wished they could build a fire and use hot water to better treat the wound, but they couldn't risk the smoke, especially with Talisia absent. Leaving her fur around the wound also concerned him. He thought that a doctor (or possibly a vet?) would have shaved around the wound to keep it clean, but he didn't have a razor, and doubted that Will did either. There was an Ace bandage in the kit, so Barrin put several gauze pads on the wounds in front and back and wrapped the bandage around to hold them in place. He had liberally applied Neosporin on the first pad he applied to each side of the shoulder, and he hoped that the antibiotic would shut down any infection.

She seemed to be sleeping more comfortably now, so Will sat down near her, and Barrin cleaned up as best he could, put everything away, and then sat near Will and leaned back against a tree. Toby had been very nervous of the newcomer at first, especially because she smelled like blood, but he had decided she was not a threat, and he went back to chomping away at the grass where he was picketed.

Now that the adrenaline of the battle and medical work was over, Barrin felt shaky. He blinked as hot tears began to form and then he wiped both eyes, trying to hide the tears from Will.

"Have you ever killed anything before?" Barrin tentatively asked.

"No," said Will. "Have you?"

"No," replied Barrin. He paused, then said. "I didn't know he was human. Not that I guess it would have mattered."

"He would have killed us both if he could," Will said. "Her too, I guess."

"Yeah," said Barrin. They sat in awkward silence for a while, letting the gravity of their adventure sink in. Both felt somewhat sad, but with a hint of pride in their saving their feline patient.

"I didn't know the hammer would break his head," said Will. "I just swung as hard as I could. I've only hit metal before."

"It's okay," Barrin replied. "You saved her life."

"We saved it," Will said.

Another few minutes went by. Off in the woods a bird twittered, and Barrin saw a ground squirrel pass by on some secret mission of its own.

"Do you know what her race is called?" Barrin asked.

"No, I've never seen anyone like her before," Will answered. Then he added, "She's not from Saldringal. I'm sure of it."

Barrin glanced at her. "I think she will be okay. She lost some blood, but I think the wound didn't damage anything important. Well that's assuming her important things are in the same place that they are on humans." He went on. "I think she collapsed from exhaustion as much as from the injury. It seems like a simple puncture wound. I don't know why she is so out of it."

"I'm glad we helped her," said Will. "I think she's fascinating. I can't wait to talk to her." He looked at the girl and smiled.

Barrin smiled to himself. "Good," he thought. "You fall for the cat-girl and let me have Talisia." This thought made him feel happy inside, but also guilty. She was helping him for the good of king and country, and he was thinking about hitting on her. Still, she was fun to be with, and he liked how she was pretty without trying. He also liked how she took charge and didn't act all helpless to impress the guys.

"What in Aeric's name?!" Talisia suddenly exclaimed, appearing right beside them and shaking him from his private thoughts. Neither had heard her approaching as her ranger skills helped her be all but silent as she moved through the woods. "I ask you two to lay low and watch a pony, and I return to find this?" Her eyes blazed as she gestured to the sleeping girl. "Who is this?" Then she looked again and, taking on a perplexed look, she calmed down a bit and said, "What is this?"

Even though she was annoyed, and he was a little embarrassed by his recent thoughts, Barrin was happy to see her. He jumped to his feet and quickly told her the story of their battle with the wraith, and their saving of the feline person while showing her the now cleaned crystal gem. As he continued, he led her to the body they had moved from the road. She took a quick look and her eyes misted with tears.

"That's Gareth," she said. "My master."

Chapter Five:
Mind of the Dragon

"What's his mood today?" Ancillon, captain of the King's Guard, asked the young man standing at attention by the door to the King's chambers. He couldn't remember this kid's name; it was Darrin, or Dabbin, or something.

As the captain, and the most senior guardsman, Ancillon really should have known the name of all of the others under his command, but the reality was that the turnover rate in the king's army in general was pretty high, and new troops in the king's personal guard usually didn't last very long before they moved on to a new assignment, especially if they had any say in it.

"He's in a dark mood, sir," the young man replied. "He threw something at the last person to go in, and I heard him pacing."

"Just what I need," Ancillon thought to himself, but he said, "Well, I have to go speak with him anyway," as he pushed the door open. The captain greeted Ishthmar politely, but the dragon just hissed at him and glared coldly, annoyed at the interruption and awaiting what he expected to be an unnecessary report.

"Your Excellency," the captain began, "You asked for any news of unusual activity in the realm." He stammered a bit, nervously, then said, "There was a great fire in a home in Wagon's Crossing last night. It raged against all efforts to put it out, and it still burns today." He paused. "We believe it may be magical in nature. Sir." He added the "sir" on quickly at the end, hoping the reaction wouldn't be too rough. Ishthmar had killed the previous captain of the Guard in a fit of rage over a taxation issue, so Ancillon had a right to be nervous.

Ishthmar was frustrated in general. After almost one hundred years in Castle Brackhaven, it was harder and harder for him to feel satisfied. He was bored, and antsy. He had needs, and they weren't being fulfilled.

All dragons have a certain level of natural lust for gold and treasure, but Ishthmar had an overwhelming desire for these precious things. He ached for more gold, more gems, more everything. Like other dragons before him, he liked to just sit in his hoard and run his fingers through the coins and the gems. He even liked to sleep upon it. But unlike most dragons, he also felt a strong, deep-seated lust for power. He wanted to rule. Everything.

For centuries Ishthmar had pushed these desires down and played the role of vizier for his brother, Ragnussen, but the suppression of his desires began to glow as an ember of hatred – a spark of contempt for his siblings and the dragon king. Centuries of waiting fanned the flames. The ember became a blaze, and then an inferno.

Suddenly, he hated the other dragons and their "non-dragon" way of living. He knew dragons were the superior race. They should rule Saldringal, not the humans. They should own the gold of Xantos and the entire wealth of the realm, and he was the dragon to lead them to their – no, to his rightful place as ruler of all the realm.

He began to see his brother and sister dragons as traitors to their kind. Theirs was the superior race, yet they chose to serve the humans. It was like they had given themselves over to bondage, and it galled Ishthmar. Even worse, instead of taking more and more treasure for their great hoard, they actually gave items away every time a halfling did its job. It disgusted him to no end. They were the all-powerful race. They should be gaining treasure, not losing it.

He knew he could never challenge Ragnussen one-on-one for the crown. Ishthmar was not only the smallest dragon, but also the youngest. Even with his copious magical abilities, the others would all oppose him peacefully taking the crown from his older, larger brother. None of the others were full mages as he was, but they all had the typical magical abilities of all dragons, one of which was a very high resistance to magical attacks. He would have to resort to physical violence if he were to overthrow the others.

So Ishthmar formulated a plan. He would interrupt the dragons' cycle of re-birthing. He would destroy the others one by one, and when he was the only one left, he would become the ruler, not only as the king of the dragons, but of the entire realm of Saldringal.

Ishthmar began watching for the perfect moments to eliminate his siblings. One by one he caught the dragons alone, fell upon them unexpectedly and killed them. He collected their heartstones and created a secret cache to hide the stones where they wouldn't be found by the others.

The tension rose in the dragons' lair as their numbers dwindled, but oddly, none of the others suspected that the danger was from within. Centuries of living together had raised their trust levels so high that it wasn't until he attacked the last two, Styvestant and Ragnussen, that any of them realized that Ishthmar was the villain destroying their clan.

He had to admit that killing the last two at the same time was a careless mistake. He had jumped on Styvestant and was finishing him off when Ragnussen unexpectedly turned the corner, and discovered him completing the task. The absolute shock of his betrayal is the only reason Ishthmar survived. He was able to greatly wound the much larger dragon before he could react. Still, Ragnussen had almost killed him, too. Ishthmar was barely able to survive long enough to fly down to the halfling village where his stone would be collected for re-birth.

Ishthmar had long known of the ability of dragon heart-stones to animate dead creatures. He had read about this phenomenon in the library of scrolls that the dragons kept in their lair. If more of his idiot siblings had studied as he had, they may have deduced and foiled his plan, but their lack of continued learning was another of the many individual hatreds he had developed for them over the years. Once his mind had turned to hate, it had begun multiplying and growing little seeds of annoyance into seething tendrils of contempt. By the time he acted, the madness of desire had fully corrupted who Ishthmar was.

His ascension to dragon king was not enough; he wanted more. He created eleven loyal followers, dragon-born Saldrant wraiths, using his siblings' essences in the heart-stones. These mindless slaves would do his bidding without qualms or compassion. The first wraith he had created on a whim, when he killed the halfling who had brought him back to life. He couldn't let the little thing tell its friends what it had seen, so he allowed it to "join the cause" as the first of his private army. He sort of regretted making a wraith of the halfling; it was not a very good fighter. Still, he kept it around out of vanity. It was a marker of his success overthrowing the others.

After that first use of the heartstones, Ishthmar was selective about whom he chose to become a wraith. He wanted strong, trained warriors, or gifted fighters to be in his private army. The stronger the human body, the stronger the wraith. Over time, some of the wraiths became too damaged, so he replaced them with another "donor." The heartstones were the important part of the wraith. He saw the host bodies as disposable.

Killing the human king was easy. By pure luck, Pallindor actually was killed by his horse. The nag startled when the dragon dropped from the sky just in front of it. The heavy warhorse reared, and rolled over backwards crushing the king. The dragon was delighted that the horse's weight had killed him when it fell. It made explaining what happened so much easier. No one would question such an accident, or the obvious, unfakeable injuries to the king's body.

Of course, he ate the pathetic princling brother just to permanently hide its body. After that, it was just the matter of replacing Prince Arkendor, and the dragon had the power he desired.

Unfortunately, Ishthmar was an addict. Once he quit suppressing his desires for gold, gems, and power, and he gave in to these needs, he found that, like a drug addict, it took more and more to give him the needed feelings of fulfillment. He struggled to satiate his desires. He wanted more all the time. More of everything. And so, he pushed the people of the realm to their breaking point with taxes and required service to the realm.

After nearly one hundred years controlling the throne, Ishthmar realized that he had taken almost all that could be taken from the people of Saldringal, and he feared what would happen when there was no more to take. Perhaps war was the answer. If they were to conquer another realm, maybe he could double, or even triple his hoard. Perhaps he should start a war.

His plans for war were underway, and for the first time in a decade, Ishthmar felt hopeful about a real growth for his hoard and his fledgling empire, but there was a problem nettling him like a thorn in an animal's paw: Thallinius the Wise.

He knew the old fool of a sorcerer was working against him, but he couldn't divine how. He had felt the old man's presence in the court recently, and he believed that the curse he had cast may have caught the old man. Maybe his worries were already over, but he wasn't sure.

The old man had hidden the heir from him. The whelp should already be dead. The wraith he sent to kill the child had been accidently discovered by a guard, or it would already be dead. He had personally destroyed the wraith in his anger, and of course replaced it with better source material.

He had tricked the Queen into marriage, promising he would make sure her child was adopted and that her brat kept his place in the line of succession. He had also personally impregnated the Queen so that the dragon spawn growing inside her would end her life. It was the simplest way to get rid of her in a plausible way. Lots of women died in pregnancy. If only her first child had just died too, Ishthmar's life would be so much happier.

"Stupid wraith," he thought to himself.

Just a few days ago, he had scryed a tear in the fabric between worlds and shoved another one of his wraiths through in hopes that that was where the heir was hidden. It had not yet returned, so he was uncertain of the outcome yet, but the return spell had been used, so he had high hopes for a word soon. Maybe the heir was already dead too. He felt a moment of glee at the thought.

Ancillon came into his chamber and interrupted his thoughts. He listened to the report of a magical fire.

"Did they discover any bodies in the fire?" he asked.

"The fire still burns, and it is too hot to check yet, sir," Ancillon replied.

"Who lived in this home?" the dragon asked.

"The village blacksmith. An older man named 'Thallon,'" he paused. "Oh, and his apprentice, a young man named 'William Ironsmith.'"

This was the one. Thallon must be Thallinius. The dragon wondered if perhaps this Ironsmith was the heir himself.

Was Thallinius's magic strong enough to prevent another person from aging? That would be impressive if it were true.

"Put out an arrest warrant for the boy, William Ironsmith, in the name of the King." He added, "He is wanted for questioning." The dragon thought for a moment, then directed. "Send forty troops into the field to find him. Have them hang 'wanted' posters all over the realm. We want anyone else traveling with him as well. He must be found at all costs."

"Yes sir," Ancillon said, bowing deeply to the dragon. Then he turned and hurried out of the room, happy to be leaving under his own power.

For the first time in quite some time, Ishthmar smiled.

Chapter Six:
The Long Way

Barrin helped Talisia carry her fallen master back to their clearing. Toby snorted at them as they brought in the body. He rolled his eyes, and moved to the far end of his picket rope. Will joined them, carrying the wraith's bow and quiver.

"He was armed with this," the young smith said, showing Talisia the bow. "I thought you might want the quiver since you've lost your own."

Talisia smiled and said, "I haven't lost my quiver, I just don't need one." She slipped the bow off her back and lightly drew the bowstring, as she did an electric arrow crackled to life, nocked and ready to fire. She eased the string back down and the arrow fizzled back out of existence. "It's a lightning bow," she said. "The magic arrows pierce like regular ones, but they also do shock damage to the target. It was a gift from Thallinius when I was accepted as a ranger apprentice. I thought you already knew about it since you were his apprentice then."

"I didn't even know he was a magic user," Will mumbled.

She studied the bow and quiver that William held and said, "This is Gareth's bow and his wolfhunter's quiver. These arrows are treated with a sleeping draught. It isn't a poison per se. The arrows do plenty to kill the wolf without any help, but we found that when we shot the night wolves, they wouldn't fall quickly enough to prevent them from attacking us first. The sedative helped put them on the ground faster. Your friend here doesn't look nearly as heavy as a night wolf, so she will probably sleep for a couple days or more before the sedative works its way out of her. She's lucky that the arrow went on through her. If the tip had lodged inside, she probably would have fallen out there," she pointed towards the cabin, "and never made it into the woods at all."

"How are we going to travel if she sleeps for days?" asked Barrin. "We can't just leave her here."

Talisia looked frustrated. "We can't stay here either. When I was scouting I found lots and lots of tracks. It looks like soldiers have been through here repeatedly the past few days. Other groups, too; probably bandits."

"I might be able to carry her," Will offered.

"You probably could for a while," replied Talisia, "but it would really wear you out, and it would make it awkward for you to help us fight if we were to run into bandits. It wouldn't be the best for her wounds either, being bounced around as we walk."

"Could we make a travois?" Barrin wondered aloud.

Will and Talisia stared at him, not knowing the word.

"It's two poles lashed together on one end," he explained. "You attach the separate ends of the poles to the sides of an animal, Toby in our case, and you wrap fabric over and around the gap between the poles. When Toby walks, it would drag along behind him, carrying her. Native people in my world used to use them."

"Do you know how to lash poles together?" Will asked.

"Not really," replied Barrin.

"Wait! I know how to do it," Will excitedly burst out. "I pictured what I wanted in my head, and all of a sudden I knew exactly how to make it!" He beamed. "I guess my ring knows more than just blacksmithing."

They set about building the travois. Will borrowed a small axe from Talisia's pack and found two small saplings which he cut down and quickly limbed. He used a piece of rope, which he cut into lengths to lash the poles together on one end and to the sides of Toby's pack saddle on the other. Together they wrapped a couple of their blankets to complete the sledge and carefully loaded the feline girl on it. She seemed to be resting comfortably.

While they worked on building the travois, Talisia removed the Ace bandage from the patient. She left the gauze pads in place, and replaced the bandage with a length of linen fabric from her own pack. She apparently carried this material for emergency bandaging. She rolled the foreign bandage and placed it on Barrin's pack for him to put fully away.

Talisia looked at the feline girl. "She's pretty," she thought, with an unexpected rush of jealousy. Ironic that she would feel catty toward the pretty feline who slept before her. This puzzled her. Why was she feeling jealous? She had just met Barrin. This puzzled her again. Why did she assume it was Barrin that made her jealous, and not Will?

She watched Barrin work for a few minutes. She liked the way he moved, and his quiet intelligence. She had never felt this way about anyone before. As she watched, she realized that the guys were almost done.

"Dragging this thing through the forest won't work at all," she warned them. "We are going to have to risk using the roads for a bit. I have an idea of where we should go to find help, but it's a good bit out of our way. It's really our only option, though." She knelt and smoothed out the dirt in a dusty grassless spot.

"Saldringal is a peninsula, and it is roughly shaped like this." She drew a rough shape in the dust with a small stick. "The King stays in his capital city, Cantigal, most of the time, which is all the way down here, near the tip," she said, pointing to the bottom of her drawing. "And the only other large city is the port, Bardhaven, which is here," she pointed to a spot on the coast in the upper left side of the peninsula about two inches from the top.

"We started out here at Wagon's Crossing," she said, pointing about an inch above the capital city. "And we are going here." This time she pointed to a spot at the top of the map which was also in the northwest, a couple inches above and to the right of the port city.

"Where our peninsula connects to the mainland," she sketched on the upper right end of the drawing, "there are mountains running right along the border, and down the east side of the realm, most of the way. They curve inland a bit when they peter out, roughly pointing towards Cantigal. The south is heavily forested, as are the north and the mountains down the east side. The central area is all open grassland as we saw, and the northern and southern forests connect here in the mountains, down the eastern edge, to totally surround them.

"Standing where we are now and looking northwest, you can't see the end of the plains." She paused, then continued. "We could go that way, but it is the obvious route if they have divined where we are going, and that way is very exposed. There's nowhere to hide, and no cover for escape. We would most likely be caught within a day."

She paused again. "I suggest that we move east. We go right back into the forest and skirt the plains altogether. I wanted to go across the grassland to save time, because the forest route is much harder walking and more mountainous terrain too, but now we have a reason to go that way."

"My master, Gareth, is from a small village east of here at the foot of the mountains," she said. "We should go and ask his family to shelter us while our new friend here heals."

Both young men nodded their approval at her suggestion. "I've been to two places in my life," Will said. "Here."

He pointed to Cantigal. "And here." He pointed to Wagon's Crossing. "So I am leaving how and where we go up to you." He smiled.

"Yes," Barrin said. "You know a lot more about this land and travel here than either of us. I trust you to lead the way. Besides, it's a good plan. We can let her sleep the potion off, and then go on from there north around the grassland." He continued. "Stopping for a couple days has an added benefit. Will and I both need to rest and heal up our feet too. Neither of us is used to walking like this."

"Umm," Will started. "Do you think Gareth's family will welcome us? We might have just killed him."

Talisia looked mournful again. "I am certain that Gareth was dead long before your battle. He could not have lived with that gem stuck through his heart, and besides, the Gareth I knew would never have attacked any person the way you describe. He was gentle and kind. Being a Ranger for him was about helping protect people and keeping the forest balanced for the good of all." She continued. "I am certain that it was some unholy reanimation spell at work to make him only seem alive."

They debated what to do with Gareth's body. Ultimately, they decided that it would take too long to dig a true grave. Talisia removed all his personal items. She took his knife, belt, and coin bag from his waist, and then they wrapped his body in his own cloak and lay him in among the exposed roots of a great tree. They covered him with as many stones as they could find in the area. It wasn't a proper burial, but better than leaving him exposed to the weather and the forest scavengers.

It was late afternoon before they finally got back underway. Talisia led the group, with Barrin leading the confused Toby from close behind her. Toby wasn't too sure about the new attachments on his sides and the dragging noise close behind him. He was jumpy at first, but settled down a bit once they reached the road where the way became less bumpy, and the ride of the travois smoothed out. Will walked along beside the sleeping girl, keeping a close eye on her and making sure she didn't roll off of their makeshift stretcher.

They followed the road around the edge of the meadow and the now-ruined cabin. Where Barrin had noticed the road curving off to the northwest across the plains they found a smaller, less-traveled road turning off to their right. There was a small signpost here, pointing the way to Willet Cliff Falls.

"Gareth's home is at the falls," Talisia said as she rounded the turn onto the smaller path. On their new way, the road was obviously much less used. It was smaller, and here and there clumps of grass had sprung up between the wagon wheel ruts, which were also much shallower than in the main road. The path to the falls stayed right by the edge of the woods, and after about a half mile or so of their walking, it quietly reentered the forest.

While they were in the open, they could see the mountains over the trees, off in the distance, but once they were under the canopy of the trees again, they lost even that reference point. As they walked, Barrin picked up his pace a little and came up beside Talisia.

"Tally," he said, tentatively trying a nickname. "Do any of the animals in Saldringal talk?"

She laughed at him and replied, "No. Of course not." Then pausing and gesturing with her thumb behind her she said, "Well, that one probably does." She giggled again. "Why would you ask that? Do they talk in your world?!"

It was his turn to laugh. "No," he said, "but in a lot of our movies they do. Some of our stories are about crossing into other worlds where they can talk. I just wanted to make sure. I mean, it could really be embarrassing. What if I went to pet a dog and it said, 'Hey! Quit it'?"

She giggled at the thought. "What's a movie?" she asked. It was really hard for him to explain, but in the end she got the idea. He wished he could take her to visit his world and show her all the things that he missed from there. He was happy here, and he knew that staying to help these people was the right thing to do, but he missed his home, his Aunt Allie, and the comforts of the modern world. This land was so far behind his own in technology.

"What is it like, being a Woodland Ranger?" he asked her.

She answered, "It's a good job." She took a breath, then added. "Technically we work for the king, but we never see him, and he mostly ignores us. The only reason we say that we work for him is that we are paid through the king's treasury." She continued, "As an apprentice, I stay with my master until my training is complete, but after that, I'll work three moons, and then have one moon off." From context, Barrin assumed that a "moon" was approximately equal to a month. As he thought about it, she kept talking. "Our Head Ranger works from the Ranger Lodge near Stavanger, which is a larger town in the north of Saldringal. He gives us assignments, but mostly, we just wander the country and look for problems with wildlife, predators, and habitat. We plant food plots, thin overpopulated herds, remove problem animals, which are usually predators, and just help keep nature in balance. Newer and growing human population areas are usually where we are needed most."

Some of the words she used sounded a little prepared to Barrin. He suspected that she had memorized parts of her answer, either for her training or because she had answered that question so many times before.

She turned her head to look at him as they continued to walk. "It doesn't pay well, but it gives me the freedom to travel and meet new people." She paused, turned back to the road, then went on, "I could never have just been a housewife. My dad was starting to talk about 'finding an arrangement' for me. I knew he meant a marriage. Arranged marriage is the normal thing here, you know?" she asked.

"No, I didn't," said Barrin.

"Oh, yes," she went on, "most women marry at about fifteen. Unfortunately, marriages are more often about resources than relationships. The family finds the man who offers the most for the girl, and then they agree to the transaction, sometimes making the betrothal agreement when she is as young as ten." She glowered. "They sign a pact and then just wait for her to be old enough to complete the marriage ceremony."

"I couldn't do that," she stated, "so I joined the Rangers. They accept women as often as men." She sighed. "I love the freedom and the travel, but it was more of a solution to a problem than a true calling."

The shadows lengthened, and in the woods, darkness was coming on fast. Ahead of them, they saw the glow of a campfire off the trail in the woods. It was to their right, and about thirty yards or so from the road.

"That could be simple travelers," Talisia said, "but it could be bandits. Wait here while I check it out, and I'll be right back." She ghosted off into the woods, quickly disappearing in the darkened forest.

In a few minutes she was back. "It's only one man," she said. "He looks familiar. I believe that I've met him while traveling before. I think we should risk asking him to share the fire." She continued, "If we camp on our own, he will know we are here, and he may wonder what we are hiding. The friendly approach may create fewer problems than trying to be sneaky or standoffish." She paused then added. "It is very common for travelers to stay together for their mutual protection."

"I'm okay with it if you are," said Barrin.

"Alright," said Will. Both of them were well past ready to stop walking. Their feet were sore, and they were now feeling every bruise from the fight with the wraith.

Will held Toby back on the road as Barrin and Talisa walked towards the camp. They made no effort to go quietly, and so as they approached, the solitary man sitting by the fire heard them and looked their way, waiting for them to arrive.

Once they were in the woods, Talisia whispered to Barrin. "There's a traditional greeting amongst travelers here. Just stay quiet and let me handle this."

While they were still several yards away from his clearing, Talisia cried out, "Hello, friend."

"Come in with my blessing," came the reply.

They continued into the clearing. The man was older than any of their party. He looked to be in his early thirties, with straight, dark hair cut short, and a black close-cropped beard that sort of came to a point under his chin. He was tall and lean and dressed in dark green breeches, with a lighter green tunic. Upon seeing him, Barrin immediately thought of Robin Hood.

The man sat on a fallen log on the other side of a neat fire, upon which sat a pot of what appeared to be stew. A rich brown traveler's cloak was carefully laid across the log next to him. His brown leather belt matched the cloak, and it held a longsword in a scabbard on his left and a knife on his right. There was a small pack leaned against the log, and Barrin noticed a buckler between the pack and the log. A much larger pack lay behind him, and Barrin wondered how he carried it in addition to the smaller one. He thought maybe the man had a pony hidden in the dark woods behind him.

"Welcome to my camp," the stranger began. "I am Gawan of Elmwood Shire. Would the rest of your party like to join us? It's probably lonely out there on the road in the dark."

Talisia looked at Barrin. "You go get them. I'll introduce us and fill him in about our hurt friend." Barrin went to help Will maneuver the pony and travois through the dark forest to the camp, and in just a short while, the pony was secured, the injured girl was comfortably resting on a blanket roll, and they were all situated around the fire sharing the stranger's stew and their own bread. The three companions sat together across the fire from the stranger, not yet completely trusting him.

Gawan told them that he was also traveling toward Willet Cliff Falls, but he was a little vague about his business there. He seemed friendly, and he was full of funny stories and tales of travel and adventure. The friends kept Barrindor's true identity secret. They gave his shortened nickname, Barrin, which wasn't that uncommon, and left it at that.

Gawan had some knowledge of healing, and he dug in his pack and came out with a packet of herbs that he insisted they take in case their friend developed a fever from infection. They thanked him profusely, and Talisia put them in her pack.

Through the evening they had a wonderful time chatting and exchanging stories. Finally their revelry began to fade as they grew tired and ready for bed. There was a short silence as everyone wound down from the fun.

Talisia spoke, "This has been pleasant, Gawan, but how about the truth now. Why are you really here?" Barrin and

Will were suddenly very uneasy. Will quietly stood and slid a hammer part of the way out of his belt, and Barrin casually put his hand on his saber hilt.

"My dear," he said. "I have no idea what you are talking about. I am a simple traveler…"

"You are Rowan, creator and organizer of the resistance movement," she quietly interrupted. It had taken her a while to place him, but now she knew.

"Shhh. Let's not say that name out loud now, Miss," the stranger said. "You looked familiar to me too. I'll drop the act. How did you know me?" he asked.

"I am an apprentice ranger, bound to Gareth of Willet Cliff Falls," she told him. "My master and I met you at a certain gathering about a year ago far north of here. We were in the back room of a certain tavern at midnight on a certain day to discuss some business with a certain group of people who, shall we say, share common interests. I remember you from there."

"Well, I am glad to know that we are truly friends then," he started. "Please continue calling me Gawan. Other names are not safe right now." He paused, then said, "I guess I can trust you enough to share my other surprise." He turned to his left to look over his shoulder toward the trees on the edge of the clearing and said, "Come on out, Grum."

To their absolute shock, the air rippled and suddenly there was a giant sitting behind Gawan. He was round and huge. Even seated on the ground, he was easily taller than Will who was still standing. His hair was light and disheveled, with bits of hair sticking out all over his head like straw from a scarecrow. He wore a simple dark blue shirt and gray pants with large hobnail boots. Over the shirt he wore a furry vest which appeared to be some sort of wooly animal hide, and he was wrapped in an immense silvery cloak.

Will dropped his hammer in disbelief. "Whoa," is all he could stammer out.

"How?" popped out Barrin.

Gawan laughed out loud and said, "Never a dull moment in this life." He laughed again, then went on. "That, my friends, is a giant. His name is Barlgrum, but that's a mouthful, so I call him 'Grum'." He looked very proud of himself. "Grum was banished from his own lands and sent over the mountains to Saldringal. The other giants saw this as an execution, but they didn't know about the dragons disappearing, and so Grum just walked right on by the dragon lair and into the forest on the other side, which is where I found him." He paused. "Now for the funny part." He chuckled again and continued. "My friend Grum, here, was banished for stealing a cloak of intention. It turns out he really did steal it, and he took it with him when he came here!"

The three friends just looked at Gawan.

"What does a cloak of intention do?" asked Will.

"Well, just like its name, you see," Gawan replied. "When you wear it, it makes everyone else see whatever you intend for them to see. Like just now, Grum intended for you not to see him, so you didn't." He smiled again, amused. "To reveal himself, he just had to think that he wanted to be seen again, and 'BAM!' there he was." They jumped a little at his excited sound effect.

"Can I have something to eat now, Gawan?" asked Grum. "I've been starving over here watching you have all you want."

"Yes, yes, my friend, eat up!" he replied, passing the rest of the stew over to Grum. Will bravely walked around the fire and gave the remaining bread to the giant as well.

Going right back to his story, Gawan said, "So there's Grum being walked off to execution for theft, and he is wearing the cloak he stole the whole time. He just intended that they not see a cloak, and guess what? They can't see it!" He laughed again, truly enjoying himself. "The thing is damned useful. Especially when we go into towns for supplies and whatnot. Grum might even have been at the meeting you mentioned. He might have 'intended' to look human-sized."

"So what is really going on?" asked Talisia.

"We are on our way to see your master's wife, Gwyn," he replied. "We have reason to believe that Gareth was taken by the king's men." He hung his head mournfully. "I am going in person to break the news to her."

"We have worse news than that," Talisia sighed. "We know for sure that Gareth is dead. We have seen his body for ourselves." Gawan shook his head defeatedly. She continued, "We are going to ask Gwyn for refuge for a few days."

"It's a terrible time for Saldringal right now," replied Gawan.

They all paused for a moment in solemn silence. The revelry of the storytelling was replaced by the frustration of the unfairness of death and the resolution to fight for justice. Whatever happened to Gareth, it was the king's doing.

"Tell me about the resistance," broke in Barrin.

"Our group is called Eagle Watch. We number about thirty trusted men and women who are spread all around Saldringal. More than anything we keep our eyes and ears open and gather as much information as we can. Then we pool our combined knowledge, information, and rumors to try and see the big picture of what is going on in Saldringal. We are constantly piecing together what the King is plotting, with the intention that if we ever have the force enough to do it, we will rise up and remove his filth from the throne." This last part he said with powerful intensity and at just a barely audible whisper.

"Well," said Talisia, "we have some good news for you."

Chapter Seven:
New Connections, New Plans

They traveled together the next morning, rising with the sun, eating a cold breakfast, and breaking camp with a sense of urgency. Talisia assured them that it was only going to be a few hours of walking today to reach the village at the falls. The young ranger still led the way, with Barrin leading the pony and Will staying beside the travois. Will was very concerned about their patient, and he doted on her, trying to keep her comfortable and secure. Gawan and Grum followed right behind the travois.

Grum was appearing human-sized today, and his cloak appeared to be dark brown. Barrin assumed that he thought the silvery material was too flashy for a common traveler to wear. There had been a moment where Grum had stood next to Will and Barrin in the camp, before he assumed a human look. Barrin thought the giant was about twelve feet tall. He was proportioned like a human, but was very thickly built. He reminded Barrin vaguely of Hagrid from Harry Potter, but taller and without the beard. He was quiet, but once you got past his intimidating size, he seemed good natured and friendly, as well as just a little shy and reserved.

Barrin found it amusing as they walked to watch the lower hanging limbs swing themselves out of the way, far over the human sized Grum below. The cloak did not change the giant's size, just the way others saw him.

The companions walked at a steady pace, not exactly hurrying, but not dragging along either. They paused every hour or so for a few sips of water, and a brief break from walking. As the sun reached mid day, they pulled out dry foods and shared a quick meal where they quietly chatted some more about their mutual quest.

The night before, the three friends had revealed Barrin's true identity and brought Gawan up-to-date on all they had learned from Thallindor before his passing. Gawan regretted the death of the old magician. He had hoped to locate the old man and recruit him to the cause. He was happy to know that the wizard had been working for the same goal all along. They shared Thallindor's theory that a magic-using dragon was behind the imposter posing as king and possibly the disappearance of the dragons as well, and they let him know about their mission to the Barrows to retrieve the Keys to the Kingdom.

After lunch, they continued along their way. Within an hour, they began to hear a rush of running water. The sound grew steadily louder, and within a few minutes, they approached and then crossed a stone bridge over a small river that wound off to the south. On the other side of the bridge, the path curved slightly to their left and when they ventured around the bend, the forest opened up, revealing a signpost exclaiming "Welcome to Willet Cliff Falls."

Beyond the sign, the road continued about a hundred yards across another smaller bridge and into a rounded cul-de-sac where the road ended. Half a dozen cabin-styled houses spread out in a fan shape around the cul-de-sac. Above and behind the cabins was a grassy slope that went up so far and then leveled off in a steppe. The hillside showed signs of having been cleared of trees, probably for cabin-building. Lining the top of the hill was a line of rocks and at the end of the steppe was an outcrop of larger boulders through which water fell, cascading off the right side of the mountain edge and into a wide pool behind a solitary house that sat much farther behind the other six. A creek came from the pool and curved around the circle of houses to join another one that came from the woods to the left of the village to form the river they had crossed earlier. The second bridge crossed only the right hand creek.

Barrin thought it was a beautiful little community. Children were playing around the cabins, and smaller livestock grazed abundantly around the homes. Looking to the forest to the left, he saw more small cabins amongst the trees. He wondered how many families in total lived here.

Talisia led them across the small bridge, through the cul-de-sac, and down a well-worn footpath to the lone cabin by the waterfall's pool. She motioned for them to wait, and she approached the door, where she softly pulled the bell rope hanging beside the solid wooden door.

The cabin was somewhat like the one that Will had lived in with Thallinius. It had a stone foundation and chimney, with thick log walls. The glass in the windows was an old-fashioned kind, full of imperfections and small bubbles. The casement windows were hinged on both outer edges so they could swing into the room like small doors to allow fresh air in. A woman's head popped out the window nearest the door and then quickly retreated back inside. They could hear her exclaiming "Bless my soul, Tally is here!" inside as she quickly undid a couple of audible latches and threw the door open. Immediately she grabbed Talisia and pulled her in for a big hug.

The woman had light brown hair with strands of gray just beginning to show. Her hair was pulled up in a tight bun on the back of her head, but a couple wisps had pulled their way free, and they fell down both sides of her round face. She was short, plump and motherly, and about the same age as Gareth had been, which was just old enough to be any of the three friends' mother. She wore a simple, light-blue house dress with a soft white apron over it. The apron was wet and showed signs of constant use. It was worn from washing, had several small stains and a light rip or two. It was a work outfit, daily wear, and probably not her best clothes.

"Gwyn," Talisia began, breaking off the hug. "How have you been?"

"I'm getting by, my dear," the older woman replied. "Where is my Gareth? Is he out with your friends?"

Talisia didn't say anything at first. She looked solemn and made eye contact with her friend. Gwyn seemed to read her mind.

"What happened to him?" she quietly asked, pulling out a straight chair from her table and dropping heavily into it.

"We believe that he was taken by the king's men and killed," Tally answered, leaving out his transformation into a wraith. "I have seen his body myself. My friends and I buried him as best we could about a day's walk from here." She continued. "We brought you some of his things."

Gwyn was quietly crying now, and tears were dripping down Talisia's face too. They were quiet for a few minutes, mourning Tally's friend and mentor, and Gwyn's partner, lover, and friend. After a bit, Gwyn wiped her eyes and blew her nose into the hem of her apron. She sniffed, and stood up.

"Well," she sniffed, "your friends have waited long enough. The living go on with their lives. Let's invite them in." She stood and stepped back through the door onto the front stoop. "Welcome, to all of you," she called to the waiting travelers. "There is a barn and a privy around the back. You can help yourself to both as needed, then please join us inside, and I will see if I can find us something to eat. You all must be tired."

Grum and Will led the pony around to the barn. They led Toby into an empty stall and gave him a couple of scoops of oats in a feed bag they found there. The greedy pony began happily chomping the delicacy right away.

The barn was just tall enough for the now visibly giant-sized giant to stand inside. He chose to stay there with the animals for the time being. He knew that his size would crowd the cabin, and it would probably be best to warn Gwyn before she saw him anyway. Grum lay down on a pile of hay and closed his eyes, hoping to nap. His huge bulk crossed most of the barn's center aisle, so Will had to carefully step around the giant's feet to walk to the back door of the small house.

When Will entered, he saw that they had laid their feline patient on a small bed in the corner of the room nearest the back door. Gwyn fussed over the "poor dear," as she called her, and changed her bandages out for fresh ones that she dug out of a cupboard. She looked with some consternation at the gauze pads Barrin had used, then, at their direction, she tossed them into the low fire in her fireplace.

Will looked around the small cabin. It was similar in construction to Thallon's cabin. The walls here were also plastered, but in a pale yellow that was warm and happy. There was a kitchen corner of the room dedicated to the storage and preparation of food. There were cabinets built against the wall, and also a large table with six chairs. The patient's bed shared a wall with the large stone fireplace. There were four comfortable chairs in the room circling the hearth, and a single door led off to another room, which Will assumed was a bedroom. The ceiling was vaulted with exposed beams. Gwyn had arranged several clumps of flowers around the large room. Altogether, there was a homey feel to the cabin, and they felt at ease and comfortable here.

Will took over tending to the patient as Gwyn went to the table and began preparing food. When he had finished making her as comfortable as he could, he carried a chair from the table over, and he sat next to her bed.

Gwyn had thrown together a batter of corn meal, wheat flour, egg and milk with a bit of onion, and she was preparing to bake a cornbread in a dutch oven in the fireplace. A bowl of fruit that Barrin thought resembled apples was on her table, and she offered them around. The travelers had only eaten about an hour before. They ended up slicing up a couple of fruits and distributed the pieces to all takers.

Will slipped out the back with an apple for the giant. Grum was snoring away, so he left it on top of an upside-down bucket where the giant would see it. He also slipped a couple of apple slices to Toby, to the pony's great delight.

Inside the cabin, Tally asked, "Gwyn, where are your kids?"

The older woman beamed. "Gregor is twelve now, and he just was apprenticed to be a stonemason. He moved to Stavanger to study with his master." She smiled again, then continued. "My Ginny is up on the hillside. I sent her to gather wild strawberries for a pie just before you arrived. It's been so warm that we have been finding them already."

Gawan had never met Gwyn, but he knew of her through her husband, who had been an active member of Eagle Watch. He didn't know what to expect when he arrived, but in conversation he quickly found that Gareth must have shared everything with his wife. She seemed to know everything that Gareth had known.

He sincerely hoped that Gareth had not also shared his knowledge of the Eagle Watch with the king's men before they changed him into a wraith. If he broke under torture, soldiers could arrive at any time to arrest and execute them all. He sincerely doubted this would happen. He knew that Gareth was a strong man, with a great love for his family, friends, and kingdom. Sharing what he knew would have damaged all that Gareth had cared about, so Gawan felt fairly safe here in the cabin and trusted that Gareth had held his tongue.

Once everyone was settled in, they all expressed their sympathy for Gareth's passing, and then they caught Gwyn up on all they were planning to do.

"We are truly suffering in the small villages," she told them. "We are taxed heavily. Every household is expected to pay five silver coins every three moons." She paused. "Now realize," she said, mostly for Barrin's benefit, "most families only earn about six silver per moon, so saving five out of eighteen is very hard." She looked sad. "If you can't pay, they beat the man of the household, and they have been known to take items of value to cover the debt."

"I've seen that," Will said. "When I was a child, the soldiers beat my dad and then took all of our chickens. I was too young to understand why, but I remember my mom holding me and crying, and I missed the eggs."

"To make matters worse," Gwyn continued, "we are suffering a shortage of actual coins. We have to send out wagon loads of anything we can sell, to have actual coins to give the soldiers. We don't have a bank here, and most local commerce is done by barter. With the high tax rate, we literally don't have the silver to give them, even if we had the wealth."

"They conscript young men into their army as well," Talisia said. "I saw it in the northern villages. I think they try not to do it in the south as much. They don't want word to reach the nobles of the capital, but it is happening."

"Well," Gawan broke in, "we are in a better position now than we have ever been to put a stop to these injustices." Looking around the table, he added, "In the morning, Grum and I will head for Bardhaven, where we will spread the word that the Eagle Watch is finally on the move. All able members should come prepared to fight. We will assemble and march with you on Cantigal."

"We welcome your help," began Barrin, "but we can't assemble a large enough army to win a pitched battle. We will need to work through stealth to achieve our goal." He looked directly at Gawan. "Have your force trickle slowly into the area around Will and Tally's hometown. It is called Wagon's Crossing, and it is just north of Cantigal. Come a few at a time, and camp in small groups, out of sight in the woods around there." He continued, "Watch the tavern for me. When we arrive, you will find me there, and we can create a plan together of the best way to take the throne."

· · ·

Their discussion turned to happier things. The cornbread finished baking, and they devoured it quickly with butter and fresh honey. Gwyn's daughter, Ginny, returned with a large batch of strawberries, which inspired Gwyn to promise a nice pie in the near future. Gwyn and Ginny went to the barn to meet Grum, who had awoken from his nap and eaten his apple. Ginny was thrilled to meet Toby as well. They didn't have a pony here, only goats and chickens, so she was very excited to pet him, brush his mane, and feed him, in hopes that she could get a ride later. The seven of them enjoyed a carefree evening; all thoughts of the king, injustice, and soldiers were pushed aside for the night as the new friends became better friends.

Through the evening, Grum stayed out of sight in the barn, and eventually they all ended up out there, with hanging lanterns lighting the old barn. Gawan told stories as he had the night before. He knew amazing tales, both from around Saldringal and, even though he had never been there personally, some from the outer worlds across the sea as well.

Barrin took a turn at storytelling, and carefully recited the story of Snow White and the Seven Dwarfs. He had watched the Disney movie many times as a child, and he knew it well. They all cheered when the wicked queen was destroyed, and Barrin was proud of his storytelling. When he finished the end of the story, Tally snorted. She thought it was far-fetched that a prince just happened by and just happened to decide to kiss the apparently dead girl.

"Ridiculous," she said, turning up her nose.

Barrin laughed. "Some people thought it was romantic," he said.

"Some people are wrong," she replied. "If you saw a strange dead girl in a glass coffin, would your first thought be, 'Ohh. I want to kiss that corpse"?

"I don't know," Barrin teasingly argued. "Maybe we'll find a dead girl in the woods on the way north and we can find out!"

They paused for a moment, Talisia's eyes flashed for just a second with what he hoped was jealousy, and then they both broke down laughing.

Tally did feel a flash of jealousy thinking about Barrin kissing someone else. What was wrong with her?

• • •

The next morning, Grum, who was looking human again, and Gawan said their goodbyes as they left on their mission to rouse the Eagle Watch. Gwyn baked the pie and set it out to cool, then she called for Ginny to help her, and she went out past the barn near the pool to wash clothes.

With Gareth gone most of the time, Gwyn raised money for the household by taking in washing from all the families in the area. She had the best access to water, and she had built fire pits for heating the wash water, and drying lines for the clothes to hang dry. She had a massive iron cauldron to heat the water in and two big clay pots for agitating and rinsing the clothes. She didn't charge very much, and she had been known to let a needy family or two slide with the payment from time to time. Washing kept her busy, and it was a way she could help the community.

She insisted that the adventurers should give her their clothes for cleaning, but they didn't have a change of clothes with them. They had decided to carry as little as possible and a change of clothes was one luxury they had decided to do without.

Unlike Thallinius' cabin, this one had a bedroom where Gwyn and Gareth slept. The small bed in the main room of the cabin was Ginny's, but she had shared a bed with her mom the night before since the unconscious girl was currently asleep upon it.

Gwyn took the young men into her room and opened a trunk there. She found two pairs of breeches and two tunics for them to wear. They had been Gareth's and they were too large, but they couldn't refuse her hospitality. She sent them off to the waterfall to bathe with the clean clothes and a chunk of what appeared to be homemade soap.

When the boys returned, laughing and holding their too large pants up she sent Tally along the same way. Barrin watched Tally walking away to bathe, and had a brief flash of wanting to go with her, then a burn of embarrassment for the inappropriate thought. He turned away and went with Will to cut lengths of rope to use as belts to tie up their pants.

Tally returned in a short while wearing one of Gwyn's simple frock dresses. It was also too large, and as Barrin watched, it slid down off her shoulder. Her damp hair, which was usually up, hung down to her shoulders, her natural curls re-energized and bouncy after cleaning.

"Wow. She's beautiful," Barrin thought to himself. Her eyes met his, and she smiled. This time he fought the embarrassment off and smiled back. Her eyes lit up.

Gwyn and Ginny took a break from washing and joined them as they ate a light lunch of bread with vegetables, followed by slices of strawberry pie with fresh cream. Barrin was happy, actually happier than he could ever remember. This beautiful, quiet village was somewhere he could see himself living forever, especially with good friends.

After lunch, Gwyn said that she and Ginny had to get back to work.

"I think I'll take a walk and look around some," Tally said.

"I'll watch the house, and our patient," offered Will.

"Can I join you, Tally?" Barrin asked.

"Sure," she replied, flashing a smile.

Together the two set out into the woods north of the town. There was a trail that roughly followed the smaller creek that they had noticed earlier. Together they followed the trail past several cabins and a clearing with a small garden, and eventually their path came to a second waterfall. It was smaller in width than the first, but the water fell a greater distance. There was a much smaller pool at the foot of the falls, and no one had built a house near here.

They paused to appreciate its beauty, and then climbed the hill to the top of the falls, to find that this creek joined the larger flow at the top, which continued down to form the waterfall near Gwyn's house. They followed the stream downhill toward Gwyn's and in a short while they reached the rocks at the top of the cleared hillside that overlooked the small village. From the hill they could look down over the valley below and out over the woods. They weren't quite high enough to see all the way out to the plains, but it was still an impressive view that was worth savoring.

Tally sat on a boulder and hung her legs over the side to admire the sight. Barrin walked over and joined her. As they sat together, he built up his courage, and gently took her hand in his.

"What are you doing?!" she snapped, snatching her hand away. She glared at him, and pulled farther away from where he sat. "Why would you grab me like that?"

"Oh, I was just…" Barrin began, embarrassed, and a little angry, but what she had said suddenly hit him, and he realized that it was a cultural difference. He said, "In my world, holding hands is a symbol. It means that you really like someone, and you want to spend more time with them."

Tally relaxed and went back to how she was sitting. She watched the smoke rise from the cabins below. Cautiously, she reached over and took his hand in hers.

• • •

Barrin and Tally spent the entire afternoon together, casually chatting and learning more about each other. For two people who grew up in two different worlds, they found that they got along very well and enjoyed each other's company. By now, Barrin was head over heels for her, and he hoped she felt the same way.

As they shared all they could about their pasts, she was amazed to learn that he knew how to use the saber he carried around. She asked why he hadn't used it on the wraith,

"I don't know," he replied, hanging his head. "It just happened so fast, and I was holding the staff." He was a little embarrassed and looked down the hill to the cabin. It was then he noticed that Will was outside frantically waving to them, and motioning for them to join him.

Barrin showed Tally, and the two jumped up and quickly descended the hill and hurried towards the cabin.

"She's waking up!" Will called, and then he ducked back inside the cabin.

• • •

Barrin and Tally excitedly burst through the cabin door and approached the bed. They saw that their patient was stirring around. Will sat right next to the bed, in what had been his normal spot for the last day. He had bathed the patient's wounds and changed the dressings and generally taken care of her since they had arrived at Gwyn's home. Even though she slept soundly, he had quietly talked to her and told her all sorts of stories and all about himself and his companions.

Gwyn was preparing a soft gruel of some sort by the fire. The two joined Will at the bedside, but stayed a step behind him to be less intimidating for the waking patient.

Suddenly, the girl's eyes blinked, revealing catlike eyes of a striking electric blue. She began to thrash her arms a little, then her eyes were fully open and aware, and she mewled something in another language. Worried about communicating, the three friends shared a nervous glance then turned back to her. Will gave a shrug to show they did not understand.

She sat up, struggling to do so with her injured shoulder. Will helped her and got her comfortably propped up against a stack of pillows.

She smiled at him and said, "Where am I? Who are you?" in Saldrani.

WIth a sigh of relief, Will began to fill her in on what she had missed. "I am Will, apprentice blacksmith," he said, pointing to himself. Then he gestured to each of the others as he added, "This is Talisia, who is an apprentice ranger, and Barrin, who is our friend, and we are in the home of Gwyn, the washerwoman, who is the wife of Talisia's master in the rangers. Her daughter, Ginny, is around somewhere as well. We have rescued you from the wraith that pursued you, but you were injured, so we brought you here to recover. Please tell us who you are." In his excitement, all of this flowed out of Will as one long, rapid stream of information. To her credit, the girl seemed to catch it all.

"I am Alexia, Envoy of Queen Adaliya of Neferkala, across the sea," she began. "I was sent by her majesty, who is my aunt, to resolve a mysterious happening here."

"Why was the wraith chasing you?" asked Will.

"Right after I landed in the port, I realized I was being followed," she continued. "I began asking questions around Bardhaven, but I was very careful since I knew a couple of agents were following me. I didn't know they were those creatures, 'wraiths' you called them?" She paused, then continued. "They tried to get into my room the first night there, but the inn had strong doors, and I had used both a chair to block the door handle and a sealing spell I know, as well." She paused for a breath. "I found out very little in Bardhaven, so I decided to travel to Cantigal, but shortly after leaving town, I was attacked by two of the creatures, the wraiths. I damaged one greatly. It should have died, but it didn't! It just kept attacking. I knew that if I couldn't kill them, then running was my only chance, so I abandoned all my belongings and fled."

Again she paused and took a deep breath. Barrin wondered if her pausing was because she was still recovering from her injury and the potion, or maybe she wasn't certain how much to tell them, and was trying to buy some time.

"Go on," Will said, caught up in her story.

"The one I hurt was slow," she continued. "It couldn't keep up, and I eventually lost it, but the other was... persistent. It never stopped. I couldn't rest. I had to keep moving. I ran for a couple of days before I saw the cabin and thought maybe I could barricade the door like I did in the inn and finally rest, or maybe that thing would miss me and pass right by." She shook her head. "I never expected the fire. I guess I'm only alive because of you."

"Please tell us about your mission," Barrin said.

Alexia looked unsure. She wasn't ready to trust them yet.

"Am I your prisoner?" she tentatively asked.

"No, of course not," Talisia retorted. "We helped you," she added, angrily. "And at great personal risk I might add. We delayed our own mission for you, and you insult us in return!"

"It's ok, Tally," Barrin said. "We have kind of known her for several days. She has known us for five minutes." He laughed. "She will trust us in time."

Alexia hung her head. "I'm sorry," she said. "I greatly appreciate what you have done for me, but I am obligated to my queen to keep private matters private." She went on, "If there comes a point that I can tell you, then I will. I promise."

"My dears," broke in Gwyn, "this poor girl has not eaten for several days. We need to give her some food!"

"Thank you!" Alexia said. "I am famished." She looked at the table. "I think if you help me up, I can sit at the table to eat."

Will and Tally helped her up, and soon she was using her uninjured arm to eat a big bowl of Gwyn's corn mash. It was early evening, so the others ate with her. What Barrin thought was gruel was ground corn with lots of butter and cheese melted in, and cut up chunks of bacon stirred through. Barrin thought it was what Southerners in his country called "grits." He had grown up in the northern United States, and he had never had grits, but he had heard them referenced several times. He thought these were good and wondered if they were the same as in his world. Gwyn refilled Alexia's bowl with a smile as soon as the Neferkali girl emptied it. The girl slowed down, but continued to eat sparingly as the others finished their meal and turned to conversation.

"Alexia," Barrin began, "we have a mission too." Looking at Will and Tally, he continued, "I am Barrindor, the true heir to the throne of Saldringal." Alexia froze with her spoon halfway to her mouth and looked at him. "William here is truly an apprentice blacksmith, but he is also descended from my family's most loyal guardsmen." He paused and looked right into her eyes. "We are on a mission to obtain what we hope to be magic swords from my family crypt, so that we can attempt to overthrow the pretender who is currently ruling Saldringal and end his reign." He took a deep breath. "Now. I have shared with you our mission; one which is treasonous and punishable by death. We would like to invite you to join us in this mission if you like, and if not, we hope you will keep our secret. We also hope that you will trust us with your secret." He smiled. "The more we know, the less likely we are to be surprised later."

"You are reckless," Tally said.

"I trust easily," Barrin replied. " And I see the best in people."

Alexia lowered her spoon back to her bowl. She was lost in thought for a moment, then she said, "You have trusted me, so I will trust you." She sighed. "I am trying to prevent a war."

"Go on," Barrin said, intrigued.

Alexia blinked her bright blue cat eyes, and looked at them one at a time. This was the first time that Barrin had really looked at her face. Seen head on, her eyes were gorgeous. The blue was shimmery and bright, and her eyes themselves were ringed in black with long, thick luxurious lashes that made them pop from her white face. Barrin felt a rush of surprise. No wonder Will thought she was pretty.

"What I tell you is a great secret," she said. "If the king were to discover my mission, I fear that I would at least be imprisoned, and probably put to death. Please do not repeat this to anyone, as I promise not to repeat your secret either."

They all promised to keep her secret, too; then, she continued, "About five months ago, our queen sent an ambassador from Neferkala to Saldringal to negotiate a trade with your king." She interrupted herself. "You should know that our country is rich in gems. We have diamonds mostly, some beryls too, but we have no precious metals to speak of. Your country, of course, has the Xantos Lode, and copper mines as well."

Barrin looked searchingly at Tally, so she broke in, "Xantos Lode is a massive gold mine due east of Cantigal."

Alexia continued, "Our ambassador was supposed to arrange a trade with your realm; diamonds for gold. We needed to replace and expand our coinage, and we didn't have the gold to make the coins. The ambassador returned victorious, with news that your king had agreed to an impressive trade. All of us in the Diplomatic Corps were so excited, because we felt that we had achieved the better end of the deal. As an envoy, I am an assistant to the ambassador, so I was there. Oh! How he gloated and paraded around our offices reveling in his 'amazing' deal! He commissioned one of Her Majesty's ships and requested a platoon of soldiers to guard the trade package. The package contained four hundred large diamonds of high cut and clarity, and one hundred near-flawless beryls of assorted colors. All the stones were of good size; nothing tiny. We expected two hundred dayweights of gold in return, which was almost twice what we had hoped for."

Tally broke in for Barrin, "A dayweight is roughly what one man could mine in one day's work," she explained.

Alexia sighed. "The best part of the package was a special diamond called 'The Eye'. It is a blue tinted diamond roughly the size of an eye. It is flawless, perfectly clear, and beautifully cut. It's truly a one-of-a-kind gem. It has passed through several generations of our nobility. Our queen inherited it from her mother, and she included it in the package as a gesture of goodwill to your people."

"So, what happened?" Will interjected.

"The entire shipment disappeared," Alexia said. "All of it." She paused. "The ship, thirty of our finest warriors, the Ambassador, and all the gems. Just, gone."

"Wow," Tally sighed.

"Are you sure they made it across the sea?" Barrin asked.

"That's the only reason that I am here," she continued. "When they never returned with the gold, the queen's military advisors recommended that she prepare an invasion force. They were sure that we had been betrayed. Our nobles had hand-selected the delivery team and knew that their men had no fealty to the ambassador. The lieutenant in charge of the platoon was ordered not to take orders from the ambassador, but to simply provide escort and guard for him. They did not know each other and were unlikely to work together. Our leaders have absolute trust in their men, and they are sure there was no foul play from our end."

"Sooo," Barrin asked, "they sent you to make sure that the shipment made it here, and that your country was truly betrayed?"

"Yes," she answered. "The queen was not convinced that the ship had arrived. She asked me to come here and find proof of what had happened. If there was a betrayal, I should also find, if possible, the current location of the stones. You see, she didn't want to start a war over a misunderstanding."

"So what did you find in Bardhaven?" Tally asked.

"Well, there is no manifest showing that the ship arrived in port," she answered. "However, the king himself was in town right around the time that our package should have arrived. He brought the largest honor guard that he had ever used, and the townspeople were still talking about how many 'wraiths' had been around." She turned to Will. "I wasn't sure what a wraith was until you told me. Apparently, they work for the king." She paused, then turning to speak to the entire group, she ended with, "I believe that the King went to Bardhaven to personally oversee the delivery of the stolen gems. I have no idea where our ship, soldiers and ambassador went, but I suspect they are at the bottom of the sea. I was headed to Cantigal to see if I could confirm that the king has the gems."

They all were quiet for a moment as her revelation sunk in. Barrin spoke first. "We could use your help, and I promise that we will help you in return." He went on. "Help us find what we need to overthrow Arkendor, and when we get to Cantigal, we will help you search Castle Brackhaven for the gems. Whether you help or not, I swear that when I am king, the gems will be returned to you."

Alexia smiled, "Okay," she said. "I'm in."

Chapter Eight:
Wanted and Not Wanted

The next morning, with many thanks and hugs for Gwyn and Ginny, the four set out northwest for the Barrows. It would be several days' travel to reach Rathsmar, especially because they chose to stick to traveling through the woods and avoiding the open plains.

They had replenished their provisions in the village before they left. They now carried a few pounds of dried jerked meat and a few crusty loaves of bread, and they had refilled the large water skin on the pony, as well as their own individual ones.

Gwyn had cleaned Alexia's cloak as best she could and had removed most of the blood stains. She had also darned the material to close the arrow hole in the back. It was still stained, but it was not so obviously stained with blood now. They had also managed to purchase a new tunic for her from a local seamstress to replace the ruined one she had been wearing.

Alexia's shoulder was healing very well. Barrin thought that her race must heal faster than humans do. Still, it was stiff and sore, and so Gwyn provided fabric for a sling to help her be able to travel with less pain.

When they were leaving, Talisia gave Gwyn the small bag of coins that Thallinius had given her. The older woman tried to turn it down, but the friends insisted. She had been a great help to them, and with the loss of her husband, they knew she would need it. She knew it, too, and so she eventually relented and kept the coins.

They made great progress and camped for the night with no problems. As they were making camp, Barrin realized that he had left his staff at Gwyn's house. It was behind the door, and he had neglected to pick it up. He told the others, who sympathized with him, but then Tally pointed out that he was more skilled with the saber anyway, so it wasn't a great loss.

The next day, their travel took them to the edge of the forest, where they could see out into the plains. In the distance, they noticed patrols of soldiers that seemed to be keeping guard.

"I think they are looking for us," Tally said. "We'll have to be more careful." They retreated deeper into the forest and moved along north. Talisia encouraged the others to follow her path and mimic the way she moved through the forest. Over time, with practice, they began to move more quietly. Alexia had a natural grace, and she picked it up very quickly. Barrin's training with footwork for fencing also helped him be a fast study, but Will really had to work at it. By afternoon, Tally was praising all of their progress. Of course, Toby the pony wasn't having any of it. He just trudged along, but Will, who held his lead, was careful to guide him through the most open paths and away from dead limbs and other debris that would make a lot of noise.

As shadows lengthened and dusk approached, Tally froze and held up her hand in a signal to stop. They all stopped in place.

"There are soldiers ahead," she whispered. "Not many. Don't move. I'll be right back." Like a ghost she moved into a shadow, and slipped stealthily forward while they waited. In a few minutes, she was back.

"There are six of them," she said. "They are spread out in a rough line. We can't go around, so we have to go through. None of them had bows, so we have an advantage even though they outnumber us." Becoming more solemn, she added. "None of them can get away. If they sound the alarm, we will be overrun." She looked at Alexia. "You stay here with Toby. I'll have Will and Barrin draw their attention, and I'll pick them off with my bow."

"No," Alexia replied, slipping off her sling and sweeping her cloak behind her shoulders. "I can fight."

"You don't have a weapon," Will pointed out.

"Don't I?" Alexia smiled. Raising her uninjured hand, she spread her fingers and claws showed at each finger tip. She gave a slight shake, and fiery blue magic extensions crackled to life extending her claws to about eight inches.

"Whoa," Barrin said. He thought even Wolverine would be jealous.

"Okay, then," Talisia quipped. "You get to fight." Looking at her friends, she said, "These are trained soldiers. They are dangerous. Don't take chances you don't have to take. I'm quick with my bow, and I'll do my best to end it quickly." She paused. "The king's men won't have mercy. They will kill you if they can. Don't give them a chance."

While Talisia was talking, Alexia withdrew her magic claws. When she finished her directions, Tally slipped ahead to get in place, then Alexia, Will and Barrin left Toby tied to a tree, and continued as quietly as they could on their way.

The soldiers were in three groups of two. They were spread out, but they were within eyesight of each other. There was a bit of a clearing where the central two were standing. Barrin drew his saber, and Will his hammers. Alexia exposed her own claws, but did not bring out the magic ones yet.

With a cry, Barrin and Will charged the central soldiers. Before they could even reach them, the outer two groups reacted and began to run to join the central squad. The central soldiers took up combat stances. Barrin heard the thrum of Tally's bow string and the chest of one of the soldiers coming from his left exploded in a shower of sparks. Seconds later, the other left-hand soldier fell with another blast of electricity.

Barrin crossed swords with the soldier in front of him. Will crashed into his man with a whirlwind of flying hammers. One of the hammers connected with the soldier's shield, shattering the wooden buckler. The soldier countered with a swing of his sword that nearly landed, Will dodging to the side just in time. They faced each other and circled looking for an opening.

In the meantime, Barrin's soldier was down. Barrin thought his man was trained but sloppy, not a true swordsman. He made quick work of the soldier and turned to the right to face the last two men. He found he was not needed. One of them was encased in ice, the other was torn to ribbons with Alexia standing over him. He turned back to help Will just in time to see Tally's next arrow blast the soldier's chest apart.

The four friends looked at each other and assembled in the small clearing.

"Is everyone okay? Anyone hurt? All good?" they all seemed to ask and answer at once. It turned out that they all were unharmed. Barrin thought that Will had had the closest call, but he didn't say so. He silently vowed to himself to begin teaching Will how to spar every time they had a chance.

Tally pointed at the soldier encased in ice and said, "Neat trick, that." She turned to Alexia. "Any other special surprises we should know about?"

"You are probably guessing by now that I am somewhat of a sorceress," she answered. "I know some basic spells, like making fire, and I can do light healing. Also, I know a few defensive spells like the ice. The amulet on my cloak is what allows me to lengthen my claws. It was a gift from my mother. Everyone in my family has one like it."

"So is the iceman alive?" Will asked.

"Yes. Probably," Alexia replied. "I don't really know. I've only used that spell in practice before, not on a real person." She sighed, and seemed to sag a little. "That spell took a lot out of me. I'm really tired now."

The adrenaline rush of battle was wearing off, and they were starting to become awkward with the new reality of combat.

"We can't leave him here alive," Tally said. She quickly drew her bow and blasted an arrow into the frozen man. Then she walked off by herself in the direction of Toby. Will sat down and leaned against a tree and sighed.

Barrin slowly followed after Tally to where the pony waited. When he reached the place where Toby was tied, Tally was on her knees with her head in her hands. Quiet sobs shook her. Somewhat embarrassed, he walked up to her. She stood and turned to face him. Seeing it was Barrin she said, "Hold me," and fell into his arms. He wrapped his arms around her and let her cry it out. He kissed the top of her head and held her tight.

When she was done, Tally looked up at him and gave him a light kiss on the lips. Her eyes grew wide and she said, "Ohh. I'm so sorry. I presumed."

"No. It's okay," Barrin interrupted. Smiling, he added, "I liked it."

"You probably think I am a silly, weak female for crying over our enemies," she said, "but I've never killed anyone before, and I was so scared for the three of you fighting hand to hand." She added, "Not that you needed it. You were all wonderful."

"I felt the same way after we fought the wraith," he replied. "We tried not to let you know, but both of us felt pretty bad after." He paused, then added, "It gets better." Then he added, "We did what we had to do, you know?"

She hugged him again. "Thank you," she said. They made eye contact, and then they kissed again. This time they were both ready, and they kissed with passion and emotion.

When their kiss ended, Tally smiled and Barrin hugged her to him again for a minute. They untied Toby and led him back to the others and they all continued on. By now it was mostly dark, but they were afraid to stop so close to where the patrol had been. They traveled until it was too dark to see at all, and then huddled the blankets close together around one tree and slept with no fire and no lights of any kind.

The next morning they awoke early and started walking before breakfast, hoping to put more distance between them and the battle site. The day was uneventful, and they saw no more soldiers. They stopped in the late afternoon within hearing of a winding brook, calling it a day a little early since they had not slept well the night before. Tally scouted the area and decided that a small fire would be okay.

They collected a small pile of kindling and some larger pieces from around the camp, and Alexia amazed them by murmuring an incantation and setting it ablaze. It was a small fire, about the size of a hat. It was for warmth and security, not for cooking anyway. Their jerky and bread didn't need cooking.

Alexia stretched out near Will on one side of the fire, and Barrin and Tally snuggled together on the other. Barrin put his arm around her and she leaned against him.

"Tomorrow we should reach Stavanger," Tally said. "We can go into town and get a good meal at a tavern if you like, but we shouldn't linger. Seeing so many soldiers yesterday makes me think that maybe the king knows about us."

"Do you think that was really just for us?" Barrin asked.

"Maybe so," Tally said. "If I'm right, they greatly under-estimated us. We can't count on that happening again." She continued, "The soldiers usually just collect taxes. They don't normally patrol like we have been seeing."

"I've been wondering," Will said. "Alexia, you were amazing in our battle. Why didn't you just freeze that wraith that was chasing you so you could get away?"

"I tried," she replied. "Understand that magic drains your energy." She paused for emphasis. "I mean, really saps your energy. I can only do one big spell, like the ice spell, per day, and I have to always be aware of the danger of overusing my power. I could injure myself or even die if I use too big a spell." She continued, "Little spells aren't too bad, like a spark of fire, or healing a scratch, but big spells are exhausting." She sighed. "So I waited on the wraith to catch up. I summoned all my strength, and threw a blast of ice at the wraith."

"And?" Will said.

"Nothing," she replied. "It kind of absorbed it. If any-thing, the magic energized it. It's why I was so exhausted that I tried to hide in the cabin in the first place." She thought for a moment and added. "I guess I didn't use a complex enough spell, but actually, I'm afraid to use anything stronger. I've never cast a really strong spell before. I could, in a desperate emergency, but I'm not really sure what would happen."

"Wow," Barrin said, "I wonder what makes the wraiths so powerful." Hopping to his feet, he dug the gem that he had taken from the wraith out of his bag. "Could it be this?" he asked her. "Have you seen one of these before?".

Alexia took the gem. As it touched her hand, she react-ed. "This thing is surging with power." She wondered at it and added, "I feel energized just holding it. I wonder where it came from."

She closed her eyes and slipped into a sort of meditative trance. A minute went by. They were just starting to worry when she startled and awoke.

"It's a dragon heartstone," she said. "We must return it to the Falkans in Falkshire Hamlet at the foot of Mount Dragon." She went on. "It spoke to me. The essence of a dragon still lives in that stone!"

"That's where the dragons went!" Barrin said. "They are trapped in their stones, and their essence is being used to create the wraiths." He took a breath. "They aren't 'lizard men', they're 'dragon men!'"

"So what are we going to do now?" Tally asked. "We can't abandon our task to run off on this other."

"Just suppose," Barrin said, "that Thallinius is correct, and there is a dragon behind the king's power." He paused. "Would it follow then, that somehow that dragon betrayed and captured the others in these stones?" He thought for a moment, and then continued. "At first I thought we may want to awaken this dragon to help us fight, but dragons are huge and obvious, and even if it helped us, it might be fighting a foe that already beat it once." He thought again for a minute. "I think we should keep the stone safe, and return it after we finish our mission. Maybe we even leave it with someone in case we lose, so it can still go back."

"What kind of talk is that?!" Tally scolded him. "I don't plan to lose, and you shouldn't either."

"I agree with Barrin," Will said. "Defeat the king first."

"I should probably share a little more with you," Alexia meekly admitted, appearing a bit embarrassed. "We have a bit of a time constraint. You see, our nobles were incensed that the gems were stolen and that our people were theoretically killed or imprisoned." She paused. "So they started planning an invasion force."

"Yes. We know," Tally said.

"What you don't know is that I had three weeks to report back, or by default the invasion would begin."

Everyone was silent as the news sunk in.

"What are you talking about when you say 'invasion'?" Barrin asked.

Alexia deadpanned her expression. "Probably four hundred troops, and another two hundred cavalry. Maybe some siege engines," she replied.

"And how long do we have till they arrive?" Tally whispered.

"It took me two days to sail to Bardhaven. I was there for two more. I was chased for two, then unconscious for three. Now it's been three more. That's twelve total. Nine days until they expect me back. It will probably take two more to mobilize and an additional two to sail here. So we may have two weeks if we are lucky."

They were all quiet.

"Is there anything you can do to communicate that we need more time?" Will asked.

"Nothing guaranteed, and even if I ask, they may say 'no'."

"Well, anything you can try is better than nothing," Tally snapped. "What is with you guys being so negative?" she scolded. "What can you try?"

Alexia pulled her cloak away from her left side and gingerly reached with her injured arm for an interior pocket. She pulled out a dark, polished stone. It looked to Barrin like lodestone, or hematite, but it was about two inches square and about a half inch thick with smooth rounded edges. It was stone, but looked like silvery, gray metal.

"It's a scrying stone," Alexia said. "Some can be used to reveal secrets, see the past, or spy on enemies, but this one is for communication. If Her Majesty is near her matching stone, I can speak with her." She rubbed her hand over the face of the stone and murmured an incantation. The stone seemed to light up as it connected magically with its mate in Neferkala. Will saw movement on the face of the stone and almost immediately Alexia bowed her head and said, "Your Majesty."

"Alexia, my dear girl," said the voice from the stone. Barrin noticed that they were speaking Saldrani. He appreciated Alexia keeping them in the loop of what was going on. "What can I do for you?" continued the voice.

Alexia carefully explained about her belief that the treasure was indeed stolen. She went on to tell about the wraiths that identified and tracked her upon her arrival and her new friends' rescuing her when she was injured. She then looked to Barrin for permission and fully explained their mission and their hopes to overthrow the king and reclaim the throne for Barrin, as well as the treasure for Neferkala. She ended her message with a plea for more time.

When Alexia was done, the queen paused. She spoke the Neferkali language and had a quick conversation with Alexia alone. They mewled, growled, and rumbled guttural cat sounds back and forth for several minutes, and then the queen returned to Saldrant speech.

"Very well," she stated flatly. "I will tell the nobles that we will not sail until you return or we are certain of your death. They may resist, but I believe that I can convince them." She went on, "Your friends are here with you now, aren't they?"

"Yes, ma'am," Alexia replied.

"Please show me the young king," the queen said. Alexia turned the stone to face Barrin.

"Good luck to you all, and especially to you, Barrindor," the queen said. "Our history speaks of a great friendship with Saldringal and with your father. I hope we can rekindle our friendship very soon." After this, the stone blinked out and was just a stone again.

"Wow. That went really well." said Alexia.

The others all expressed relief and happiness with the results.

"Good thing we tried," Tally rubbed in.

Alexia gave her a dirty look.

They were quiet for a few minutes, then Alexia said, "Barrin, you don't know it, but I can sympathize with your situation pretty well." She continued. "You see, I should be in line to be queen of Neferkala."

The others expressed surprise and then looked at her and waited.

"My mother was the heir," she explained. "In our country, the position usually passes from the mother to her first-born daughter. We don't ever have a king, unless a queen only has male offspring, and that hasn't happened in centuries." She paused for a breath. "So my mother was the first born. Our queen is her younger sister."

"What happened to make your mum be skipped over?" Tally asked.

"I happened," Alexia murmured. "My mother fell in love with a human man. A man from Saldringal actually." She smiled. "She gave up her chance at the throne to marry my father. She loved him very much, and they had a wonderful time together. She says giving away the throne was worth it."

"What happened to him?" Tally quietly asked.

"He died of a fever," Alexia said. "It was after my aunt was already queen. A plague passed through about five years ago. I was only thirteen. It hit him worse than any of our race. He started coughing, and he just got worse and worse. The coughs led to fever. He was so hot to the touch, and then he was just gone." A tear trickled down her cheek. "So I decided that it was my new purpose in life to be an ambassador to my father's world. I spent the last five years training for that role. Sadly, this is my first time coming to Saldringal. I wish it were on happier terms."

Tally got up and moved around the fire. She plopped down next to Alexia and hugged her tight.

"Thanks for sharing that with us," Tally said. "I'm sure it is hard to talk about."

"Yeah, Lexie, thanks for telling us," Barrin said.

"Thanks, Lexie," Will added, and he reached out and rubbed her shoulder. Both girls sniffled a bit as they continued to hug. Then they all retreated to their own blankets and faded off to sleep.

Will's last thoughts before sleep were how beautiful Alexia was and how he hoped she would one day fall in love with a human too.

Alexia's thoughts as she drifted off were of Will. She loved how handsome and strong he was. In a small way, he reminded her of her father. She understood now how her mother had felt around a handsome human man, and she smiled.

•••

The next morning, it was a bit windier, and there was a light drizzle of rain. They all pulled their cloak hoods up to shield their faces and they trudged along through the woods. The rain made everything damp, uncomfortable, and miserable. Tempers were a little short through the morning as they walked. They were almost silent through lunch; the bonhomie of the previous evening was a distant memory now. Shortly after lunch, Tally dropped back until she was walking next to Barrin.

"We will be approaching Stavanger soon," she said. "I've been thinking, and we might need to consider leaving Toby there."

"Why?" Barrin asked.

"A few things really," she started. "He slows us down. He isn't quiet. We have to arrange to feed him, and I don't think we really need to carry that much. He mostly carries food and extra water, and most of the time we are camping without fire or cooking, so we aren't using that much water anyway. Please think about it." She took bigger strides back to the point position.

Barrin felt bad about possibly losing the pony. He was a sweet old thing, and he suspected Will would be very resistant to the idea, since he had grown up with Toby. Barrin wondered if they could pay boarding for the pony and collect him back later.

In about an hour, they stopped for a rest. They were a dreary and bedraggled lot as they sat under the trees, sipping water and resting their legs.

"Could we possibly stay in an inn tonight?" Barrin asked. "I mean, Stavanger is a big town, right? Couldn't we just blend in?"

"Maybe," Tally said. "Is it worth the risk?"

They all looked at each other. Water dripping off their noses, running down cheeks, and soaking through clothes.

"Yes," Barrin said.

"I think so, too," said Will.

"Tempting," said Alexia. "Do you think I could blend in enough? I don't exactly look like you."

"If you all want to try, I'll go along," Tally said. "Lexie, you are going to have to keep your hood up and hope."

The rain slacked off to a mist in the late afternoon, and the sky began to clear. They arrived in Stavanger just as the sun was setting, its rays lighting up the sky as if it were on fire. The remaining clouds picked up various colors, and the dazzling sunset lit up the town with a deep orange glow.

Pulling their hoods up and their cloaks tight about them, they emerged out of the woods onto the road into Stavanger and trudged downhill into the valley hamlet. As they descended into the deep valley, Barrin noticed a large, lighted building high up on the side of the mountain behind the town, and he asked Talisia what it was.

"That's the Ranger Guild Hall," she replied. "We need to avoid the rangers, though. If they notice me, and they've heard about Gareth's passing, I'll be given orders to go with someone else to complete my training."

The town was the largest that Barrin had seen in Saldringal. There was a main street that, like Willet Cliff Falls, ended in a circular central town square. What appeared to be a town hall building, and possibly a jail, stood in the middle of a ring of shops that circled the common area. The town hall was strategically placed so that travelers on the road saw it first as they approached. It was plastered and whitewashed, with a wooden shingled roof and a small bell tower at the top.

There were multiple retail shops offering various wares, a blacksmith shop, two taverns, and a third building that appeared to be a tavern, but with a sign advertising it was an inn. A larger building advertised rooms for rent, but this appeared to be more of a boarding house for longer-term guests. More commercial buildings and many single family homes ringed the town, and various workhouses and assorted workshops were intermingled with the homes. The road was dirt out of town where they were, but when they reached the town limits, as marked by a sign, it changed to flat paving stones. The entire town center was paved, as well as several smaller streets and alleys offshooting from the central circle.

The mountainside surrounding the town had been cut into steppes, and the travelers saw various crops growing at multiple levels, including a vineyard, assorted grains, and several varieties of fruit trees. The Ranger Guild Hall was the highest up, sitting about halfway up the mountain.

Trying to remain unnoticed, the four approached the inn. A wooden sign hung from the front that said, "The Purple Pony: Inn and Tavern." Will passed the blanket rolls off to Barrin, Tally, and Lexie, then he led Toby around a walkway to the rear of the inn where he assumed he would find a stable. He was in luck, and he unsaddled the pony, turned him out into a small stall and fed him from the supplies there. He hung the saddle and their large water bag in the stable and, unsure of the location of a rear door, he brought the bag of food with him back around to the front.

The others had already entered the inn and were speaking to the proprietor at a tall desk to the left of the entrance. The right side of the room was a seating area with tables and chairs for meals. Several of the tables were occupied, and there was a bustle of noise from the various patrons eating and drinking from the crockery bowls and pewter tankards.

The back wall of the downstairs room was a long bar with rows of bottles and kegs on a counter behind it. A door at the far end of the bar led to what had to be a cooking area. Beside the high desk area where his friends stood were steps leading upstairs to the sleeping rooms.

As Will approached, the proprietor was saying, "The room will cost you one silver for the night. The meal tonight and breakfast are one copper each. Stable and oats for the pony is another copper, so two silvers in total. You pay up front." He smiled, "You can pile your belongings there beside the stairs and eat first. The kitchen will close soon and you don't want to miss your meal…"

The proprietor went on talking about breakfast procedures, but Will's attention was drawn to a poster hanging on the wall behind the Innkeeper. It said, "Wanted: Will Ironsmith of Wagon's Crossing, and all companions of the same. For questioning, by order of the king. Reward 10 Silver." Underneath the words was a rough sketch that wasn't entirely accurate, but did show some resemblance to him.

Will's eyes grew wide and his heart raced. He felt an urge to turn and run, but Barrin was handing over the silvers, and his friends were on their way to sit and eat. Will joined them, but he felt a little sick to his stomach and didn't know if he could keep anything down.

They sat and a buxom server woman brought them each a plate of stew and a tankard of mead. She seemed to be the proprietor's wife, though she was easily ten years younger than him. She smiled at the travelers as she served them, and tutted at their being so wet and miserable. Alexia still had her hood fully up, and she pretended to be searching her pocket for a lost item so she could turn her face away until the server left the table.

The food was good, even though Barrin was unsure of exactly what kind of meat was being served. It was filling, and the still-wet travelers appreciated the warmth of the food as well as the excellent flavor.

After an initial period of serious eating, they slowed and Will whispered, "Did you see the poster by the desk?"

"No," they all replied.

"I have a price on my head," he whispered. "The king wants me for questioning!" He was careful to keep his voice very low so that the others in the tavern would not over-hear.

"Wait till we are upstairs," Talisia whispered back.

Barrin had never really drunk alcohol before. His Aunt Allie had offered him a taste of wine once, but he hadn't cared for it. He sipped the mead carefully and found that it was palatable. It wasn't very strong, and he could drink it. He remembered hearing somewhere that in the past in his world, people had drunk alcohol like this when they couldn't trust the water. He assumed that this was why they were serving mead. What he really wanted was a Coke. He was desperately missing sodas, and candy bars, and pizza... he was getting tired of jerky and cheese.

As soon as they were done, the four gathered their gear and ascended the stairs. At the upstairs landing, there was a long hall with only one door to the left, which was the inn-keeper's personal dwelling, and three doors to the right for renting out. At the end of the long hall was a door which led to what Barrin would have called an emergency exit. The innkeeper had explained to them that his first wife and child had been lost to a fire, so he had insisted on building the ex-ternal set of steps when he rebuilt the inn.

The key they had been given was for the central room, so Tally turned it in the iron lock, and they all piled in. It was a reasonably sized room for sleeping. The only furniture were two wooden framed beds with straw-filled mattresses and one wooden chair. They turned the key behind them to lock the door and then used the chair to further secure the door by propping the chair under the handle.

"I'm wanted!" Will said again. "The soldiers we fought were looking for me."

"The king must know that Thallinius was up to some-thing, but he can't be sure of what." Barrin said. "The only thing he knows is that you lived with Thallinius, and now you are gone." He paused. "He might even think you are the heir," he added.

"The drawing on the poster isn't good," Alexia pointed out. "No one will know who you are from that. We just need to remember not to use your name."

"It will be okay, Will," Tally said calmly.

Looking around at the two beds, Barrin asked, "So how is this going to work?"

"I'm with you," Tally said, smiling. "But we are sleeping in our clothes."

"I'm okay with that, too," Alexia said, smiling at Will, who grinned from ear to ear.

They all sat on the edge of the beds.

"I spoke with Barrin earlier," Tally said. "I think we should leave Toby here. He will slow us down, and we don't really seem to need him." She continued. "I thought we would be cooking more, and carrying more gear, and I didn't expect them to be after us this quickly."

"Can we afford to board him and come back?" asked Will.

"At a copper a day, I don't think so." Barrin replied. "We have no idea how long it will take us to come back either, so how much do we pay? You know the owner will want it in advance."

"Okay, then," Will pouted. "I guess we can let him go."

"Barrin, why don't you come with me and we will talk with the innkeeper about a sale?" Tally suggested. They slipped out of the room.

The innkeeper agreed to purchase Toby for the two silver they had paid for the room and food. He returned their coins and asked them to sign a receipt showing the purchase was complete.

"Apparently the transfer of livestock is a big deal in Saldringal," Barrin thought to himself.

Tally signed the bill of sale, and their task completed, the two returned upstairs to their room. As Tally swung the door open, Will and Lexie scrambled apart from each other. Barrin smiled and looking at how red-faced Will was, he suspected that they had caught the other couple kissing.

Barrin opened his coin bag and was about to put the silver coins in, when he noticed that they were already there. Puzzled, he added the two he had been given to the bag and counted the contents. He had four silver and six copper. The others were chatting together, but he was intrigued by the bag and zoned out. He removed one copper and closed the bag tightly. He lay the coin on the bed and held the bag for a few minutes as his friends talked. Then he re-opened the bag and counted. He now had two silver and six copper again. He laughed and interrupted to show his friends the magic bag. The others were amazed and Will tried his bag to find that it was magic too. Tally was very happy that she had left her bag with Gwyn. The washerwoman should have no tax worries now.

"Notice that the coins are old and used," Alexia said. "I bet this bag is connected to a chest or a cache somewhere. The coins already exist and are moved to and from the bag." She paused for a moment. "I would expect that they will eventually run out, depending on how many there were to begin with." She paused. "It's not hard to do this magically, and it's a great idea, as long as your cache is safe. If someone steals it, your bag will empty too."

After the long, draining day, they were all yawning and ready to sleep early. They spread their blankets over the bare mattresses and curled up on the small beds, covering themselves with their cloaks.

It was comfortable and warm cuddling together on the small beds. Maybe it wasn't as romantic as Barrin would have liked, sleeping with his arms around Tally. They were fully dressed, and they hadn't bathed in days, but there was nowhere Barrin would rather be. He finally had a girlfriend, and he thought she was incredible.

•••

It was still dark when Tally woke. Something was wrong. She slipped out from under Barrin's arm and carefully peeked out the only window. In the street outside stood about twenty mounted soldiers. They had apparently just arrived. Their horses were blowing and tossing about, and only a few of the troops had just begun to dismount. The sound of the horses must have been what awakened her.

"Wake up, wake up!" she hissed to the others, afraid to raise her voice for fear of the soldiers hearing her. She shook her friends awake, then she grabbed her own pack and bow as they were groggily coming to. She hurried them along and within minutes they were ready. Tally, silently opened the door and peeked out. No one was in the hall yet. She led the group out of the room to the right towards the exit door at the end of the hall. As they traversed the short distance to their exit, the sound of the soldiers starting to pound on the downstairs door echoed up from the other stairs.

Once outside, they could hear the horses around the other side of the building as they descended the steps and turned away from the street. As quietly as possible, they wound their way out of the area through the surrounding town towards the road to escape from the valley.

When they cleared the last house, they saw two figures standing in the road right by the town limits sign. Beyond the two it was only a few paces to the forest and cover, but the eighty yards or so from the last houses to the sign was wide open. They broke into a run, realizing about halfway there that they were charging Saldrant wraiths. There was a shout from the horse soldiers behind them as they were noticed, but by now all of the soldiers had dismounted, and since they had to remount to give chase, the friends large head start was probably enough to escape, if they could quickly get by the wraiths.

Tally reached into a pocket and as they closed on the dragon born warriors, she pulled out one of her bolo weapons, whipped it around to build momentum and threw it at the one on the left. "Lexie, finish that one." She pointed to her target, whose arms were now pinned down. Alexia activated her magic claws, shredded its clothing and snatched out its gem. The dead wraith collapsed to the ground as the others engaged the second one.

Barrin had his saber out. Tally had drawn her knives, and Will had a hammer in one hand, while he held their food bag with the other. They were weighted down with their packs, so they weren't as agile as they would have liked to be, but with three against one, they quickly caused the wraith to overcommit its weapon to one side, and Barrin whipped his saber over its off-kilter defense to cleanly remove the wraith's head.

Its headless body kept trying to grab them, but Tally sliced open its clothing and snatched out its gem, and clutching the two new gems, they all fled into the woods. Barrin glanced back at the tree line; the first horsemen were about halfway from the town to where they were. Tally was with him. She raised her bow and sent two arrows crackling at the lead riders, who had to veer off into the other riders' way to avoid the shots. The friends disappeared into the woods as the horsemen re-corrected their charge.

The next hour Tally led them winding through the trees on a circuitous northwestern route. The horses were an advantage in the open plains, but in the woods, they were a hindrance. The four friends quickly outpaced the cavalry through the dense forest.

When she felt that they had a safe lead, Tally called for them to rest for a minute in a small clearing. She dug in her pack and brought out a vial from a protected inner bag. Removing the lid, she dripped the liquid contents around the area where they stood, then she carefully replaced the lid, returned it to her pack, and then hurried them back to running.

"What is that stuff?" Barrin asked her.

"It is a scent that attracts night wolves," she said. "If there are any around, they will come running. We use it to bait them into traps, but we usually use a couple drops. I put out way more than we normally use." She laughed. "It's likely that our horsemen friends are going to be in for a surprise."

They continued at a brisk pace until they were sure they had lost the pursuit. By now, their leg muscles were shaky and they were hurting from over-exertion. They collapsed for a meal and rest. Will opened the food bag and passed cheese and dried meat out to his friends. They all drank from their water bottles.

"Someone in the town must have alerted them," Will said between bites. "Do you think it was the innkeeper?"

"No," Tally replied. "He didn't respond to the door until we were long gone. I think if he sold us out he would have been awake and waiting on them."

"Someone had to go out to find them, too," Barrin said. "Probably by horse I would think. Anyway, someone in that tavern was a spy for the king."

"One of the wraiths we killed was the one I cut up earlier," Lexie said. "The one I pulled the stone from had stitches holding it together. Maybe it tracked me somehow."

"If it was following you, I hope it didn't bother Gwyn," Tally added.

After lunch, they continued on their trek. They slowed to a regular walking pace but kept moving as much as they could. They continued until dusk and then selected a good spot to sleep. They made two pallets with blankets and slept cuddled together as they had the night before.

The next morning they ate cheese and bread and had a piece of fruit each from their bag, then they packed up to head out.

"We will reach the Barrows of Rathsmar today," Talisia announced over breakfast.

"You both looked very worried about that at Marlin, er, Thallinius's house," Barrin said. "Tell me about Rathsmar."

"Well," Tally said, "officially it is the Royal Barrows of Rathsmar, but most just call it the 'Land of the Dead,'" she began. "No one has been inside the crypt there in centuries. The crypt is set into the base of the mountain. I am told that the barrow is guarded by a deep magic that makes the door somewhat impassable."

"What if we can't get in?" Will asked.

"We will," Tally replied. "Thallinius believed in us. He knew we could do it."

• • •

The Barrows were quiet when they finally arrived. The land itself around the burial grounds was barren and creepy. Some sort of blight had killed all the trees, and even the undergrowth, so there was no canopy overhead. Instead of the typical verdant forest to which they were accustomed, they walked through dusty, dead, dry soil and the twisted husks of what had once been great, old-growth trees.

It was early afternoon when they arrived at a stone wall with rusted iron fencing along the top and a massive wrought-iron gate in the center. They sat and rested a few minutes after arriving, and drank heavily to ease the parched feeling from their walk through the damaged land.

Like the fence, the gate was also rusted heavily, and crookedly hanging from the center of the left side was a rough handwritten sign that read, "No living soul may pass the gate of the dead." Barrin wasn't sure what had been used to paint the sign, but he feared the coppery brown letters were scrawled in blood.

Behind the gate was a cemetery grounds with many visibly decaying headstones. The rocky mountainside behind the burial grounds had been cut away to form a flat wall of stone in the back, with masonry supports to keep the upper hillside from sliding down from above. The cemetery plots started right at the mountain's edge and reached to the curving stone wall and fence. The graveyard had apparently reached its capacity before it fell into disuse. A heavy looking door was mounted into the center of this stone wall, directly opposite from the gate where they now stood.

The door to the crypt was a massive stone slab set into a stone archway which fitted into the side of the mountain. The door was etched with symbols and had tarnished brass fittings and large, dingy brass-colored hinges. It appeared to open into the side of the mountain itself.

Barrin looked through the gate to see all of this, and as he observed the site, his biggest concern was the abundance of partially clad skeletons lying around in the cemetery. Most graves had a skeleton on top of them. Many were leaning against their headstones. Several more were away from the gravestones and were leaning against the door itself or the rough stone mountainside. Almost all of the skeletons were armed with a weapon of some sort, although some of them just had simple clubs or spears. Several wore decrepit bits of armor or helms, and some had baggy chainmail hanging from their fleshless frames.

"Let's leave our gear over by the trees," Barrin suggested. They piled up everything that they thought would be unnecessary in the crypt. Tally dug in her bag and brought out a couple of torches. She gave one to Alexia. "Sorry, guys, I only have two," she said, as the girls both tucked the torches into their belts.

They returned to the gate. "Here we go," Barrin said, unlatching the gate and swinging the right half out and open with a creak of rusted metal.

On guard, they tentatively walked across the cemetery ground towards the door to the crypt. When they were just more than halfway to the door, the skeletons began leaping up and running toward them. Within seconds, the four friends were surrounded by a small army of skeleton warriors. At the first movement of the skeletons, they had all brought out their weapons, so the bony warriors were met with hammer blows, arrows, and slashes from Barrin's saber and Lexie's claws.

The battle dragged on for several minutes with almost no progress. The skeletons weren't particularly adept fighters. I mean, they did lack brains to guide their movements, but the sheer mass of their numbers made them dangerous. Also, they were hard to knock down. The magic that bound them together and animated them in death wasn't defeated by a slash to the throat or a cut to a non-existent belly. To stop a skeleton it had to be literally knocked to pieces. Only Will's weapons were designed with this end in mind, so the other three found themselves defending each other and guarding Will's back while he battered away at the grinning bony warriors.

Tally realized that this approach was hopeless. They were tiring, and it was only a matter of time before some skeleton got through their defense and seriously injured one of them. She already had a cut along her cheekbone and several other minor wounds, and they weren't making any real progress in reducing the skeleton army.

"Back to the gate!" she yelled over the fray. "Retreat!" They started pushing back in the direction from where they had come. As they passed through the gate, the skeletons stopped. One of them, after being struck by Will's hammer, accidentally fell through the gate. It instantly turned to dust and collapsed in a heap on the ground. All the skeletons were careful to stay back from the gate itself.

When they had all passed through and were back out of the barrow grounds, Will quickly swung the gate shut. Discouraged and exhausted, the four walked away and collapsed on the ground. Several of them had minor cuts, and they all had bruises. Will had a serious wound on top of his left shoulder. Barrin found his first aid kit and used butterfly bandages to hold it shut while Alexia murmured a healing spell to stop the bleeding. It did instantly look better, but Lexie collapsed in a heap, exhausted by the effort.

"So what should we try next?" Tally asked.

"Let's rest and think about it for a while." Barrin replied. He lay down on his back and closed his eyes. Alexia turned her back to them and literally began licking her wounds. Will also lay down and tried to nap. Only Tally sat facing the skeleton gate.

Suddenly she jumped up. "I've got an idea," she said. "Come with me, Barrin." She walked toward the gate, and he hurried to her side. She stopped about ten feet from the closed gate, and the skeletons bristled and brandished their weapons. She turned to Barrin and fished the necklace from under his shirt. The dagger key and the gold ring were both on the chain around his neck.

"Thallinius said the ring might help us get in. Remember?" she asked.

As the ring became visible, the skeletons visibly reacted. Barrin removed the gold artifact from his chain and slid it onto his finger. The skeletons looked at him.

"Let us pass." he commanded. Like troops falling in for inspection, the skeletons quickly formed up into two lines from the gate to the stone door. He turned and called out to Alexia and Will, who got up and joined them.

They quickly discussed it and decided to bring all their gear, so they collected their packs and the four of them swung the gate open and walked through the phalanx of skeletons to the stone door.

There was no visible way to make the door open.

"Open the door," Will whispered from the back of the line as he eyed the skeletons nervously.

"What do I do?" Barrin whispered back.

"Look!" Alexia pointed. "Stick the ring into that." There was a metal piece fitted into the stone. It was recessed with a raised pattern inside at the deepest point. Barrin inserted the top of the ring into the cavity, and it fit perfectly, the raised pattern fitting into the engraving on the ring. There was a rumbling click as massive internal bolts slid back and the door lurched as it popped free. Barrin and Tally pushed it, and the entire stone swung into the crypt on invisible hinges, revealing a dark and dusty room.

Chapter Nine:
In the Crypt of King Mortingas

Barrin thought that for its size and apparent weight, the door was easy to use. He and Tally moved into the dusty chamber, with Will and Lexie coming through behind them. Alexia lay her hand on the door as she passed it, and she recoiled from the feel.

"Wow, that has powerful magic," she snapped.

"Are you okay?" Will asked with concern.

"Yes. It didn't hurt; it just surprised me," she replied, smiling at his attention.

Inside the crypt, it looked about how one would picture a room that had been sitting untouched for hundreds of years. Thick cobwebs and dust covered everything in it. The room was about thirty feet square and was ringed with shelves upon which lay the skeletal remains of an army. There were door openings to their right and left as well as an open passageway straight across the room from the stone slab.

Alexia was still shaky from the healing spell, so Tally felt around in her pouch, pulled out the firestarter she had taken from the wraith in Thallinius's home, and lit both of their torches. The added light revealed that the doorways to the left and right led to rooms that were identical to the one they were in.

In response to their entry, the skeletons in all three rooms scrambled to their feet. Ancient dust fell from their bones as they stood. Barrin held up the ring, and the bony army all snapped to attention. There were roughly sixty former warriors in the three rooms, and they were in much better shape than the skeletons outside. "This must be the second line of defense," Barrin thought to himself. "They haven't seen action like the guys outside."

The four friends walked through the center doorway and down the long passageway beyond it. Along this hallway, they noticed sconces holding torches were set at uniform intervals. Lexie and Tally lit a few of them as they walked by, and the place became brighter and less intimidating.

At the end of the passage was another open door. This portal was very dark, and as they approached, they saw that it opened into a large chamber. Barrin passed through first, with the others close behind him carrying the lights. This room was perfectly circular. In the center of the circle was a raised round dais with an ornate stone sarcophagus sitting in the middle. It was two steps up to the top level. Each level of the dais was surrounded by a circular step so that the dais could be ascended from any position in the room. The outer wall of the room was ornate, with stones set tightly, intermingled with ancient skulls to make the walls. Rounded stone pillars stood in four evenly-spaced locations around the outer wall. The pillars were sunk halfway into the wall itself so that only part of each pillar was visible in the room. There were two tall floor sconces on either side of the door, which the girls quickly lit.

Standing against the wall, entirely encircling the room were skeleton warriors holding long spears. They wore chainmail with metal breastplates and skirts of interlocking metal leaves to protect their hips. Most of them still had short swords hanging from their waists. A few of their leather belts had let go with age and dropped their weapons to the stone floor. Rotting leather boots were falling off most of their feet. They were elbow to elbow in a perfect circle, and had the friends not had the ring, they would have been intimidated by the show of force.

"So, what do we do now?" Will asked.

"Maybe open the sarcophagus?" Tally replied.

It was decided for them. With a rumble, the sarcophagus lid slid open and dropped to the floor with a crash. It cracked in half and bumped down the two steps to the lowest floor where one piece stuck leaning against the steps, as the other fell flat.

"Let me see my heir!" yelled a voice from within the sarcophagus. A grizzled looking skeleton sat up and nimbly climbed out of the box. It looked older than the others. His spine was curved and hunched looking, and the bones looked frailer, as if they had belonged to a very old man. Sitting cockeyed across the top of his grinning skull was an elaborate golden crown with deep-set, large gems. The crown and the skeleton were as incredibly dusty as the rest of the tomb. A few wispy strands of pure white beard hair clung doggedly to his bony chin, and on his head there were a few long white hairs left amongst the cobwebs.

"My boy. My boy. Let me look at you!" the skeleton said, approaching the well-muscled Will. "You look like a fine warrior, son," he prattled, admiring Will's muscular arms..

"I am Will Stonehart, sir," Will said. "I'm not your heir, but I am with your great-great-something-or-other grandson, and I hope to be in his guard someday."

The skeleton looked disappointed.

"I am your heir, sir," said Barrin, showing him the ring. "I am Barrindor, son of Pallindor. I was sent by Thallinius the Wise to find the 'keys to the kingdom', sir."

"Ohhh. You want my keys," the skeleton king said haughtily. "Well." He paused and cocked his head at Barrin. "Then you shall have them!" he cackled. "Everyone wants the keys." He waved his arms dramatically over his head. "But only the heir can have them." He lowered his arms and pointed directly at Barrin. "And I will know alright if you are my heir!" He cackled again. Turning to the sarcophagus he said, "Let's find them, shall we?"

The skeleton carefully climbed the top steps to his coffin and reached inside. He brought out a sword belt with two attached scabbards that held short daggers in them. Everything in the chamber was filthy with age, cobwebs and rot, but not the keys. The leather of the sword belt was supple and strong and shone with careful polishing. The daggers' hilts and oversized cross guards were perfectly clean, and Barrin supposed the blades which were hidden in their scabbards would be perfect, too. The skeleton king instructed Barrin to remove his saber, and he did so, passing it to Will to hold.

"Ask your girl there to gird you with the keys." He passed the belt to Barrin, who turned and held it out to Tally. Barrin wondered how the old skeleton knew she was 'his girl'.

"Please, will you help?" he asked.

"Yes. Of course," she replied. She took the belt and wrapped it around his waist, cinching it into position. As she drew it tight, she looked into his eyes. He smiled at her, and ran his finger down the scratch on her cheek sympathetically.

"Now draw the blade on your left side," the skeleton ordered, interrupting their moment.

Barrin turned away from Tally, drew the blade and studied it. The hilt of the key was gold with a large crossguard and a black, leather-wrapped grip. The pommel appeared at first glance to be an orb of gold with a black gem set into it. Intricate patterns were carved into all the golden pieces of the hilt, and upon closer view, the orb of the pommel was actually a stylized dragon claw gripping the gemstone. The blade itself was unique. It was wide where it met the crossguard and like many blades do, it decreased gradually in a triangular shape to a sharp point, but the shape wasn't the unique feature. The metal used to create the blade was unlike anything Barrin had seen before. It was a glossy metallic black that reminded Barrin vaguely of the scrying stone that Lexie had used, but it was blacker, and for lack of a better description, more deadly-looking.

"Yep. You're my heir alright," the skeleton stated.

"How do you know?" asked Barrin.

"You didn't drop dead," the skeleton replied matter-of-factly. "Anyone not of my blood who handles that blade is instantly poisoned."

"By Aeric, I just handled that belt! What if I had accidentally touched it?" Talisia asked exasperatedly.

"Well then, sweetie, you would've gotten to stay here with me." the bony king replied with a laugh. "Haven't had a young miss around here in ages." He laughed again, and attempted a playful wink, but with no eye or skin, the motion didn't really transfer. "Besides, you would have had to draw it. Touching the handle in the scabbard wouldn't hurt you." He paused and added. "Well, anyway, I think that's right. Don't quote me on that."

It was becoming clear that a thousand years of waiting in a crypt was not good for one's sanity.

"That's not all that the blade does either," the king went on. "You can release its poison when you want with the casting word." He paused, "Resheathe the blade so you don't waste it." Barrin did as asked. "Now repeat after me, 'venox'"

"Venox," Barrin repeated.

"If you are touching the black dagger and say 'venox' it will deliver its venom to the next thing the blade touches," he said. "This venom is not to be trifled with, either. It will burn through many materials, and it kills almost instantly – size doesn't matter."

"Wow," Will murmured. "That could come in handy."

"Now for its partner," the skeleton went on. "Draw the other blade." Barrin followed the directions again. The other blade was identical to the first, but everything black on the other dagger was red on this one. In place of the black gem in the pommel there was a fiery ruby; bright red and beautiful. Like its twin, the metal of the blade was a unique color; bright metallic red to match the ruby. Also like the other blade, it was about a foot and a half in overall length, with about a ten inches of blade, and a five inch grip. The pommel and stone added an additional inch at the end.

"Whoa," Will said. "What metal are these made from?" He thought for a moment. "Even my ring doesn't know how to make blades like these."

"Beautiful," Alexia murmured.

"Yes," Tally agreed.

"Does this one have a trigger word?" Barrin asked.

"A what?" the old king asked.

"A casting word," Alexia interjected.

"Oh yes," the skeleton replied. "Say, 'extensa.'"

"Extensa," Barrin repeated. As the word left his mouth, with an audible 'shing' of metal, the blade extended to the length of a longsword. The weight changed as the blade lengthened, but it stayed exquisitely balanced.

"The length doesn't matter as much as this does," Mortingas said. "Listen to me, that blade will cut anything, and I mean anything. It can't be parried or blocked. It goes right through other blades, and right through shields. Anything you want to cut, it will cut. You might even be able to cut between worlds if you tried, but I wouldn't mess with that if I were you."

"That's amazing," Barrin exclaimed. He had found it awkward to always have his long saber strapped to his belt. This would be so much more comfortable. He turned away from the others and ran a few drills, going through his long-practiced sword techniques with ease. The blade handled beautifully. He was thrilled to have the pleasure of wielding it.

"How do I make it shorten?" he asked.

"Redux," the skeleton replied.

"Redux," Barrin said, and the blade instantly responded, quickly shortening to its original length. He sheathed the blade. "Thank you sir. They are wonderful."

"That isn't all," the skeleton king said. Turning to the nearest guard, he called, "Cyrus, come over here." The skeleton immediately animated and walked directly to his king. "Give me your sword." the king directed. The skeleton drew his rusty short sword. As the sword cleared its sheath, the belt holding his scabbard in place disintegrated and fell to the floor. The skeleton reversed the blade and offered it hilt-first to his king.

"Thanks, Cyrus," Mortingas replied. Taking the grip, he turned and drove the blade straight into Barrin's chest.

"No!" screamed Tally.

Will dropped the saber and drew his hammer, and Alexia bared her claws and growled.

"It's okay," Barrin said, turning to look at them. The blade was through him. They could see it on the other side, but it wasn't hurting him at all. To Barrin it felt cold, but there was no pain, no blood, or any damage whatsoever.

"How does this work?" Barrin asked.

"It is something to do with different worlds," the king replied. "The power comes from the belt. If you wear the belt you can't be wounded by weapons, even the keys themselves. You can burn in fire, freeze to death, fall off a cliff, drink poison, and you're still done for, but weapons will pass right through."

The skeleton king withdrew the sword from Barrin and tossed it aside. He drew himself to his full height and said, "I have been preparing for this day for centuries. I knew some day my heir would come to me in need of the keys. I didn't know who or when, but I knew you would come. I've prepared a speech about being king, and I want to share it with you." He gestured to the dais. "Why don't you all sit down while I talk." They sat on the steps to be an attentive audience.

"Before we begin, do you know anything about dragons?" he asked them.

"Not really," was the consensus reply.

"Dragons can die, but when they do, they leave behind a heartstone. If you take that stone and insert it into a dragon egg, it will hatch back into the same full-grown dragon that just died. The hatching process only takes minutes.

The eggs are produced through a mating ritual, but no genetic materials are exchanged. The egg itself does not influence the newborn dragon, only the heartstone determines which dragon comes out. Okay, now you know what you need," he said.

"We believe that we have reclaimed three of these heartstones," Barrin quickly added. "They were used to reanimate dead men into undead warriors. We have destroyed three of these warriors and removed their stones."

"Good," the king huffed. "Those wraiths are an abomination of nature. By the way, I've been dead, and sealed in here for ages, but I still know things. Through the magic of this place, I see what is happening in our world. I saw the wraiths being birthed. I already know your goals and your quest, and I believe that you can succeed. It isn't decided yet, but the chance is there. It is up to you to make it happen." He turned to face them like a professor addressing a class.

"Now," he began. "There are things you should know if you are going to be king." He paused, looked at them, and said, "I'm going to go through all of this, so just listen and don't interrupt."

• • •

"If it weren't for dragons, I wouldn't have been king, and Saldringal as we know it would not exist. I was a good warrior and a decent leader of men, but I didn't have the tools to take over and unite this world on my own. The dragons created and gave me these 'keys' and they helped me drive out the monsters and solve the problems that plagued the land. They even stayed here to guard our border and prevent these same problems from returning. They literally helped me become king, but I also learned a few lessons from them about being a ruler – important lessons.

"First, the secret I have kept for a thousand years. There were thirteen dragons, not twelve. The first dragon was the oldest and the most important. I met her first, before the others, in my travels. She was old beyond time and very magical. She was at least a couple thousand years old, and she was bored of life. Everyone wants to live forever, but you should try it! It's boring as all get out. You do the same old things, day after day. It's fine for a few hundred years, but it gets really old.

"In the dragon realm, all the dragons did was bicker and fight with each other. There were five elder dragons, and each of them had twelve offspring. Don't ask me how they created new offspring. She never explained it to me. The five elder dragons all thought that they were the most powerful, and so they fought constantly over who would rule their land. She knew this was a never ending cycle, and she wanted out.

"When we met, she gifted me the keys to the kingdom and the help of her brood with the promise that I would help her in return. She moved her twelve offspring here with the understanding that when she died, I would keep her heartstone and not rebirth her. She wanted to rest. I was to store her heartstone in a safe place and never implant it in an egg unless it were a true emergency. Her heartstone is hidden here in this barrow, which is why the magic guarding this place is so strong. She helped me build this place to protect us both, and her magic is how I am speaking to you now.

"Here is what I learned as king: gold doesn't matter. Measure your wealth in the people around you, and value your subjects like gold. Use your wealth to make your people's lives easier, and you will be successful.

"Dragons crave wealth, especially gold and gems. The need for gold intoxicates them. They hoard it and always crave more. Don't be like them. As the king, you will have all the gold you could ever need. You won't need more. Use your wealth; don't hoard it like a dragon.

"Don't get me wrong. Taxes are important. You must have a fair tax. It allows your subjects to feel ownership for their realm. They can say, 'that road was built with my taxes' and they can see the benefits of their contribution around them. The rangers, like your girl here, are keeping the forests safe and the animals in balance because of those taxes. The soldiers keep the peace because taxes pay for it, and so on. But the taxes must be only what it takes to provide for the needs of the people and the good of the community, and nothing more.

"Tax fairly and spend wisely for the good of all, and your people will love you. The people will value your honesty. Be like a dragon, give into greed, and take a little extra to hoard away, or spend on yourself at the expense of your people, and they will turn on you and plot your demise in an instant.

"Speaking of upsetting your subjects, war is for fools. Our realm is the perfect size. We have towns, farmland, and a deep port for trading. We have all we need. Saldringal is beautiful and uncrowded. No king needs an empire. Keep a force for defense in case someone else is a fool, but there is no need to try and expand. Maintain the wonderful lands we have. Remember that every soldier you sacrifice for some cause is a son, daughter, or maybe a parent to other of your subjects. Before you use your army, make sure your military goal is worth their loss.

"Now you should know that kings have to serve as judges, too. Don't be too quick to punish. Ask questions, and find out the reason behind the crime. Stealing a loaf of bread to feed your starving family is very different from stealing a loaf of bread because you hate the baker and you want him to lose income. Pursue the truth and then make the punishment fit the crime. Don't get in the habit of yelling 'Off with his head!' just because you can, and it's the easy solution. Look for situations that benefit everyone. Maybe the bread thief can be sentenced to work a job that will provide food money for the family. If you are fair and consistent in your rulings, and make the punishment fit the crime, your people will love you.

"Barrin, son, you may be wise. I don't know you that well, but even the wisest man doesn't know everything. Some would say that everything the king says is right, because it is said by the king. Don't believe that. Know your limitations. The wisest kings keep trusted advisors around them that know more than they do, especially in the subjects they know the least about. Find people you trust and then trust your people. That will make you a wise king.

"Restoring the dragons is vital to your survival as a realm. Without them, the land will return to chaos and disorder. Make it your primary goal to bring them back as soon as you can. The Falkans know what to do. Just get them the heartstones, and they will do the rest. It is their honor and privilege to do so.

"Now my last advice, about these keys. They are too powerful to just be carried lightly. They are powered by dragon magic, and dragons sometimes want things differently than a good king should. Don't carry them all the time. Use them until you don't need them, then put them aside. I believe that their magic may wear on you over time and influence your decisions in a negative way. They will feed your greed for gold.

"When you pass, and you will, as all men do, I recommend that they come right back here to sit and wait with you. I will be gone. I have served my purpose, and it is time for this magic to end and for me to rest. Follow my advice, son, and you will make a fine king."

• • •

This last statement made Barrin feel a little sad. He was growing fond of the old man and hated that he would be truly gone.

"King Mortingas," Barrin said, "thank you for your help and your guidance. I hope to make you proud."

"You already have, my boy," the skeleton croaked. "You are the first in a thousand years to come visit me. King after king wore and used my ring for generations, but they never came here to see me, only you."

"Do you have advice for us in choosing a path back to Cantigal?" Tally asked. "The imposter king's men are after us."

"I don't have a secret way to Cantigal," the skeleton began, "but there is a way for you to leave the barrow in a different place than where you came in." He cocked his head to the side. "How close behind you were they?"

"We really aren't sure," Tally said. "But they were on horseback, so we want to avoid the open plains."

"My men did not dig this crypt," the king said. "It was an old mine. The silver strike here petered out and they were abandoning the tunnels, so we re-purposed the entrance tunnel as my crypt." He turned to face away from the door and pointed to the back of the room. "There is a doorway over there. It is locked, but if you can get it open, it leads into the old mine tunnels."

The skeleton began walking around the dais, and the others followed. "The mine here was truly abandoned. Nothing should be in the tunnels, so you will be safe there. Shortly before the vein of silver ended, I had the miners dig an air shaft in case there was a collapse. We thought there would be more silver than there was. If you follow the mine to the end and find the air shaft, it will lead you to the surface. You will exit the mountain on the other side of Stavanger. You could take to the woods from there and avoid the plain."

They were nearing the back wall and the second door. It was much darker on this side of the room. Mortingas pointed to two sconces flanking the back door, and Lexie hurried over to light them.

"Two more things I can give you before you go," the skeleton said. He turned and yelled, "Percival, it's time to give it up." Then he added, "Bring it to me."

A skeleton near the back door animated and stood straight. Unlike the others, he carried a shield. It was square on top but the sides rounded down to a point at the bottom. It was dusty, but when the skeleton took a step, the dust easily fell away. There was a heraldic dragon embossed on the shield. The dragon was a bright green that popped from the recessed black background. It was reared up with white claws out and it was blowing red fire from its open mouth.

"Percival here was my Captain of the King's Guard," Mortingas said. "His shield was a gift from the dragons. It blocks much more than its size would lead you to believe." He took it from the skeleton who handed it over freely and then returned to his previous post.

Addressing Will, he said, "You hope to serve His Majesty as a guard, so I will give this to you. Guard your king well."

"I will sir. Thank you, sir," the overwhelmed, young smith replied.

"And last," Mortingas said, "I must give you this, Barrin." He removed the jeweled crown from his head. "It has no magical properties really, and it wasn't made by dragons, but it was my favorite. I asked to have it rest here with me because I enjoyed it, but my long wait is over, and it should be used, not left here to rot away." If he had had eyes, he probably would have shed a tear at this point. Alexia's eyes were already watery, and a tear trickled down Tally's cheek. "I wish you the best of luck in your quest," he said as he held the crown out to Barrin.

Barrin sniffled; he was tearing up too. He bowed and accepted the crown with both hands. "Thank you so much, sir. I will do my best."

"Make me proud, and wear it proudly," the King said. Then he turned and walked to the dais. He ascended the steps and climbed into the sarcophagus and lay down. After a moment, a slight breeze passed through the crypt, and all the skeletons collapsed into piles of dust, their weapons clattering to the floor.

"I guess it's all up to us now," Will said.

"Yes," Tally replied.

They were all quiet for a minute honoring the significance of the moment.

"Any ideas for getting through the door?" Will finally asked. "He forgot to tell us how. It's stone, so bashing it with force is out; fire too."

"Let's look closer," Alexia said. They approached the stone slab.

"Look," Tally pointed. "There's a keyhole."

There was, in fact, a keyhole. It was small and it reminded Barrin of something. Quickly he pulled his necklace out of his tunic again and slid the dagger shaped key into the hole and twisted it. There was an audible click as the bolt withdrew. He pushed the door, and like its sibling outside, it swung open on invisible hinges.

They quietly celebrated the discovery, and then they made their plans. Will and Alexia went out of the crypt to shut the outer gate, close the large stone door and search the skeleton resting rooms for anything of value that they could use.

In the meanwhile, Barrin and Tally extinguished the lit torches and gathered as many torches together as they could find. Tally suspected that they may be in the mine for a few days, and they would need the torches for light.

They decided to leave Barrin's saber there in the chamber. He carefully laid it on the dais next to the sarcophagus. Then, once all the preparations were made, they passed through the door, shut it behind them, locked it with the key, and moved on into the abandoned mine.

Chapter Ten:
The Mine and Beyond

The mine wasn't at all what Barrin had expected. It looked more like a cave than he had thought it would. He didn't notice any tool marks in the walls. The passage looked natural. The floor was the only part of the place that looked to be manipulated by man. It was the smoothest road that Barrin had seen in Saldringal. The stones of the floor were tight fitting, smooth, and flat; nothing like the dirt ruts on the plains or the bumpy cobblestones of Wagon's Crossing. Other than having to avoid the occasional outcropping of stalagmites and the enveloping darkness, the travel in the mine was easy.

Shortly after they passed through the door they found a golden chest on a carved, white stone pedestal. The stone was made to look like a sitting dragon, and it stood about waist high. There were two of the floor sconces on either side of the chest. Barrin tried the dagger key again, and it opened the chest. Inside, sitting on a luxuriously soft fur lining was another of the odd gems like they had pulled from the wraiths. This one was clear white like a diamond.

"That confirms what we thought," Barrin said, locking the chest back. "And now we know where to find the last dragon if we absolutely need her."

"I wouldn't wake her if I could help it," Will said. "I don't want to meet an annoyed dragon."

"Ummm. I think that's kind of our whole mission here," Tally jibed.

"Oh, yeah. True," Will agreed.

They moved on through the mine passage. It was an easy path to walk, and they moved along at a comfortable pace. Gradually they rearranged until the two couples were walking together in a square, two by two. Alexia was telling Will about something from her country in the back. Barrin couldn't catch it all from the front, and he had lost track of her story.

"Tally," he whispered. "Do we have to worry about anything dangerous here in the mine?"

"I wouldn't think so," she replied. "I don't think anyone knows this is here but us. Besides, Mortingas thought it was safe or he wouldn't have sent us."

"Are there goblins or demons in Saldringal?" he asked her. He was remembering the 'Mines of Moria' in *The Lord of the Rings*, and he was very nervous that they would make too much noise and attract goblins, a troll, or a balrog. He could see her soft grin in the torchlight.

"Ohh, yes. They are quite common. Shocked we haven't been eaten by them yet," she mockingly replied. He gave her an annoyed look and was about to protest when she said, "I don't know what those things are."

"In my world, there are stories about terrible monsters that live in deep, dark places like this," he said. "I am just feeling a little nervous. That's all." She laughed lightly and hugged his arm.

"It's okay," she replied. "We don't have those things here, and we aren't actually going deep. The path seems to be fairly flat. I am more relaxed here than I have been since we left home."

As they walked, Barrin tried to see evidence of mining. Finally they reached a point where the tunnel walls started to show tool marks. "There must have been caves here first, and they mined their way out of the caves," he thought to himself. He wondered how they got through the stone cave walls to get started and how they knew they would find silver if they did.

They walked for a few hours. Without the sun it was difficult to gauge time, so they walked until they eventually grew too tired to go on. There was no chance of finding firewood, so having a fire was out of the question, but they didn't want to be totally devoid of light, so they rigged a makeshift holder for one torch, and extinguished the other.

"I hope we find more torches," Tally said. "If we go more than another day in here, I am afraid that we'll run out."

They shared a quiet meal, laid out two pallets, extinguished the torch, snuggled up together in couples, and quickly fell asleep. Barrin slept incredibly soundly in the empty dark of the mine. It was still and silent, and darker than anything he had experienced before. He pushed his fears out, cleared his mind, and was quickly fast asleep.

Tally took a little longer. She was concerned that her attachment to Barrin was a mistake. What business did she have flirting with the future king? Still, he made her happy in a way she had never felt before. She drifted to sleep imagining herself as Queen Talisia of Saldringal.

That night, Barrin dreamt that he was in Cantigal in Castle Brackhaven. He had never actually seen the castle before, but in his dream he knew that was where he was. In the dream, Barrin was a lot older, and he stood high up in the castle looking out over his kingdom. He turned to look beside him and Talisia was there. She smiled at him and took his hand. She too was older, with the first few strands of gray showing in her beautiful curls. As they watched the sunset, they saw a knight ride out of the castle on a black charger. Barrin knew that this was their son, off on his first errand for the king and queen. He smiled in the dark as he slept.

The next day passed uneventfully. They walked in the dark. It felt to Barrin like the darkness went on forever. They really had no idea how long they had been walking, with no way to measure time or distance. They walked until they were too hungry to go on, or too sleepy to take another step. At first, the novelty of being in the dark made their travel an adventure, but that had long worn off and now everyone was tired of being here. They longed for light that they didn't have to hold and for fresh air that moved.

After sleeping again, they moved on to find that they had reached a fork. They decided to take the right hand fork because they hoped to exit the mine to the south. If the other passage led to an exit, they believed it might be on the wrong side of the mountains.

They walked and walked through the dark, and finally, when Barrin was beginning to despair of ever seeing the outside again, they reached a dead end.

"Mortingas said that the vent to the outside was made shortly before the silver ran out." Barrin said. "We need to turn around and head back, watching for a side tunnel."

Tally opened her pack to find extra torches so they would have more light, but there was only one more left. They lit the second one and started back through the cave searching as they went.

"Look at this," Will said. He had found a gold coin on the mine floor.

"Cool!" Barrin replied. "Don't put it in the magic coin bag, or it will disappear."

"Good catch," said Will. He slipped it into an inner pocket of his cloak.

"I wonder who lost it," Talisia mused, curious.

"How old is it? What's the date on it?" Barrin asked.

"Our coins aren't dated," Tally explained.

"Do you – er, do we have the king on our gold coins?" he asked.

"No. We don't do that. Every coin is the same," she continued.

They kept walking and looking and presently Lexie spied the vent. It was head high and just large enough for an adult to crawl through. Tally volunteered to go first. They boosted her up and she slid into the vent shaft. She took one of the torches and their spirits rose when she lifted the torch into the passage and they saw it flicker in the breeze.

The shaft was only about thirty yards long. At the end there was a thick grate, but it unlatched from the inside. Tally left her pack by the grate and crawled back to let the others know.

"How will we get the last one of us into the shaft?" Will asked. We can boost each other up, but the last is stuck, and if someone reaches down to pull them up, then they have to crawl out backwards. No way any of us can turn around in that tight space."

"I think I can do it," Alexia said. "I'll go last."

They boosted Barrin up, then Will. Both guys shimmied along the shaft. Will had the second torch, and he tried to turn around to see how Alexia was doing. As he watched, she suddenly came sliding into the tunnel on her belly, arms first.

"How did you do that?" he called back to her.

She smiled back. "I ran and jumped. I could see the outline of the shaft entry outside because of your torch. Good thing I didn't miss. I would have crashed into the rock wall."

They exited the tight tunnel, and crawled out through a clump of bushes onto a mountainside. They were maybe two-thirds of the way up a lower ridge of the Dragon Mountains. It was dusk and there was no one and nothing in sight but the forest. Tally told them to wait, and then she ran off to look around. They sat and leaned against the nearest trees as they waited.

Eventually Tally returned looking rather satisfied.

"That ridge," she pointed to the west, "is the ridge above the Ranger Guild House and Stavanger. I am certain that the soldiers that chased us will never expect us here. I think we should go east from here, maybe even all the way to Falk-shire Hamlet. From there, we can cut south through the mountains and come to Wagon's Crossing from the east."

"How long will that take us?" Alexia asked.

"Less than a week," she replied. "But I am guessing."

"Okay. Let's do it," Barrin said. "We have to avoid the sol-diers. Even with the keys, we would be hopelessly outnum-bered."

"It's getting late," Tally said. "Let's camp near here to-night and start off tomorrow for Falkshire." Pointing east she added, "We can look for a good place to sleep that way."

They found a good looking spot shortly, and after a bite to eat, they all drifted off to sleep, happy to be free of the mine and the never ending darkness.

• • •

When they awoke, Barrin noticed two things right away: Tally was gone, and someone or something else was in their camp. He started to sit up, but a rough boot shoved him right back down.

"Good morning, kind sir," grunted a rough voice. It was a mocking tone, deep pitched, and gravelly. It was the sort of voice that a pig would have, if pigs could talk. "It was kind of you to finally wake up and show us some hospitality," the voice continued. This was followed by raucous laughter that sounded a lot like pigs oinking.

Barrin opened his eyes, and raised his head just enough to see a creature standing right next to him. It was a large, grotesquely muscle-bound, human-like creature with skin of a dingy yellowish green color and black spiky hair sprouting from the top of its head. Its ugly green skin was pebbled, almost like some sort of scales, and it was dressed in a leather armor chest piece with matching gauntlets and furry pants that ended in rough hobnail boots. It had an axe tucked in its leather belt, and its face looked similar to a pig in that it had deepset, beady eyes, a porcine snout, and large lower tusks that tucked up over its upper lip. It stood over six feet tall and was very broad-shouldered.

Barrin glanced around and saw that there were eight of these beasts in their camp. One stood right next to him, but only the speaker, their apparent leader, wore a metal skull cap that fit over its massive head and ended at its eyes.

The speaker was in the center of the clearing that they had chosen to sleep in. Will and Alexia were sitting upright on their blankets to his left and about ten yards away. There were two of the pig-men beside them as well, one on either side of their blankets. The other beasts were spread defensively around the speaker.

"Good morning to you, too," Barrin said, playing along and pretending to be happy to see them.

"Shut up," the speaker snapped, unimpressed. Then he continued. "I am Obnoc Tous, leader of the orgrum, and we are here for your treasure."

"I apologize to the … did you say, or-grum," Barrin said. "But we only have a few coppers. Nothing of great value." A boot hit him in the head, rolling him over.

"Don't lie to me!" Obnoc roared. "We saw you climb up out of a tunnel in the ground last night. We know what people hide in the ground! Now take us to your treasure!"

Barrin sat back up. He thought it was quite a leap of logic to associate tunnels with treasure, but he suspected that Obnoc Tous's lack of intelligence would only make convincing him to leave them alone harder, and it would not work to their favor.

"I'm sorry, but there is no treasure," he repeated.

"Grab him," Obnoc Tous commanded. The orgrum next to Barrin bent and gripped him under the arms and easily jerked him up onto his feet. His blanket fell away as he was manhandled by the monster. The beast was massively strong.

The shape of the orgrum bodies reminded Barrin of the old "He-Man" figures he had seen in his own world. Their upper body was a mass of overdefined muscles to the point that they were top heavy. Barrin silently found their appearance amusing but also somewhat terrifying, and he suspected that their muscles were from some sort of weird genetic quirk instead of dedication in the gym.

The orgrum gripping him stood very close behind him and pinned his arms to his side. He could hear its breath whistling in and out of its pig nose, which was just behind and above his ear, and he could smell its fetid body odor.

"Look at those!" the orgrum next to Obnoc sniveled as he pointed excitedly at the keys to the kingdom around Barrin's waist. He was the smallest of the band, and Barrin thought he gave off a toady vibe. He stood near Obnoc Tous and seemed to be going overboard to please his leader.

The keys had been revealed by the falling blanket. Their gold and bejeweled hilts glittered in the morning sun and were quick to draw the eye. The excited, toady orgrum followed Obnoc Tous over to stand right in front of Barrin.

"No treasure," mocked the leader. "These knives are worth a fortune." Obnoc snatched the red blade from its sheath. The toady one tentatively reached over and took the black key. It had barely cleared the scabbard when he gasped and fell to the ground.

"What did you do!?" Obnoc growled. He turned and drove the red blade into Barrin's chest, but the young king was ready and hoping for this. As the blade entered him he said, "extensa."

Inside of him the blade jumped to its full length piercing the orgrum grasping him. The beast screamed and relaxed its grip. Springing to action, Barrin shook his arms free, snatched the sword from the startled Obnoc Tous's hand, and whipping it in a circle to cut its way out of the beast behind him, he beheaded the orgrum leader.

At that moment, the chest of the orgrum nearest to Will exploded in sparks of electricity, followed quickly by one in the clearing. With a snarl, Alexia leapt from her blanket, crashing into the orgrum next to her. As she rose, her magic claws popped out of both hands, and she slammed them into the belly of the creature and pulled up, slicing him wide open as she knocked him away from her. With a squealing grunt he collapsed in a pile, his guts leaking out of his eviscerated stomach. The remaining two turned to run, but Barrin was already in motion, he split the nearest one from shoulder down before it took a step, and the other caught a lightning arrow from Tally, who must have been close by in the woods.

"Good morning, guys," Will quipped. "What's for breakfast?"

They shared a grim laugh as Talisia walked in from the woods.

"Sorry," she said. "I awoke as they were walking into the camp. I didn't have time to warn you. It was still dark; just as dawn was breaking, and I could slip off without them seeing me. They were busy searching our packs." She pointed, and they saw that their backpacks had been emptied. All their belongings were scattered about in small piles. It appeared that the orgrum were already dividing the spoils.

"No problem," Barrin said, giving her a hug and quick kiss on the head. "You saved us. Those lightning arrows are fearsome."

"What about those blades?" Will added. "You had three down before she fired an arrow."

Barrin gave a dry laugh. "I only get credit for the one really," he said. "Their stupidity did the rest."

"What are those things?" Barrin asked after mumbling "redux" and sheathing the red blade.

"They are one of the reasons we need dragons on our border," Tally answered. "They sneak in from the north to kill and steal. This band has been giving the rangers fits for a long time."

"Well, they won't anymore," Will observed.

"We need to move," Alexia said. "We just made a lot of noise, and we don't need any attention."

"You're right," Tally replied. "We need to go."

Barrin retrieved the black blade. They quickly reloaded their packs, relieved the orgrum of what few coins they carried, and started walking as quickly as they could. They were headed due east, and they decided to drop the heartstones with the Falkans since they were going near there anyway. Falkshire Hamlet was a couple days' walk from where they were.

They were staying at higher elevations than they had on the way northwest. Talisia was careful to avoid the open areas but stayed near the ridge as they moved east toward

Mount Dragon. The home of the dragons was significantly taller than the chain that it sat in. It was the only peak that had a treeline and exposed top. It was also newer looking than the other mountains around it. While it was volcanic and was mostly covered with conifers and younger growth, the western mountains were more rounded and worn down with old-growth deciduous forest for the most part.

As they walked, they began seeing glimpses of Mount Dragon in the distance. Barrin thought the constant smoke rising from the craggy peak was ominous. He was a little glad not to have dragons there to worry about, even if the guardians were supposedly friendly.

For two days they wound their way east through the mountains. These days were uneventful, but very tiring. Traversing the mountains was hard work, and they had to be constantly alert in case they were spotted.

They saw no further signs of orgrum in the area and didn't spot any predators, although they saw several large deer in addition to the now-standard fare of rodents, birds, and other small species. The animals in Saldringal were all familiar to Barrin but not identical to what he would see at home.

Saldringal had many varieties of birds that were kind of new to him, but they could have evolved from a common ancestor. For example, cardinal birds here looked like cardinals at home, except they were deep orange instead of red. Most of the creatures were similar, but not the same. Another example were the squirrels, which were the same as squirrels he knew, but they were larger and fatter than what he was used to, and they had a black stripe down the center of their spine from head to tail.

As they walked along on the second morning after the orgrum incident, the trees began to transition to conifers, and the soil began darkening. The smoking crest of Mount Dragon looked very close now, although it was still an hour or more away at their pace. Tally led them slightly higher so they would be walking just below the tree line.

They stopped for a break when they found the trail down the mountain to Falkshire Hamlet. The trail wasn't marked, but Talisia knew it was there from her Ranger training. Their rations were getting rather low. They had run out of bread in the mine, and as they sat to eat now, they finished the last of their cheese. There wasn't much left to share, making this a snack, not their lunch.

"I hope we can buy some food in Falkshire," Will said. "Our sack is almost empty; just a little jerked meat."

"My water is very low, too," Barrin commented.

"Yeah," Tally said. "Mine, too."

"I've been thinking," Barrin began. "We can't just walk into Falkshire and say, 'Here are some heartstones,' or we will get a lot of questions that we don't want to answer."

"That is a problem," Tally said.

"In Neferkala," Alexia said. "If you want to suggest something to the queen, but you don't want to personally deliver the message, you can ask the chancellor to deliver the idea anonymously." She paused. "What if we found someone to turn them over for us after we are gone?"

"That sounds like a good plan," Barrin said. "When we get to town, be thinking about who could do that for us."

"Didn't Thallon mention meeting an old man here?" Will asked.

"Yes," Tally said. "He mentioned meeting someone who saw a dragon take his friend."

"Let's start with him," Barrin said. "If we can find him."

They finished their snack and sat to rest for a few more minutes. Barrin had been wondering about something for a long time and finally his curiosity got the best of him.

"Alexia, do you have pet cats in Neferkala?" he blurted out.

Alexia reacted with hurt and anger, but then her understanding of his ignorance of her world washed away the reaction.

"No," she replied. "In fact, that word, 'cat,' is a hurtful racial slur used against our people."

"Oh. I'm so sorry," Barrin began, but she cut him off.

"No. It's okay," she said. "I know you didn't know." She continued, "My people were once enslaved and that word was used as a way of dehumanizing us. Well, you know, we aren't truly 'human' but we are sentient, and we don't deserve to be treated as lesser because we aren't your kind of human."

"Of course not," Barrin agreed. "I'm sorry I brought it up, I didn't think it would hurt your feelings."

"No. It's good that you know," she replied. "When you are king, you will need to be aware that not all of your subjects, and especially not all of the races of your neighboring realms, will think and act like you do. You need to learn what matters to other races."

"I want to learn as much as I can," he assured her. "I want Saldringal to be a good neighbor, and I would love to visit Neferkala and meet your people some day."

"I would like that, too," Alexia replied with a smile.

"Would you mind telling me what your queen said in your language when you were on the scrying stone with her?" he asked. "It's okay if you can't tell me."

"No, I can tell you," she said. "The queen asked if I thought you could win." She smiled. "I told her 'yes'."

Barrin continued to think about their conversation as they descended the trail to Falkshire Hamlet. She was correct. He had a lot to learn to be a good king. Cats were ubiquitous in his world, but come to think of it, he had not seen a single feline since he came to Saldringal other than his Neferkali friend.

Chapter Eleven:
What the Halfling Knew

There was a stone arch over the trail at the edge of Falkshire Hamlet. The town was a small cluster of just a few buildings. Very few people actually lived here. Almost all the Falkan families ran farms that spread out across the sides of the mountain and down the valley below. Centuries of rustic farming had cleared a large amount of land, most of which was cut into steppes along the mountainside, but trees still circled the village itself, and were dotted through the downtown area so that the town was shady and comfortable.

The streets, if you could call them that, of the entire village area were cobblestoned, with pathways radiating off the central square toward the various farm communities that circled the town, but most notably, there was one larger central thoroughfare that arrived from the west. Barrin theorized that this road probably went toward Stavanger or possibly down to the central plains.

The town square was by far the most square that Barrin had seen in Saldringal, but like the rest of the town, the Falkans did not strive for perfection in their architecture, and so it wasn't really square. In the center of the almost-square was a raised platform that reminded the friends of the dais inside Mortingas's tomb. There was no sarcophagus on top, however. The platform was vacant and appeared to be unused. Barrin wondered if it had been a stage or something.

The buildings of Falkshire Hamlet were the most interesting feature of the town. It appeared that Falkan builders disliked two things: cutting wood to length and matching materials. All the buildings were oddly shaped, with curved, sloping roofs, strange, added-on rooms poking out, narrow, unsquare corners, and a hodgepodge of building materials. One building may have two stone walls, one cut block wall, two plank board walls (they weren't all square buildings) and may have round, square and triangular windows interspersed along with a red brick chimney. The Falkans built their buildings to fit the land; they didn't change the land to accommodate the buildings, and so it all worked. Their homes, stores, and government buildings fit perfectly against the mountainside and looked like they belonged there.

There was a town hall, a bakery, two taverns, an inn, a mill, and a store that sold anything and everything, depending on what the proprietor could get. On the edge of town was a farmer's market where more trading went on than sales and a permanent shelter that could be used by traveling merchants, but none were present today. In fact, there had not been a trader here in quite some time. There were a few permanent homes built in the hamlet proper. They were all nestled discreetly off the central square; most were lining the roads that radiated off of the central area.

The four friends arrived through the stone arch just before noon and passed a couple of small homes on their way into the square. A few of the Falkan residents were out tending to their gardens. They all stopped and stared at the travelers, nodding in a friendly greeting but staring in an unnerving way. It must have been unusual to see strangers walking through because everyone noticed them, and most were curious enough that they started to follow after the friends to see where the four were going. Barrin noticed that several halflings quickly called for their families and hurried them outside just to see the visitors.

By the time Barrin and the others reached the town, they had a small gathering of nosy Falkans trailing along behind them, coming to see what these 'big people' wanted.

When they entered the square they were met by none other than the Honorable Mayor of Falkshire Hamlet, who was wearing a long, dark maroon robe, cinched with a golden rope and a matching maroon hat that looked like something the Mad Hatter from Wonderland would wear. Like many of the other Falkans, his shoes were thick felt slippers with curled up pointy toes, but the mayor's were much more ornate, and, unlike his neighbors who wore earth-toned shoes, his were rich maroon in color to match his outfit.

The mayor seemed incredibly nervous and excited to meet them, and there was no way they could miss him. His wild outfit stood out against the crowd of halflings dressed in simple farming clothes. He was short, round and plump, with a bulbous nose; bushy, red, out-of-control eyebrows; and a large, bushy, red mustache to match that curled on the ends. The ends of curly red hair poked out around his hat, and his eyes were bright green.

"Welcome to the fair hamlet of Falkshire," announced the oddly dressed Falkan. "I am Mayor Grumbleton, and we are always pleased to welcome guests to our quaint village." He bent in an awkward, sweeping bow like a model showing a prize on a gameshow. Smiling proudly, he continued, "How can we be of service to you, fair travelers?"

They were all rueing the attention they were getting, and they wanted it to be over quickly. Their plan had been to just blend in and to try to get in and out of town quietly without being noticed. However, the tallest Falkan present in the square did not reach Talisia's eyes, and she was the shortest of their group. They were all head and shoulders above everyone else in sight. There was no way they could "just blend in."

"Ummm," Will said. "Uhhh. We need, um. Food."

"Right this way, right this way, young people," the mayor gushed, as he again swept his arm toward the nearest tavern.

"Hey!" yelled a voice. "You old rat, Grumbleton! Don't make them go to your tavern!" The angry one was a man in a well-worn apron standing in front of the other tavern. "Let them choose."

"Mind your own business, Prattleton!" the mayor called back. "They just want to eat."

"Sir," called Tally to the other tavern owner. "We promise to visit your tavern as well before we leave. We look forward to trying it."

Prattleton looked annoyed, but he turned with a dismissive wave and went back into his tavern. Most of the crowd were losing interest by now and were starting to wander off. A few planned to follow the group into the tavern, not ready to give up the novelty of having visitors yet.

Although the friends didn't know it, Falkshire Hamlet almost never had visitors. The village was very far off the main road and a fair distance from all of the larger towns in Saldringal. They had no significant cultural events or unique products to draw sightseers or travelers, and they weren't on the way anywhere. If it weren't for their legacy of serving as dragon healers, then no one would have cared about the Falkans at all.

Many Falkans had gone their entire lives without seeing more than one or two visitors other than the couple of infrequent traders that came to sell their wares. Having four visitors show up together was unheard of, and so the news was spreading through the community like wildfire.

The good news for the four friends was that the lack of visitors meant that the Falkans almost never had any interaction with anyone outside of the hamlet, so no one in Falkshire knew that Will was wanted or that soldiers had been pursuing anyone. The king didn't even collect taxes from Falkshire. Their service to the dragons was their contribution to the greater good of the realm. Strangely, the disappearance of the dragons had not changed this fact yet. Perhaps it had not yet occurred to the king that the status quo had changed, or perhaps he avoided the Falkans for another reason known only to him.

They stopped at the door to the tavern, which Barrin noticed was called "Beartown Tavern," and the mayor addressed Will. "Do you need a stable or a cage for your beast, sir?"

They were all dumbstruck. For a moment, they didn't know what he was talking about; then they realized that he thought Alexia was an animal and that she belonged to Will.

"How dare you." Alexia said, her voice thick with ice and contempt.

The mayor jumped with fright. Apparently, he did not know that she could speak.

"My apologies, miss! My apologies! Please forgive me!" he stammered. "I have never seen one of your kind, and I was remiss." He bowed deeply, groveling. "I promise you the best service and utmost respect during your stay."

Alexia growled, and said. "It's okay. Let's go on." But her eyes were still angry and hurt. Will gave her a quick side hug and kept his arm around her. Just in case.

The mayor led them to a round table with six chairs. There was a four seat table available, so Barrin wondered why he would choose the larger one, but then the mayor plopped down and joined them at the table as casually as if they had extended him a personal invitation.

The server came to the table with pint sized tankards of mead and small plates heaped with what looked to be a chicken stew. The server was young and cute, and she flirted a bit with Barrin and Will. Tally and Alexia glared at her, and upon catching their expressions, she excused herself and left them alone.

The food was good, but it was difficult to relax and enjoy it. The mayor kept going on and on about all the town had to offer, and he repeatedly asked pointed, prying questions about why they were there and how long they planned to stay. Finally, Barrin decided to see if Grumbleton could help them out.

"A friend of mine mentioned an old man whom he had met here." He acted like he was trying to remember. "Oh yes, this man said that he saw a dragon take his friend away, or something like that."

"Awww," the mayor sniped. He looked down his nose as if he had smelled bad fish. "That's old Jaster. He's a fool. Don't waste your time."

"Oh, you know him?" Barrin asked. "Does he live here in town?"

"He's in the small cottage just down the hill. Last one on the right," the mayor replied. "It's a tiny, one-room place. Not much to see. He sits out on the porch some evenings."

"Well, maybe we can go by and pass along a 'hello' from our friend then," Barrin said.

"So, you own this tavern?" Tally quickly asked, changing the subject.

The mayor beamed.

"Yes, my dear," he answered, "but I have given the running of it over to a manager since I am so busy with my mayoral duties." They all wondered what these 'duties' included. This was such a small town; there couldn't be much to do. Besides, he had dropped whatever he was doing to latch onto them, and now he wouldn't leave them alone.

"I am sooo busy, working day and night to keep this town going," the mayor went on. "But. It's worth it. When I see the appreciation in my constituents' eyes…"

He prattled on for some time in what Barrin theorized was a piece of a campaign speech. All four of them just ate quietly and waited for his soliloquy to end. A couple of times two of them would make eye contact across the table, and they would be on the verge of giggling. Will had to intentionally look away to regain his composure, while Barrin feigned a coughing fit to cover his snickers. The mayor passed him a tankard of mead and never stopped talking. This cheered Alexia up considerably. She grinned at the absurdity of the mayor.

"...and so I knew I had to do my duty and serve my community, and I have been mayor ever since," he finally ended. He took a big draught from his tankard. "So will you be with us for a few days? Would you like to visit our inn?"

He was totally unaware of how uncomfortable he was making them.

"We haven't decided yet about how long we will stay," Tally answered. "And we probably couldn't afford the inn. I think we would be happy to camp on the edge of town."

"Nonsense," the mayor replied. "Our inn is very reasonable. Let me put in a word with the proprietor, and I am sure you will get a fantastic deal."

The friends made eye contact and tried to silently communicate their thoughts. Tally was instinctively nervous to use the inn after their experience in Stavanger, but she did feel rather safe here. She hoped the others felt the same way. Barrin looked at her and shrugged a little. His expression seemed to say, "What do you think?" Will looked nervous. He was the most upset about the inn in Stavanger, because that was where he discovered the bounty on him. Alexia was hard to read. Stare at any cat. You will understand.

"Could we have just a minute alone to talk about it?" Barrin asked the mayor. "Please?"

"Ohh," he was a little crestfallen. "Yes, I understand, you are big, important people. Take your time. I will just step out on the front porch and wait for you there."

The four friends put their heads together and whispered.

"What should we do?" Barrin asked.

"I don't want to sleep in the inn," Will said.

"It makes me nervous, too," Tally replied, "but I don't think these people have any communication with the outside world."

"The mayor doesn't seem to want to take 'no' for an answer," Alexia added.

"I think we will be okay here," Talisia said. "I haven't seen any sign that there is anyone here in this town but the Falkans and us. I've never met a ranger who has been here. I only knew the path from a map I had to memorize, and it was wrong. It just happened to be close enough that I found it. I think we are okay to be comfortable."

The others were quiet for a minute.

"I trust Tally," Alexia said.

Yeah, me too," Barrin agreed.

"Okay," Will said defeatedly.

"It will be alright," Tally reassured Will.

The server came by the table, and they asked how much for the meal. It was one copper for each plate and one for each tankard. The Mayor had left without paying for his drink, so they ended up paying for him, too. Barrin wondered if that was on purpose.

When they exited the tavern, the mayor latched right back on to them. By now, the rest of the townsfolk had gone about their business, but the mayor did not seem to have other obligations. He led them to the inn without asking for their decision. Together they stepped across the front porch, through the front door, and into the office area.

There was a long counter to the front and right of them in the lobby area. A couple of small overstuffed chairs faced a stone fireplace to their immediate right. A short hall went straight back to the left of the desk to access a couple of rooms, and a stairwell was on the left wall leading upstairs. There was no one in the lobby but them. They stood awkwardly for a minute, and then the mayor walked around behind the counter and faced them.

"How many rooms would you like?" he asked.

"Umm, do you own the inn, too?" Barrin asked.

"As a matter of fact I do," he replied with a grin. "It is my pleasure to serve the people in many…"

"How much for each room then?" Barrin cut him off.

"The rooms are normally three silver per night, but for my good friends, I can lower that to two," the Mayor replied. The inn at Stavanger had been one silver per night for their room. Barrin looked at Tally.

"How about two silver for two rooms for one night," Tally offered.

"Ohh," the Mayor reacted as if he were literally wounded. "That is a hard bargain."

"Well, we could just camp, I guess," Barrin murmured.

"Yeah. Let's get out of this place," Alexia agreed.

"You have a deal!" the mayor erupted.

"Can you throw in hot baths for us?" Alexia asked, noticing a sign advertising them.

"You are killing me," the mayor moaned. He dramatically sighed. "Baths for a copper each." The sign said two.

"Okay. It's a deal," Barrin said. "But we each get clean water."

"It's like you want me to lose money," the mayor cried.

Barrin pulled out his purse and paid the two silver and four, knowing it would be refilled when he needed it again.

The mayor had them sign the ledger book for the rooms. Tally and Will would sign, because they weren't sure that Barrin could write in their language. He had never tried.

The mayor was looking through the cabinet for their keys, so Will paused to think of a good pseudonym to sign.

"Write down 'Underhill,'" Barrin whispered.

Will did it, then whispered back. "Why Underhill?"

"It amuses me," he replied. "It's from a story I know."

Tally and Will were each handed a key and sent upstairs to find their rooms. The inn only had four rooms upstairs and two rooms down. The rest of the downstairs was used for the hot baths. None of the rooms seemed to be the mayor's own residence, and according to the mayor, none of the other rooms were currently occupied. In fact, it appeared that none of the rooms had been occupied in quite some time; as would be expected in a town that rarely had visitors.

Finally free of the pesky Falkan, they went to their rooms and dropped their gear. The rooms were tasteful and colorful and of reasonable size, even though they were designed for the smaller Falkan race. The beds seemed short, but Barrin thought he would fit without hanging his feet over the end. There wasn't a lot of floor space, but each room had a small desk with a chair and a more comfortable chair in the corner, as well as the bed. The floors in each room were polished hardwood, with woven tapestry rugs that covered the central area. The walls were plaster of a warm, cream color, and they were adorned with unique works of art in each room.

They had arranged to bathe right away, and the mayor had asked that the men go first. Will and Barrin left the ladies upstairs and went down for their baths. They were shown one at a time to individual rooms for bathing. Each room had a stone floor, with a large cast iron tub of heated water in the center, waiting for them. The rooms were side by side with a narrow hallway in between leading to steps that went up to a platform up against the interior wall at the end of the narrow hall.

A Falkan man was there to assist with their bathing, and after he showed each of them to their bathrooms, he retreated to the central hall where he sat on a stool waiting for them to finish in the tub. He had kindly informed them that they were to bathe first and then, when they got out, they were to stand in the corner stall for rinsing and pull a bell rope to alert him that they were ready.

In the bathroom, there was a small basin of water set out with a straight razor and soap for shaving, but Barrin had no idea how to use them, as he had only used a safety razor before. Besides, he kind of liked the light beard that was growing in, and so he went straight for the tub.

The water was hot, but not too much so. Barrin had had some concerns about the bath, as the facility was intended for Falkans, but there was a reasonably long-handled brush on a small tray attached to the tub, along with a bar of what appeared to be handmade soap. The tub, like the brush, was a little too small, but Barrin fit in it, and it felt great. He surmised that the Falkans must not have been used to preparing the tub for someone his size, since water overflowed the top of the tub when he sat down.

Until this moment, he had not realized quite how dirty he was. He scrubbed away the dust from the mine, bits of blood from the Orgrum battle, and the detritus of the last week. When he finished, the water was noticeably darker. He hoped that the Mayor would be true to their deal and would have his staff change the water for the girls.

Barrin finished cleaning himself and laid back to rest for a minute. He almost fell asleep, so he decided he had better move on. He climbed out of the tub and carefully plodded over to the corner and pulled the bell rope. He heard a bell jingle just on the other side of the wall.

Nothing else happened at first, but he heard the Falkan outside thumping up the steps. Barrin looked up and noticed the ceiling just above him was a grating. He couldn't see much through it, but he saw the edge of a bucket come out from the center and then warm water cascaded down over him to rinse away the bath water.

He waited, but no other water came down, so he padded back across the room and shook himself as dry as he could, then put his dirty clothes back on. He dearly wished that he had thought to buy another set of clothes, but then he thought that it was likely that the clothes sold here were too small anyway. Compared to his freshly clean self, his clothing smelled bad, and it felt a bit greasy. He promised himself that he would buy a new set as soon as he could.

Barrin reached their room before Will got back. Tally was gone, and so, after he knocked on Will and Alexia's door and got no answer, he left his door open to wait. Pretty soon Will came in on his way back. His hair was wet and though he looked cleaner underneath, his clothes were still dirty just like Barrin's. He had managed to trim up his beard.

"Do you know where the girls went?" Barrin asked.

"No I don't," Will replied. "Want to go out and explore the town a bit, and maybe look for them?" he asked.

"Sure," Barrin agreed. He stood and slung his cloak over his shoulders.

When they reached the lobby, the worker who had helped them with their baths was at the counter. He assured them that their ladies were bathing now and that his wife was helping them. They told him that they were going out for a walk, and asked him to please tell the girls to meet them at the other tavern, not the Mayor's, when they had finished. The Falkan was happy to oblige them.

Will and Barrin casually strolled to the tavern owned by Prattleton and took a seat inside in a corner. It was midafternoon, and with it being between meal times, the place was empty except for the barkeep and the proprietor himself. Prattleton rushed over to take their order and seemed disappointed when they only ordered two tankards of mead. They had had a large meal at lunch, and they weren't the least bit hungry.

Prattleton was the most weaselly looking Falkan they had seen. He was lean and tall, for a Falkan anyway, with close set eyes and a thin mustache. He seemed friendly enough, but Barrin kept thinking of Snidely Whiplash every time he saw the man. Prattleton appeared with their drinks, and to appease their host, Barrin asked him what time breakfast would be served in the morning. The tavern keeper gave them the time and a rundown of what would be available.

As Prattleton left the table, the girls walked in. The transformation to the pair was so astounding, that without realizing it, both young men stood up. Both the young ladies wore sleek dresses of a soft fabric that flowed with their natural curves. Each dress had short sleeves and a lace-up bodice over a soft white slip underneath. The dresses were identical, with swooping necklines that displayed a tasteful bit of cleavage behind the lacing without being too revealing. The dresses were solid, rich colors, and they had chosen them to match their eyes: Tally's was a warm green, and Lexie's was bright blue. Their hair was cleaned, brushed out and styled beautifully, and for the first time, Tally was wearing makeup. Her eyes popped, and her lashes were darkened and long.

Barrin always thought she was pretty, but now, she was gorgeous. He suddenly felt really bad about having to wear his dirty clothes.

The girls reached their table and smiled expectantly.

"Wow," Barrin said. "Tally, you look amazing. You're so beautiful." She blushed and looked a little shy.

"Lexie, you are so gorgeous," Will stammered. She batted her eyes at him and he grinned ear to ear. Her white hair was brushed out and straight. She hadn't pulled it back, like she normally did, and it fell over her ears and almost to her shoulders. Will couldn't take his eyes off of her.

"Where did you find these?" Barrin gestured to the dresses.

"The store in town had them," Alexia gushed. "The lady from the inn told us about them, and we hurried over and got them before we bathed. She helped us with our hair, too. She is really nice."

"Alexia did my face with her make-up," Talisia said. "I'd never seen make-up before! What do you think?" she asked.

"It's amazing," Barrin said. "But you were already beautiful." Tally beamed.

They revelled in their surprise for another minute, then Tally changed the subject.

"I need to not look like a ranger for a while," she told them. "I'm sure the horsemen at Stavanger got a good look at me, and between my ranger clothes and my lightning arrows, I am sure that by now they have wanted posters up, with my name on them. I need to look different. I want to go look for some different clothes at the store when we have more time."

"Well after seeing you two beauties, I'm feeling self conscious in these dirty clothes," Barrin said. "Would they have something for me too?"

"Maybe," Tally replied. "Shrilly – that's the lady from the inn – told us that the shop owner had purchased an assortment of clothing from a trader that turned out to have a few human-sized dresses mixed in. The salesman at the store hoped we would buy them all, but even if we wanted to, we don't have a way to carry them all."

"Let's go find out if they have something to fit us," Will said. "I need a change of clothes, too, if we can find one to fit me."

Will and Barrin both tossed back the last swallows of their drinks, and the group paid, then left the tavern and crossed to the local mercantile. Barrin and Tally held hands as they walked, and Alexia took Will's arm. They relaxed and took their time visiting with the shop owner and buying a few items.

Barrin found a new tunic that fit, which he quickly put on. He folded the old one up and set it aside to return to their room when they were done. Will found pants, but his strong muscled biceps were too large for any of the few human-sized tops they had in stock.

Tally had the best luck. At her height she was just a little taller than the Falkans, and so many more of their clothes fit her, giving her more choice than the others. She selected a hunter green tunic with dark brown breeches and a lighter brown cloak to replace her Ranger outfit.

Alexia wanted a new cloak since hers was still bloodstained, but clothes for travelers weren't needed in Falkshire very much, and they didn't have anything tall enough for the five foot ten girl.

After their bit of shopping, the friends dropped their extra items off in their rooms in the inn and then went out for a casual walk together. The girls grabbed their cloaks since their dresses were thin and didn't offer much warmth. It was beautiful outside, and they wanted to enjoy it. The afternoon was beginning to cast long shadows, and the perfect day was just beginning to have a touch of chill to it. The air smelled fresh, and they enjoyed each other's company as they meandered through the town.

"I could get used to living here," Tally said.

"It's fun to think about living somewhere until you remember that you need a job and a home," Alexia said.

"Wow. Lexie, way to kill the mood," joked Will.

"I know," Tally replied. "Just, everything is so pretty here and it just feels peaceful."

Their walk had led them down the hill away from the town square. At the last house on the right, there was a tiny old man sitting out in a rocking chair on the porch.

"Look. There's our man," Barrin said. "Let's go have a talk with him."

· · ·

As they approached, the old Falkan on the porch struggled to his feet and bowed as deep a bow as he could manage, which wasn't much.

"Blessings, Sire, and thank you for deigning to come see us," he croaked out. The old man was short, even for a Falkan. He had withered with age until he somewhat resembled a skeleton in skin pajamas. He shook a lot and held a cane in his left hand. His remaining hair was wispy and straggly, but clean, as were his clothes. His back arched forward so much that it was hard to tell when he was bowing and when he wasn't.

"What do you mean by 'sire'?" Barrin asked.

"I mean that you are the king of Saldringal, and that young lady," he bowed to Tally, "is your queen." He paused, "I apologize if I don't know the proper rules of court, Your Highness." His voice was croaky and had a little whine to it as well.

"I'm not the king." Barrin said. He quickly looked around, "But is there somewhere more private that we could discuss it?"

The old man gave them a quizzical look and motioned with the hand that didn't hold a cane. "C'mon in. We will see if we can find a place for all of you to sit."

"Hey," Will whispered, "Lexie and I can leave you here if it's going to be tight. You can fill us in later."

"Okay. Are you sure?" Barrin replied.

"Yeah. We can take care of ourselves. See you in a bit." Will insisted.

Barrin and Tally entered the little cabin after the hobbling old man. To say the cabin was sparse would be generous. It was clean, but almost entirely empty. Perhaps the old man had outlived his income. Still, someone took care of him. It was obvious from the clean tidiness of his home.

"My name is Jaster, by the way." the old Falkan said. "Now, why don't you two take the chairs," he said, gesturing to the only two seats in the room, "and I will sit on my bed. I don't usually have more than one guest at a time."

"Why did you think I was the king?" Barrin asked.

"Well." he took a deep breath, "people around here think I am crazy, but I'm telling you, I have visions." He looked up, "Usually it's dreams at night, but every once in a while they'll be in the day." he trailed off, caught his breath, then continued. "So, a few days ago, I was asleep and I seen you," he pointed to Barrin, "and you," he pointed to Tally. "You were at the top of a great castle, and you were dressed like a king and a queen." He paused to think, "You both had crowns on, and yours" he pointed to Barrin, "looked old and had big gems in it. You were watching a knight ride away. I think he might have been your kin, cause you were sad watching him go or maybe worried about him."

"I had that dream, too." Barrin interjected. Tally reacted to this news.

"You did?" she asked.

"Yes. The night after we got the keys." he replied.

"I'm sorry if it upset you." the old man began, "I didn't mean no harm. I just wanted to be respectful if you were the king."

"Oh, it's okay." Barrin assured him. "We came to see you about something else. I just wanted to know why you said it."

"Well." Jaster said, "what did you need with an old guy like me?"

"I am Barrin, and this is Talisia." Barrin began, "We had a good friend named Thallinius. Some called him Thallon. He was very old, and human, so he was taller than your kind." He paused to see if the man showed any hints of recognition. "He came to see you some time ago, and he said that you saw your friend carried off by a dragon."

"Yes. I remember your friend. He's a magic man of some sort," Jaster said.

"That's him," Barrin confirmed. "He was a magician. He has passed away now."

"Oh, that's too bad," the old man said. "I liked him."

"We would like to hear the story of what happened from you," Barrin continued. "Also, anything more you can tell us about the dragons."

"How long've you got?" the old man laughed. "I could tell you an awful bit about the dragons."

"Well," Barrin added. "Maybe give us the basics, and we can ask from there."

"Okay," Jaster mused. "You probably know that dragons die and are reborn. Well, most of the time, when they are ready, they fly into our town, land on that stage and suck their life force into their heartstone. Poof, they die; their body burns up, and their heartstone is left laying on the stage there." He checked to make sure they understood.

"Now this doesn't happen often," he continued. "They live about a hunnert years or so each time, but there are," he caught himself, "er, were, twelve dragons, and the rebirths are kind of spread out, not all at once, so most of the time we have two or three Dragon Healers trained up, just in case. Well, we noticed that we weren't seeing the dragons around much, and then one day, Ol' Ishthmar, the black dragon, comes to town. He's all raggedy and beat up-lookin', and blam!" They jumped at his sound effect. "He's gone in a blast of flame." He paused with his story and looked at Tally. "Could you be so kind as to pour me a cup of water?" He pointed to a cup and pitcher. "I'm not used to talking this much."

Tally picked up the pewter cup, filled it, and brought it to him. The water was cool and fresh. "Someone must come look after the old dear," she thought. Jaster took a drink and continued.

"It was my best friend, Bringle's, turn to go place the stone. It was his first time, and he was crazy excited about it. It was all we talked about for a couple days afore we went. I went along to help, but I wasn't going in the cave with him. See, the dragons are fussy, and they don't want more than one person coming in. They threatened to eat us if we brung more than one. Now I'm not saying they could eat us in one bite, but it wouldn't take more than two!" He laughed. Obviously this was a joke he had used repeatedly in the telling of the story. Tally and Barrin both smiled and waited while the old man laughed to himself.

He went on. "Anyway, we got up there and Bringle went in. I felt something was wrong afore he ever set foot inside, but he wouldn't listen to me. Anyway, he didn't come out for the longest time, then the black dragon came out carrying him, and he flew away. We haven't seen a dragon on the mountain since."

"Wow," Tally said. "I'll bet that was scary for you."

"Well, Miss Queeny," Jaster laughed. "Thanks for noticing that. Most people don't."

"What do you think happened?" Barrin asked.

"I think that Ishthmar killed his brethren for some reason and took their stones," Jaster replied matter-of-factly. "I think he killed 'em, and then got my friend to rebirth him, and then he took him off so he wouldn't tell nobody what he saw in there."

"Why do you think that?" Tally replied.

"Well it makes sense, don't it?" Jaster said. "They're all gone, and he still lives, wherever he is."

"We think we know where he is," Barrin said.

"Really?" the old man replied.

"I'm afraid we may know where your friend Bringle is, too," Tally said. Barrin looked at her. He didn't think he knew.

"He's probably dead by now," Jaster retorted. "Even if that dragon didn't kill him, most Falkans don't live past about seventy."

"You did," Barrin said.

"Well, yes." Jaster replied, "but I'm a special case. So, where do you think the dragon is?"

"We are pretty sure that he is in Castle Brackhaven. He is the power behind the king, who is an imposter pretending to be Arkendor," Barrin told him. The old man looked thoughtful.

"We think he helped this imposter slay the true king, my father, Pallindor, and his brother, Arkendor, so that they could replace my uncle and claim the throne," Barrin continued. "Our good friend Thallinius the Wise worked in the court, and he believed this to be true."

"How could that be true?" Jaster said. "About you being the son of Pallindor. He died almost a hunnert years ago."

"Thallinius used his magic to hide me where I would not age. I am Barrindor, son of Pallindor, and I have come to regain the throne," he insisted.

"Well, that's something!" Jaster said. "And I guess since you shared your secret, I should share mine. I don't know for sure, but I'm pretty sure it's not an accident that I've lived to be this old. There's a good reason I'm still goin' on after all these years. I've never told anyone before, and to be honest, it'll feel good to say it."

"We can keep your secret," Tally said.

"I stole from the dragons," the old man whispered.

They were quiet. Not sure what to say.

"When that black wurm flew off with my friend, I went on into their lair. I was angry, and I was worried." He paused, then continued. "I found Bringle's cloak and I got that to bring home. Then I looked around a bit, and I found this." He pulled up his sleeve to show an armlet of gold circling his withered upper arm. It was three solid strands of gold that were braided together. There was a rounded ball at each end for comfort. It was permanently shaped to fit around an arm, and the soft gold could be bent for size to help it stay in place. It was simple, but beautifully made.

"It was laying on the floor behind the dragons' sitting area; over by the wall." he said. "I figure that old Ishthmar dropped it or forgot it somehow. Anyways, I found it, and there tweren't nobody around." The double negative made their head spin for a moment, but they powered through as the ancient Falkan continued. "So I put it on, and I've worn it ever since. I was gonna sell it, cause, you know, it's gold and all, but it was soon after I got it that I started having my premonitions, and I think it's 'cause the band is magic. I think it has given me this long life, and probably my seein' eye too." He opened one eye wide and rolled it around, then smiled. It reminded them a bit of Mortingas. "My momma, bless her soul, died at seventy three; my daddy, sixty seven; and me? I'm a hunnert and twelve. It's magic, I tell ya."

The more Jaster talked to them, the less he tried to appear formal and respectful, and the more he lapsed into dialect and became harder to understand. Barrin wasn't completely sure that he really understood everything the man had said, but he caught the important parts.

"Hey. What do you think happened to Bringle?" Jaster asked, circling back to their earlier conversation.

"I'm sorry to tell you, but I think the dragon used a heartstone to kill him and turn him into an undead servant," Tally told him. "I think we met him a couple of weeks ago, and unless I'm mistaken, his body was consumed in a fire. I believe he may truly be at peace now."

It had not yet occurred to Barrin that the first wraith may have been a Falkan, but now that he thought about it, the first one was significantly smaller than the other three. It being created from a late Falkan's body made perfect sense, and it was unlikely that the dragon found a second Falkan to make into a wraith without the whole village knowing about it, so it probably was Bringle.

Tally brought her hand out of her pocket and showed Jaster the fire starter that the wraith had carried.

"Do you recognize this?" she asked.

"Yes," he sighed. "That was Bringle's. It was a gift of the dragons to someone in his family. I think 'twus his grandfather."

The old man hung his head. "It's one thing to think your friend is dead. It's another to know it," he said.

They sat quietly for a moment.

"Bringle was supposed to be mayor, you know?" Jaster mused. "That idiot, Grumbleton, his father bought the businesses and took over being mayor from Bringle's father. Bringle was his old man's only son, and when Bring disappeared, the old guy just fell apart. He was never the same." Jaster sighed. "He sold off the bakery, the inn, and the tavern and just withdrew." He paused. "Next election, he didn't even run, and he died not too long after. Grimbleton became mayor and passed it on later to his son, Grumbleton."

"So Grumbleton owns the bakery, too?" Barrin asked.

"Yes, he does," Jaster answered. "He pretends to be busy as mayor, but he really just sits around and feels important. He's harmless, though. An idiot, but not anyone to worry about."

"Are there any trained dragon healers now?" Barrin asked.

"No," Jaster said. "Not any who are trained and ready to go. Usually the dragon healers were young adults, and we aren't training our younguns like we used to, but there are old people left who were trained. They still know how to do it."

"So if I were to give you, say, three heartstones, you could see that they are delivered to the dragons' lair?" Barrin continued.

"Are you saying you have three heartstones?" Jaster asked incredulously.

"Yes," Barrin said.

"But," Tally jumped in, "the reappearance of dragons right now would draw unwanted attention to us and our companions, and it might bring the wrath of the faux king down on your people."

"Yes," Barrin added. "We want to leave the stones with you, but we ask that you hold them for a short while. Give us about seven days. We want the king brought down and the other stones out of his grasp before he realizes that we know what the stones do."

"We don't know how vindictive he is," Tally said, "and we don't want him to be able to cause problems for us or for your village. We need the element of surprise on our side, and the sudden reappearance of dragons would let him know that we are acting behind the scenes."

"I'll do it," Jaster said. "Just leave them with me, and I'll wait a week before I put 'em to use." He laughed. "If I could climb the mountain, I'd put 'em in myself, just to surprise Grumbleton."

"Thank you," Tally said.

"Yes. Many thanks," Barrin added.

"Now," Tally continued. "We will be on our way, but we'll stop by with the stones tomorrow morning on our way out of town."

"I'll be waitin' for you," Jaster said. "Please see yourself out. I need to rest after all this excitement."

Barrin and Talisia stood and slipped out as the man lay back on his bed.

Will and Alexia were nowhere in sight, so the couple linked arms and meandered down to a creekbed that they noticed just south of the town. It was mossy and green, and the first few fireflies of summer were twinkling under the trees. It felt magical and romantic. The area must have been considered a park. There were a couple of benches around and evidence that children played here.

Barrin and Tally sat down and watched the small flow of water swirling through the rapids and falls of the creek. They shared a kiss and just enjoyed being together.

"Barrin," Tally shyly said, "I've got something I need to tell you."

A lurch of fear struck him. Was she breaking up with him already?

"I really like you, but…, I don't want us to move too fast." She paused, struggling to say what was on her mind. "I know we have a room, and we are alone…" Again, she was searching for what to say. "I mean, I don't want to be…, you know, physical yet… ."

"Ohhh, it's okay." Barrin breathed a sigh of relief. "I am perfectly fine with that. Don't worry." He kissed her, relieved. "Look, this is new for me, too," he said, then hung his head, embarrassed. "You're my first real girlfriend."

"What do you mean girl friend?" Tally asked. "Are we just friends?"

"No," Barrin quickly replied. "In my world, a girlfriend is a girl who is very special to you. You spend time together, you kiss each other, sometimes a little more, and sometimes you end up getting married."

"We don't really have that here," she told him. "I mentioned before; if you are a girl, your parents arrange a marriage, you get married, and that's that. Afterwards, you are expected to, you know, be a wife and have babies, but a lot of married women also have a lover on the side. Someone they really care about. Some fall in love with their husbands, but most don't. A lot of husbands have lovers too; usually someone else's wife." She stopped and they were quiet for a minute.

"Was there anyone in the Rangers that you…" He didn't know how to say it either. "You know, you were close too?" he finished.

"No way," Tally replied. She chuckled and added, "Women who join the Rangers are usually more interested in each other than the men they work with. The male rangers don't even ask. They just assume."

"So, why did you join?" Barrin said. He was very pleased to hear that Tally hadn't been with anyone else. He felt a very strong attachment to her, and it made him jealous to think of her with someone other than him.

"I told you. I didn't want my father to arrange a marriage for me." She leaned against him. "I was always what other people would call 'headstrong'. My Dad wanted a boy, and he got me instead. He and Mum weren't able to have more kids, and Mum died when I was still pretty little, so he raised me by himself, like you would a boy, I guess. Without Mum, I never really learned how to be a 'lady.' Dad did the best he could, but I knew what I wanted, and being a housewife wasn't it. So I was off to the Rangers. Dad probably thinks I want a woman for a mate, and he probably thinks it's his fault. Some day when I marry, I'll convince him of the truth." She smiled up at him.

It was almost fully dark, and so they shared one last kiss and then got up and walked back to the town square. Will and Lexie were sitting on the front porch of the inn. They joined Barrin and Tally and the foursome walked to Prattleton's tavern, which was called "The Iron Bell," and together they shared a wonderful meal of roasted meat and root vegetables.

After dinner, the four of them all went to Barrin and Tally's room. It had become their tradition for Barrin to entertain the others every evening by telling them a story. He always just repeated the main plot of a movie from his own world. He had a good memory for dialogue, and he could recall many of the pertinent conversations from many films. He was working his way through the *Star Wars* saga right now, and tonight he would tell them *The Empire Strikes Back*. Barrin was a pretty good storyteller, and when he got to the famous moment when Han says, "I know." he noticed a tear in Tally's eye. The big reveal by Darth Vader drew gasps from them all.

When he finished the story, the others were all disappointed. They were excited to hear more about who they called "the Star People," and they didn't like how he ended with no resolution to the heroes' stories.

"Is it true?" Will asked. "Is Dark Vader his father?"

"It's 'Darth' not 'Dark'" Barrin laughed, "It's a title, like 'Lord'"

"Ohhh." Will said, looking expectant.

"Yes. He really is." Barrin admitted, "I'll tell you the conclusion tomorrow."

Will yawned, and he and Lexie gave their apologies and went on to their own room.

"Alexia had a talk with Will tonight, too." Tally whispered after their friends had left. "She is worried that she will have a baby and her family won't let her come home. I worry about that, too," she added.

"You don't have to worry," Barrin said. "We can wait until the time is right." He hugged her and kissed the top of her head.

He slipped off his tunic, and asked if it was okay to sleep in his underwear. The underwear were knee length with a drawstring top. They were much baggier than what he had been used to in his old world. Tally agreed, and he dropped his trousers and wriggled under the blanket onto the bed. Tally carefully removed her dress and slid in next to him in her slip. He hugged her to him, and they cuddled and kissed.

"Am I your girlfriend?" she asked, teasingly.

"I hope so," he replied.

"Good," she said.

"Tally," he was serious. "I am so happy that I came here to your world. Being with you is the best thing that has ever happened to me. You are very special, and I don't want this to end."

"I know," she replied grinning. Then she giggled, kissed him, and closed her eyes.

He lay his head down and slowed his breathing. A couple of minutes went by as they drifted toward sleep.

"I love you, too," she whispered.

Chapter Twelve:
The King at Rest

King Arkendor sat on his throne in the great hall. The throne itself was encrusted in gold and gems, and it made the king happy to bask in its opulence as often as he could. It wasn't particularly comfortable, but about as comfortable as human furniture of their realm could be.

Ancillon entered the room and approached the throne. He bowed low and greeted the king politely, then waited for a reply.

"What is it?" His Majesty snapped.

"Good news, sire: we have received a message from the Northern Squad," he said excitedly. "They encountered whom they believe to be Will Ironsmith and three companions in Stavanger." He paused hoping for praise. The King only stared at him, waiting for more.

"A loyal servant of the realm recognized the fugitive and rode out to find our troops. They thought that they had him cornered at an inn in Stavanger, but he and his companions escaped and fled into the woods." He hurried to go on. "Our men are tracking them even as we speak." He smiled. "We will have them for you, sire, very soon."

The King stared at him. Ancillon became very uncomfortable.

"Good news! Right, sir?" he stammered.

"So you come to me to tell me that my troops, not our troops as you seem to think, but my troops failed to capture a sleeping boy, and you come here to brag about it?" the King hissed.

"Well, we are right behind them. And they are on the run... ." Ancillon trailed off.

"Do you have any real news to report?" the King sneered.

"Well, we did identify one of his companions... ." he said, sheepishly. Again, he trailed off and waited.

"Well?" the King replied.

"Well, what, sire?" Ancillon asked. The king grabbed a heavy goblet of wine off the side table next to his throne and hurled it at Ancillon. The heavy cup bounced off Ancillon's face and fell clanging onto the floor, leaving behind a cut along the poor man's cheekbone. The guard captain clutched his wound and trembled with fear.

"You idiot!" screamed the King. "Who is the companion?"

"Talisia, of Wagon's Crossing," he stammered. "She is an apprentice ranger." He quickly added. "She was recognized by her ranger uniform and her magic bow; a gift from, well, from someone. We are not sure who gave it to her, but the ranger captain thought it was a gift."

"Put out 'wanted' posters for her as well as more for the blacksmith apprentice. We need to catch them!" the king bellowed. "You make sure the posters mention the other two in their party. We want all four of them." He glared at Ancillon. "I want patrols covering every part of my realm. These four are very dangerous, and they must be found. Send out another platoon if you have to; just find these four!"

Ancillon quickly turned to leave.

"Oh, Captain," the king said.

"Yes, Sire," he replied, turning to face his master.

"I will be holding you personally responsible if they aren't captured," the king hissed.

"Yes. Sire," Ancillon sputtered. Then he scurried around a couple of chests and out of the room.

The king stewed in his anger. Why couldn't he find men of intelligence to help him run this place? Dragons were intelligent and efficient. If only he could have a few more dragons to help him run the kingdom, but he knew that was impossible. Even if he made it possible for more dragons to be created, they would side against Ishthmar. He was sure of it.

He really needed to capture and destroy Pallindor's heir. It galled him that a simple blacksmith could elude him for so long. "It is probably the ranger girl's doing that he has made it this long," he thought. Well, he would take care of her, too, in due time – if his bumbling soldiers would do their job.

Maybe if he stepped up the tax schedule, his subjects could be persuaded to assist in capturing the fugitives, or at least be pushed to give them up. He was sure that they were being helped by some of the peasants in the realm. Pressure might be the way. He picked up a sheaf of parchment and a quill and jotted out instructions for his tax-collecting soldiers. He made four copies, one for each quadrant of his realm. More pressure, and more tax; that would help. He signed the notices and marked them with his seal.

Another frustration, his seal. When he took the throne, the official seal of the king, the ring which Pallindor had worn religiously, disappeared. He had been forced to make a new seal to replace it. Pallindor's seal was a heavy golden ring that had been used by the Kings of Saldringal for centuries. He suspected Thallinius was behind its disappearance, but he hadn't been able to locate the old man to find out. He sighed at the endless frustrations of being king.

Fuming and feeling sorry for himself, he bellowed for a guard and sent the letters to be delivered to his troops, then he went back to sulking away the day, sitting on his bejeweled throne in his Great Hall.

Chapter Thirteen:

The Battle of Willet Cliff Falls

The next morning, the adventurers slept later than they had in a week. By the time they dragged themselves out of their covers, the town was going about its business, and the taverns were about to switch from breakfast foods to luncheon. Yawning and stretching, they packed their bags and checked out of the inn, then had a quick breakfast at the Iron Bell. They purchased a few loaves of bread, chunks of dry cheeses, and with Barrin's direction, they prepared four large sandwiches from smaller loaves, stuffed with leftover roast meat from the previous evening's meal. All the food was carefully wrapped and stuffed in their food bag for travel.

They purchased jerked meat from the general store and also a package of dried fruits. Barrin especially was happy to have the fruit. It was the closest thing to candy he had eaten in ages, and he missed the occasional sweet treat.

Their last task was quietly dropping the three heart-stones with Jaster on their way out of town. With that accomplished, they were on the march due south. Their path followed the ridge of the mountains down the eastern edge of the peninsula of Saldringal. Starting out of town, there was a genuine, though little used, trail leading in their direction. It was probably only used by the occasional traders who visited Falkshire Hamlet.

The previous night's sleep had left the four invigorated. The beds in the Falkan Inn had been incredibly comfortable, much more so than the ones in Stavanger. If it hadn't been for the mayor's ugly remark about Alexia and his insufferable attachment to them, Barrin probably would have given him the extra silver he had asked for as a sign of thanks. Instead he had slipped an extra silver to each of the couple that ran the place. They had been very gracious hosts, and he wanted the money to go to them and not the mayor.

Barrin had had memorable dreams again during the night. In the first one, he was in battle with a great black dragon. It was blowing fire, and flames were all around him. The dragon turned to face him, glared an evil snarl, blew fire into his face, and as the flames engulfed him and the world went dark, he startled awake. It had been very real to him. Shaken, he went back to sleep, to drift back into another dream.

This time he was attending a wedding. He was far off to the side of the main aisle, just a face in the crowd, and he could not see who was getting married. There was a mass of people cheering all around him, and he struggled to get a glimpse of the celebrants. Through the crowd he saw a female form and a beautiful elaborate dress, but her face eluded him. The dream ended with him never seeing the elusive wedding couple.

As Barrin walked, he pondered the meaning of the dreams. Were these glimpses of the future or just the workings of his tired mind? If they were the future, was what happened in the dreams already decided, or were these just possible happenings that changed with the present? He kept these things to himself and just let his mind work on them while they traveled.

The next day was devoted to walking. Their relaxing visit in Falkshire was behind them, but its memory pulled at them, and all four were tired of traveling, tired of walking, and ready to return to a stationary existence, living in one place for a while.

The weather was nice, and even if they were tired of walking, it was pleasant to be outside. They were also happy to follow a path, as it was much easier than finding their own way through the primeval forests of the realm.

Eventually, the path cut hard to the west, and Tally instructed them to continue south. They left the trail and had to climb a steep hillside to continue. It was a tough climb but with several rests they made it to the plateau above them.

They camped that evening on a grassy open area on the side of the flat level of the mountain; then, the next morning, they walked farther south along the plateau. A stream cascaded down a rock face to join them, and in a little while, it split with one portion falling off to their right. Talisia and Barrin had been here before.

Tally dropped back to walk astride of Barrin, and she took his hand in hers. He looked at her and smiled, and she grinned back. In a few minutes, they reached the rock wall above Willet Cliff Falls where they had shared the quiet afternoon together and looked down over the community.

They had only been gone for a few days, but much had changed. One of the homes around the cul-de-sac had been burned. Its heavy log walls stood but were charred, and the roof was gone. Gwyn's washing pots were overturned and the drying lines were cut. No one was outside; no children and no livestock were in sight, though thin smoke rose from almost every chimney.

They hurried down the hill to Gwyn's and knocked on the door, worried that she was injured or worse. The Gwyn that answered the door was not the same woman they had encountered before. Her hair was disheveled and her face lined with worry.

"Oh, you shouldn't be here," she wailed. "Hurry inside." She threw the door open and waved them quickly in.

Ginny lay in the bed where Alexia had recuperated on their previous visit. She was asleep and was heavily bandaged.

"What happened?" Tally asked.

"The king's soldiers are what happened," Gwyn replied. "They came to town in a terrible mood," she continued. "Twelve horse soldiers leading several extra horses behind. They had three big black wolf pelts laying across three of the extra horses." She paused. "All the soldiers were wounded. They must have been in quite a battle. Most of the wounds were superficial, but that seemed to just make them angrier. They wanted us to pay our taxes, but they were early. We hadn't expected them for two more weeks, and many of us did not have it all collected yet.

"Stauer went first, and he only had one silver and four copper. Well, they beat the poor man and took his fowl. The next was Lassersmith; he only had one silver. It went on. I had all of mine, but the worst was the Mellon family. They only had a few coppers. The soldiers put the torch to their home and stole their child! Their little girl is just gone." She sobbed, tears running down her face. Tally and Alexia were crying too, and both Will and Barrin were blinking back tears of anger at the injustice as well. "After that, the soldiers just started breaking things. They struck at anyone they could catch and then rode off. One of them cut my Ginny with a sword. It isn't that bad, but she needs time to heal."

"The worst of it," Gwyn said, "is that they told us they would be back in a few days for the rest." She paused. "These people have no way of making money that fast."

"Yes they do," Barrin stated. "They will have the money if that's what they want." He took Gwyn's hands. "Gwyn, I promise you that this will not stand. Go gather your neighbors. Bring them here, at least one from each family. We need to talk with them."

Gwyn left and Talisia fell against Barrin sobbing. "This is all my fault." she managed to get out. "If I hadn't used that lure, the night wolves wouldn't have attacked the soldiers, and this wouldn't have happened."

Barrin held her until her crying subsided. "This isn't your fault," he said. "This is on the soldiers. They chose to hurt these people, not you." She sniffled and then wiped her eyes.

"What can we do to help them?" she asked.

"I've got an idea," Barrin said. "We will help them if we can." Speaking to Will and Alexia, he said, "Let's see what resources we have available." They counted their coins and prepared for the meeting together.

The townspeople began filtering in. They looked suspiciously at the four young people and found places to sit; mostly on the floor. Finally Gwyn arrived and squeezed into her now packed cabin.

"I think we have at least one representative from each family now," she told them.

Barrin stepped up on the hearth and spoke.

"Friends, I am Barrindor, the son of Pallindor, who was your king." Everyone started grumbling and conversing at once. "Please. Hear me out," he continued.

"People!" Gwyn yelled. "For me. Please listen to this young man." The noise slowly subsided.

"My father and my uncle were murdered, and their killer sits on the throne, pretending to be your king," he stated. "His soldiers did terrible things to your community in his name; well I say that enough is enough!" He paused, and added, "This cannot stand!" There were light cheers.

"My friends and I are on our way to Cantigal to try and take the throne back, but I don't want to leave here until we help you get back on your feet." They were listening now. "Before we leave here, we will see that each of you has two silver pieces for when the soldiers return, and from now on Gwyn will give you two silver every time they come asking." They all cheered.

"I don't have that..." Gwyn began.

"Don't worry," Barrin cut her off. "You will." He continued, "Tomorrow, let's all pitch in together and fix Mellon's home. We can do it if we work together. They deserve a place of their own, and they didn't deserve this."

A man they didn't know by name stood up. "I don't always get along with Mellon, but that could have been any of our homes. We all were short. So I say, let's do it! Let's pitch in and fix it together." There was a chorus of agreements from various families.

A man quietly stood and said, "Folks. I appreciate you all, but you don't have to do this for us. We'll get by somehow."

"Are you Mellon?" Barrin asked.

"Yes," he replied.

"We aren't just fixing it for you and your family," Barrin said, "It's for everyone here. You all love your village, and you deserve to live in a nice town."

"We saw a beautiful, happy village here just a short time ago." Tally said.

"And we want the soldiers to know that they haven't broken this town," Barrin added. "They knocked you down, but you aren't broken. We put it back and show them that they broke a house, but they didn't break this town."

"What about my Arelly?" Mellon asked.

Barrin assumed this was his taken daughter.

"I'm sorry, but I don't know what we can do for her yet," he said. "But don't give up. We will try our best to get her back if we can."

"Now, who is our best carpenter?" Barrin asked. The rest of the meeting was spent planning for the following day. The townspeople grouped together by skills and discussed plans to rebuild.

The next morning, the town turned out early and set to work. Will took over from the local smith, who was self-taught, and churned out beautiful hinges, nails, brackets, shelf hangers, and anything else needed for the construction. He continued making pieces for anyone who asked, enjoying his new skill level and the added endurance provided by his ring.

Alexia and Talisia organized the women and children into moving the debris from the ruined home and seeing what could be salvaged. They, along with the other women, provided light manual labor, and the children served as "runners," moving supplies and essentials around to the various builders. Early in the day, Tally sent two of the older girls to go well out of town and watch the road. The soldiers were expected, and they didn't want to be caught flat-footed.

Some of the women finished their jobs and started working to correct some of the other damage done around the village. They fixed Gwyn's washing equipment and cleaned up broken and damaged items around the town. They also dug up and repotted wildflowers in various vessels to place around the town.

Barrin was everywhere helping with anything he could do. If someone needed a hand, he was there to help, and quickly the town members started looking to him more and more. He had good ideas, and every plan for the construction was run by him to see if he thought there was a better way.

By late afternoon, the roof was solid again, and the carpenters were putting the finishing touches on the interior of the home. Most of the town members were still outside laughing and visiting and reveling in the pride of a job well done.

"Tally!, Tally!" One of the girls who Tally had sent to watch the road appeared. She was running for all her might into town. Talisia ran out to meet her. "The soldiers are coming! We saw them!"

"Where is your friend?" Tally asked worriedly.

"She couldn't run as fast as me, so she ran off to hide in the woods," she said. "Don't worry. She's a good hider."

"How many soldiers?" Tally asked.

"About ten horse riders, and at least twenty on foot." the girl replied. "We saw them far off, and I ran here. We didn't wait to get a good count because they would be too close."

"Okay," Tally said. "You did great!" She smiled at the girl encouragingly. "Everyone, the soldiers are coming now. Meet me at Gwyn's to get silver for your family," she called out.

All day, Alexia and Tally had used the magic coin bags to generate a stack of silver coins, but to her surprise, no one headed for Gwyn's to get them, instead three of the men of the village came to talk with her instead. Barrin saw them and came hurrying over.

"Ma'am," the spokesman of the group said. "We appreciate you trying to help us, but we have decided that we need to help ourselves. If we don't stand up to these soldiers, we may as well not have a village. You helped us see that this is a place worth fighting for." He stopped, looking uncertain and awkward.

"How many men do you have ready to fight?" she asked.

"We have fifteen men with hunting bows," he replied.

Tally looked at Barrin. "What do you think?" she asked him.

"Spread the bowmen around the village," he said. "Out of sight where you can shoot from the woods." He paused. "You lead the archers and take out the horses and bowmen if they have them, first. Will, Lexie and I will meet them at the bridge. Try to get them before they cross. Anyone that cross-es the bridge, we will have to stop."

"I'll put two archers on each side of the path into town in case some try to get away. We can't let the word get out of what is happening here," Tally added.

"Good plan," Barrin agreed. Turning to the townspeo-ple, he added. "I would like to ask everyone in town who isn't an archer to find anything that looks like a weapon and have it in hand…" He went on to explain his idea.

• • •

The soldiers came into the clearing on the other side of the small bridge. The riders were light cavalry; their horses were more for transportation and scouting than combat, so they brought up the rear. The foot patrol was led by one mounted officer, followed by four Saldrant wraiths. There were closer to thirty infantry, six of whom were archers. The consternation on the soldiers' faces as they saw the repaired home, and the beautiful little town put back to order so quickly was obvious.

Barrin hoped that Tally could see the archers too, and he hoped they would fall quickly. He waited till the mounted captain approached the bridge. The wraiths were just behind the captain followed by the footsoldiers, then the archers. The light cavalry brought up the rear and they spread out to surround the foot patrol.

"Your filth is not welcome here," Barrin said, stepping forward. Will and Alexia stood on either side of him. When he said this, behind him, every house door opened, and the entire town piled out. Each person carried an improvised weapon: a pitchfork, an axe, or even a poker from their fire-place were fair game. They walked out and made a rough semicircle behind the three friends.

"Who are you, to think you can tell us, loyal agents of the king, where we are welcome?" asked the captain.

"I am Barrindor, son of Pallindor, and I am your rightful king," Barrin asserted.

The Captain laughed. "Barrindor died almost a hundred years ago. You are a lunatic, and you will be taught a lesson." He kicked his horse to charge and as it stepped forward, Tally's first arrow hit him. The shock of the arrow strike knocked the captain over backwards, and the shock of the lightning shook his arms like a puppet master shaking loose a tangle. He keeled completely backwards, his feet jerked free of the stirrups and he rolled off the horse and fell over its rump to the ground. Before he even left the saddle, soldiers were falling all over the field.

The hunters of Willet Cliff Falls were very skilled bowmen. Years of over-taxation had left them desperate for food to feed their families, and whether they ate or not often depended on their making a good bowshot on game. These men practiced, and they were skilled. They sent flight after flight into the terrified troops.

These soldiers had not seen real battle before; in their experience, no one had resisted the king's will, and many of them froze in panic at the attack. But not the wraiths.

The arrows did not phase the wraiths. The four came steadily after Barrin and his friends, arrow shafts sticking out of their dead flesh.

They crossed the bridge and the three friends prepared for combat, but the townspeople weren't going to let anything happen to their heroes. They charged en masse, swarmed the wraiths and pulled them down, beating away their weapons with the force of numbers and iron determination. One by one, Will, Barrin, and Alexia pulled the dragonborn warriors' heartstones free and watched the dragon born immolate.

When it was clear that it was going to be a rout, a few of the infantry tried to run away. They were cut down by the reserve archers that Tally had sent to line the trail into town. None of the king's men walked away from the battle. The people of Willet Cliff suffered one casualty. One of the teenagers in the crowd twisted his ankle chasing the retreating troops. He would have to rest it for a few days.

Mellon came up to Barrin after the battle and said, "I recognized the piece of trash that took my girl. Those horse soldiers were the same ones from a few days ago."

Tally was just arriving at Barrin's side. He turned to her. "Would the soldiers have had time to return to Cantigal and back here in the time they were gone?"

"Not unless they ran their horses all the way there and back," she replied.

"So they probably have a camp nearby," Barrin said. "Maybe they have Mellon's daughter and the livestock there."

The four friends caught four loose horses and mounted them. They called Gwyn over and let her know what they were up to, then they rode out of town along the road back toward the central plains. They had walked this way some time ago, but it was much faster on horseback. The horses were excellent, and they made good time. Barrin had never ridden a horse, but after a bit he found the rhythm, and then it was fairly enjoyable, despite the urgency of their task.

When they saw the edge of the forest ahead, Tally motioned for them to slow, and she pulled up, dismounted, and walked into the woods and out to the edge of the field. She was back in a few minutes.

"I see tents out there in the grassland," she said. "I watched and there appear to be only one or two guards, but they have several horses and a good assortment of livestock."

"Should we rush them?" Barrin asked.

"Let's approach them slowly," Alexia said. "They will probably assume that anyone on a horse is an ally. No one else has horses. By the time we are close enough for them to see our faces, it will be too late."

"Alright by me," Barrin replied. Tally nodded.

They remounted and rode out in a two-by-two block. They headed straight to the tents. One of the guards ran out to meet them.

"What brings you back?" he called, right before Tally raised her bow and fired. The other guard heard the commotion and ran for a horse. He got one foot in a stirrup before her arrow caught him and he fell.

The four friends dismounted and searched the camp. They gathered all the coins and anything of value they found and used the captured horses from the camp as pack animals to carry their bounty. In one of the tents they found the stolen girl. She was terrified, and when Alexia found her, she burst into tears. She cried more once she was free than she had in her bonds, as she had attempted to hide her fear from her captors. Since Alexia found her first, she was the one to hold Arelly as she cried and cried from the relief of being saved. When they were ready to go, the girl insisted that she ride back with Alexia, and she clung to her new friend all the way home.

The last thing they did before leaving was to pile the tents, the two bodies, and the massive wolf pelts together and set them ablaze. They didn't want any evidence left of who had destroyed the camp. Hopefully, the other soldiers and the king would never find out what happened to this particular patrol.

By the time the four reached Willet Cliff Falls with their bounty, driving the livestock before them, the townsfolk had cleaned up almost all signs that a battle had taken place. Once again, the community had pitched in and worked together for the common good. The dead bodies had been relieved of their coins and had been removed to a communal grave in the woods. The living horses were in a freshly-created corral to the north of town, out of sight, and the fallen horses had been butchered, and their meat was being prepared for drying in the smokehouse. Buckets of water had been taken from the creek to wash away any remaining blood stains in the grassy area around the bridge, and the arrows had been collected and fairly redistributed to the hunters of the town.

All the coins taken from the soldiers and the camp were dumped on Gwyn's table. Barrin added those taken from the orgrum to the pile. Gwyn asked several ladies to help, and they made equal stacks for each family. Gwyn convinced them to divide the silver equally amongst the adults and the coppers equally among the children so that the larger families got a little larger share. She now knew the secret of the coin bag Tally had given her, so she didn't keep a portion for herself, only a few coppers for Ginny, who seemed to be feeling better and was excited to have a few coins of her own.

Mellon came up to Barrin and thanked him awkwardly; then realizing it wasn't enough he grabbed Barrin in a bear hug where he cried a bit and said, "Thanks for saving Arelly." He said it over and over again, until Barrin finally pulled away and told him it was okay.

Barrin called several of the men together and met with them privately.

"Of course you know there may be retaliation," he said. The men nodded and looked worried. "I am very proud of you and all your people today," Barrin told them. "If I am able to drive out the imposter, I will be counting on good people like you to help make Saldringal better for everyone. I will use your community as an example of what is right in our realm."

The men were flattered. "But be warned," Barrin said. "If I lose, and he remains king, I am counting on you even more. You showed today what teamwork can accomplish. You have ignited the spark of revolution here. If I can't take down the king, you can, and I would ask you to make it happen."

"We would do our best," Mellon said. "But we believe in you, King Barrin. We know you can win, and we would gladly follow you."

• • •

The next morning, the four friends left Willet Cliff Falls early, headed for Wagon's Crossing. Most of the town turned out to say goodbye. The townsfolk lined the road, cheering as the friends walked across the bridge and on their way, waving to their new friends as they went.

As they were preparing to leave, Will walked over to Mellon and held out his hand. Mellon grasped it to shake hands and a puzzled look came over his face. He withdrew his hand and looked at the gold coin Will had given him. It was the one he had found in the mine.

"It's my gift to you," Will said. "Your family has had a bad time lately. Use this to replace the things you lost, and do something special for Arelly."

"I can't..." Mellon started.

"Yes. You can," Will cut him off with a smile. With lots of hugs and promises to visit again, the four left town and cut south through the woods.

Talisia expected it to take about three days to get to Wagon's Crossing. She wanted to stay deeper in the woods this time, but as she knew these woods very well, she did not think it would slow them down very much. They also didn't have the pony to contend with anymore, so, even with the longer path, she expected three days to be enough.

Chapter Fourteen:
Strike of the Eagle Watch

The days spent traveling to Wagon's Crossing were tense and nerve wracking. Even with the deeper route through the forest, they encountered several patrols of soldiers. They were fortunate enough to see all of the patrols before they themselves were seen. Tally had taken to leading from a great distance out in front of the others. She had created a hand signal, and when she gave it, they would take cover and freeze, barely breathing until she gave the "all clear" signal. Patrol after patrol passed them by, probably because the soldiers didn't really expect to find anyone this far off the beaten path.

The first evening they camped in a thicket where they could conceal themselves while they slept. They kept quiet and were careful not to disturb any more of the underbrush than they had to as they made their way into the briars. All of them ended up with minor scratches, but they felt safer from the soldiers inside.

They lay down for sleep early and Barrin reflected on their recent battle. It had been too easy for their ragtag group of villagers to beat the larger force of the king's soldiers; especially with civilian weapons against a military force. At first he thought that it was some sort of ruse – a trick to make them think they could win and give them overconfidence. Now he didn't think that was it.

Now he suspected that the king's army was cocky and overconfident. They had never been opposed, and none of their troops had seen actual combat. Over decades, their training must have become sloppy as they trained for battles that never came. They seemed to expect everyone to just appease them because they were soldiers, and until Willet Cliff Falls, everyone always had. Fear, and their sheer numbers, made them feel invincible, but now Barrin knew they were not. After that battle, he liked their chances better than before. They were facing barely more than amateurs, not professional warriors.

More than anything, Barrin realized that the soldiers had disconnected from their mission. They had supposedly sworn to protect the people of Saldringal, but instead, they themselves had become the enemy of the populace. He decided that when he became king, he would work to correct this problem. The soldiers should work with the people, not against them.

The second evening, they came to a place where two small ridges jutted off from the mountainside to their left, creating a hollow. There was a dry drain that ran down the mountain and across the forest floor in front of them. Tally turned into the hollow and told them that it was a good place to sleep for the night.

"What's that?" Barrin asked her, pointing to a small mammal he had spotted in the woods. It looked very much like a raccoon from his world, but it's head was a bit larger, and it didn't have the expected raccoon mask and tail. Instead, its head and tail were both mottled black which contrasted against the animal's furry gray-brown body.

"That's a 'coriacc,'" she said. "It's a minor predator." She further explained, "They spray a soporific to immobilize their prey, usually ground squirrels and other rodents."

She led them into the hollow to a flat area near the drain, and they spread their bedrolls to prepare to sleep. As they moved around preparing their beds, Will kicked a few bones loose from under the leaves that turned out to be an entire skeleton. It was mostly intact, but the various pieces were scattered about as if the body had been pulled apart. Tattered clothing was rotting around the remains, and a rusted sword and bag of coins were lying where they fell when the belt gave way.

"Look," Alexia said, "the bones are chewed on." She was correct. Many of the bones showed teeth marks.

"I wonder what happened to him," Will said, yawning.

"It wasn't bandits; he wasn't robbed," Tally pointed out. She yawned too.

"Suddenly, I am really tired," Barrin said. He walked over to his blankets.

"Yeah," Will agreed, yawning again. "Good nigh…" He trailed off as he fell over, sound asleep.

Alexia saw a coriacc on the hillside behind them. Barrin was lying down then. Talisia fell to her knees. Another coriacc was across the drain from them. Alexia heard a noise and saw another one, and then another.

"Tally!" she screamed. "Get up!"

Tally looked at her, a foggy look in her eyes.

"We are being attacked!" Lexie yelled. "The coriaccs!"

Tally struggled to her feet, groggy. They pulled Barrin up, and walked him out of the hollow. He staggered along, barely awake enough to walk. They got him a fair distance from the coriaccs and sat him down where he could lean against a tree.

"I'm feeling a little better," Tally said. "Let's go get Will."

"Take a deep breath, and try to hold it," Lexie said. They ran into the hollow. A coriacc was approaching Will as they arrived. It hissed at them and skittered off as they approached. Together, the girls lifted Will and half-carried, half-dragged him out of the hollow and out to where Barrin was.

Barrin was more awake when they returned, and he was able to help them move Will farther away.

"I guess we know what killed the other traveler," Tally said. "I have never heard of them working together like that. I'll need to let the Rangers know about this as soon as I can." She looked at her friend. "Lexie, thank Aeric that the coriacc's spray didn't affect you as strongly as it did us. You saved all of our lives."

"My pleasure," she replied with a smile and a nod. "Anything for my friends."

Barrin continued the storytelling that night after they had regathered their gear and moved on to a safer location. His friends had grown accustomed to discussing the stories throughout the day as they walked. Of course this depended on how many patrols they had seen recently.

He had finished the *Star Wars* series and was working his way through the Harry Potter stories, but his friends weren't nearly as fond of those tales as they were of *Star Wars*. Apparently Harry Potter isn't as amazing in a world that already has and accepts magic.

The travel was slow because of the foot patrols in the area. When they finally approached Wagon's Crossing, they were about a day behind their expectations. Barrin had been thinking about what to do next, so he opened a discussion with the others looking for ideas.

"I'm nervous to just walk into town," he said. "We know that soldiers frequent your tavern, Tally." He paused. "But I told Gawan to watch for me in the tavern. I didn't know that there would be so many soldiers out looking for us. What should we do?."

It turned out that their worry was unnecessary; the woods around Wagon's Crossing were riddled with campsites. The Eagle Watch must have gained several recruits since they had last seen Gawan.

They approached the first camp that they found and repeated the ritual greeting that Talisia had used before. The two men by the fire asked them to enter. Walking into camp, Barrin feigned surprise.

"Oh, I was looking for my friend's camp," he said. "His name is Gawan."

"I used to know a Gawan," said one of the men with a wink. "I think he might be staying on the other side of town." He pointed in the approximate direction. The friends made their apologies and moved on.

They repeated this process a few times until they finally found the man himself. Gawan was well and had a campsite set up that was large enough for all of them. Grum looked human-sized and when they found them, the two were sitting by the fire together, roasting two whole fowl over the flames.

Gawan was thrilled to see them. He jumped to his feet to welcome them personally and was beside himself with excitement. He grabbed Barrin, Will, and Tally in an embrace and then introduced himself to Alexia.

"It is wonderful to meet you, Miss," he said bowing deeply. "I mean meet you awake and well, of course." He laughed.

Turning to Barrin he said, "Have you seen the army we have put together?" He beamed, then went on, gushing. "We ended up with more than sixty! That beats the thirty I expected to bring any day!" He continued, "The king's men have been really pushing the subjects hard lately, and the realm is primed for revolution. Everywhere I went to gather the Eagle Watch, new recruits volunteered to join and came along too."

"Are you concerned about the possibility that some of the new recruits may be agents for the king?" Talisia asked.

"Well, to be honest, that is always a concern with our new recruits, but I think we are okay," he replied.

"I'm concerned that this many camps will attract attention," Barrin worried.

"Me, too!" Gawan replied. "That's why I am so happy you are here. We need to plan our attack and move immediately, tomorrow if we can."

It was currently evening. The sun was starting to set, and the fires were becoming more noticeable. The four friends gathered around Gawan, and they began discussing a plan of action.

"Castle Brackhaven is at the center of Cantigal," Gawan began. "The town has a wall, but it isn't well-guarded, and the gates on all four sides are left open all the time. It has been so long since we had a threat here that I am not sure that they even know how to close them." He paused for a moment to remove a scroll of parchment from an inner pocket. He spread it out to show them.

"The castle is more or less square in shape with only one gate, which faces north towards us. The wall surrounding the castle has battlements with walkways for archers to patrol, and they do patrol it." He pointed to two squares at the front corners on either side of the gate. "There are guard houses on these two corners, and a small guardhouse built around the gate itself. We will need troops near these three places to counter the guards as they respond to your attack. And we will need to deal with the archers on the walkway under the battlements, here," he pointed.

"There is a wall down the center of the castle that divides it into two halves." His finger moved to the center of the square and traced a wall there. "The wall connects to the keep in the middle, and there are gates through the wall on both sides of the keep. Behind the wall is a smaller town unto itself that provides the servants with living quarters, barracks for the castle guards, an armory and smith shop, and the keep's kitchen as well. There may be a few guards off duty in that area, and they may respond, so we need a few men at each of these gates just in case, but I suspect that the majority of the guards will be in the guard buildings, assuming that we hit during the day." He looked at each of them to make sure they understood, then he continued.

"The keep is in the center of the castle, and it is the tallest building; the one with towers and parapets. There is a lower balcony on the side that leads to the king's living quarters. He seems to enjoy addressing his people from the balcony, mostly just announcing new taxes, declaring verdicts, and that sort of thing." He pointed to the location on his drawing. "If he won't come out, you might get to him through the balcony. Grum could toss you that high if it comes to it, but I think the king will want to confront you personally."

"The courtyard has become a bazaar of sorts," he said, refocusing on the map. He pointed to the right side of the courtyard near the wall. "Over here is a corral for the soldiers' horses, but the majority of the courtyard will be full of tents with various vendors hawking their wares. The people who live around the castle are the only ones left in the realm that really have any money to speak of. More and more businesses have tried to move inside the castle in order to actually sell their products. You should expect a lot of people shopping and selling." Finally he pointed to the center of the courtyard right in line with the balcony. "The Arkenstone is here," he said. He made eye contact with Barrin and added, "We need to get you to it before we are discovered."

"We estimate the entire force of the king to be about two hundred fifty soldiers," Gawan continued. "And we know that more than a third of that force is out in the realm gathering taxes and searching for something – probably for you." He laughed. "We are expecting about one hundred twenty soldiers; maybe a few more, which means we are almost one-to-two with them. Good odds, especially since we have Grum." He nodded to his giant friend.

"We have battled the king's men," Barrin said. "They are poorly trained. We have a good chance of success."

"Well don't take it for granted," Gawan countered. "The king's personal guard may be better than what you saw out in the realm, and we haven't trained as an army would. We are but an assemblage of willing fighters who really care."

"True," Barrin agreed.

They discussed their plan of attack and ironed out as many details as they could; then Gawan slipped off to communicate the plans to all the others and make assignments for the next day.

The Eagle Watch leader had just returned to camp when a commotion broke out at the group campsite that was nearest to them. A man came running over to Gawan and collapsed to his knees by their fire. Blood flowed heavily from a wound in his side, and he had a cut across his scalp as well.

"Wesson!" Gawan exclaimed. "What happened?"

"Wraiths…" the man croaked. "Wraiths…" and he pitched forward on his face.

Everyone scurried to draw weapons, but it was too late. Even as Gawan drew his sword, three wraiths materialized out of the night behind him. The first one ran his sword through the resistance leader from behind as the other two swung unnecessary hacking blows at Gawan on their way to attack Will and Alexia. Will raised his shield in time to fend off the wraiths' attack as Alexia prepared her claws. Barrin jumped to help them and within a few minutes, he had cut one wraith down to pieces with the red key while Will and Alexia had dismantled the other with his hammer and her claws. They pulled both the wraiths' heartstones, then turned to go after the third one. Their help was unnecessary.

Grum had the remains of the third wraith in his grasp. He was raising it over his head and slamming it into the ground over and over, and over again. Tears ran down his giant face and he was wailing with anger and grief. The wraith was no longer distinguishable as a being. The tremendous blows had changed it into an amorphous mass of tissue. It appeared that just about every bone in its body was broken, and yet, through the magic of the heartstone, it was still twitching and attempting to move as the giant pounded it into oblivion.

The four friends quieted Grum and got him to stop pounding the wraith. He dropped the pulverized beast, and howled in grief as Will carefully retrieved the wraith's heartstone. The danger averted, they hurried to Gawan's side. Their friend was barely alive, but he was fading fast, and there did not seem to be anything they could do for him.

"I'm not going to make it," he said.

"Sure you will," Barrin replied. "Hold on."

"I really wanted to ... to see the tyrant fall," Gawan whispered, then he looked at Barrin. "Don't ... let me ... down. You are the king." His eyes slid shut and he was gone. Grum wailed again.

Barrin and Tally visited every camp that night. They counted their losses and let everyone know that Gawan had fallen. All in all, the wraiths had killed eighteen. Four others lived, but were too injured to fight. The Eagle Watch bemoaned the loss of their leader, but all swore their allegiance to Barrin and agreed to proceed with the attack tomorrow. Their army was down to about forty. The odds had changed.

When they returned to their own camp, Barrin spoke with the others. "There is a good chance that they know we are coming tomorrow," he said. "Obviously, they knew we were here, or those wraiths wouldn't have shown up.

"I don't think they know that we are here," Alexia replied. "Remember, the wraiths targeted Gawan." She paused. "Shouldn't they have gone after Will, or possibly Barrin first?"

"I'm not even sure that the king knows that Barrin exists," Tally said. "We know they want to talk to Will, and they are probably after me, but I think every soldier that has seen Barrin died at Willet Cliff Falls."

"But the wraiths didn't go after Will first. They targeted Gawan," Alexia persisted.

"Either way," Barrin cut in. "Tomorrow we end this."

"Yes," the others agreed.

They skipped storytime that evening; they were too worried and wrapped up in their thoughts about Gawan's death and the challenge of tomorrow. Grum stayed up to keep watch. He was still feeling pitiful about the loss of his friend, and he wanted to be alone to grieve.

The next morning, the remaining Eagle Watch members packed their gear and slowly made their way to Cantigal in twos and threes, arriving in the morning hours. They visited friends and acquaintances, ate in the taverns and hung about the town, staying as casual and as unnoticed as possible. All hid their weapons under traveling cloaks, and did their best to blend in.

Barrin and his friends waited. Per the plan, they timed their arrival for just after noon. They had heard that the king's troops ate a meal at high-sun, and they planned to arrive when hopefully the soldiers were experiencing an after-meal spot of lethargy brought on by their full stomachs. Grum was with them, appearing man-sized, and carrying a massive war club under his cloak of intention. He displayed a new level of anger on his countenance, and secretly Barrin was very glad that he did not have to face the enraged Grum in battle today. Four other members of the Eagle Watch were with the friends as they slipped through town and into the courtyard of the castle.

As they passed through the gate, two of the Eagle Watch were "distracted" by the nearest booth. They wandered off to take up a position near the gate house.

Tally broke off to her left with Grum and one of the remaining Eagle Watch soldiers. They made subtle eye contact with a few other Eagle Watch members as they approached the guard house on their side of the courtyard. Barrin looked to his right and saw several clusters of Eagle Watch troops, who were appearing to shop at tents on the other side of the market, which put them near the corral and the second guard house.

Together, Barrin, Will, Alexia, and the remaining Eagle Watch troop, meandered their way through the crowded marketplace to the Arkenstone in the center of the courtyard. As Gawan had predicted, there was a large crowd of people milling about and carrying on their daily business. There were sellers shouting advertisements for wares, shoppers milling about, and even livestock wandering in and out of the crowd with their owners; either freshly bought, or about to be sold.

The Arkenstone stood on a pedestal in the central courtyard. It was white, soft-looking stone cut into an obelisk shape. It had engraved runes running down along the edge of one side, and the stone stood atop a pedestal, in a holder that kept it upright, with its narrowest point aimed at the sky.

"The stone contains at least one magic spell," Alexia whispered. "I can feel it." Then she added, "It's powerful magic, too; be careful."

Just then a murmur went through the crowd. The peasant shoppers around them randomly started turning to face the keep as if they had noticed something of importance. "The king. The king," they heard people whispering all around them. Barrin looked at the balcony on the side of the keep across the courtyard from him.

King Arkendor himself stood there. The reaction of the townspeople led Barrin to believe that the king's appearance in public view was out of the ordinary. The people seemed excited to actually have a glimpse of their leader; even if they hated his iron rule.

The king was surrounded by a small group of well dressed men and a couple of guards in more ornate uniforms than Barrin had seen in his brief time in Saldringal. Barrin supposed that the men around the king were likely to be nobles or possibly advisors.

Arkendor himself had long, stringy black hair without a hint of gray, and a long black beard that hung down and narrowed to a point. His skin was pale, and he was gaunt with an angular face and deep set, black eyes that burned angrily under craggy brows. He wore black robes of the type that Barrin associated with sorcerers.

The king also wore a tall spiky crown upon his head, and the back of his cape stood up in a tall frill behind his head. He spoke with a magically amplified voice.

"You may as well reveal yourself, magic user," the king called out. "I can feel that you are here." He paused and there was no response. He spoke again. "The more that we have to search for you, the worse it will go. You may as well give yourself up now."

Barrin wasn't sure if the king sensed the keys, or Alexia, or Grum's cloak, but he wasn't going to wait to find out. He drew himself to full height and stepped to the side of the Arkenstone where the king could see him. He threw back his cloak, drew the red key and murmured "extensa." The blade jumped to life. A blaze of recognition, and then angry fear washed across the king's face.

"I am Barrindor, Son of Pallindor," he bellowed out. "And today I claim what is rightfully mine, the throne of Saldringal."

The king smiled with a grim, menacing sneer. "You fool," he hissed. "You may break my Arkenstone, but if you do, I promise that you will regret it, and you will never live to be king." Gesturing to the nearest guard house, the king roared, "Guards. Seize him!" and pointed at Barrin.

As the soldiers flooded out of the guard houses, the crowd around the friends panicked. It was utter chaos. Gripped with fear of the soldiers, the peasants began screaming and climbing over each in a scramble to get away from Barrin.

From within the mass of villagers trying their best to get away, the Eagle Watch erupted, throwing back their cloaks and moving to engage the encroaching flood of soldiers.

Above the din, Barrin heard even louder startled screams of terror break out as Grum revealed himself and brandished his club, startling the panicked throng of people that swirled about him.

Grum began swinging his weapon in great swaths, swatting away soldiers two and three at a time as they exited their guard house. Tally was at Grum's side, flinging arrow after arrow at the upper walkway that ringed the courtyard, picking the king's archers off the top of the wall. Her Eagle Watch companion stood by her side, sword bared, protecting her from ground attacks as she sniped.

On the other side of the courtyard, the larger Eagle Watch force was engaged with the swarm of king's men that were streaming from their guard tower. The rebels were outnumbered, but they were fighting valiantly, and they were holding their own.

Barrin was scanning the crowd and the castle battlements looking for the dragon. Thallinius had been sure that the dragon was here. Barrin had found the king, but where could the dragon be hiding?

"Barrin. It's now or never," Alexia called to him over her shoulder as she engaged in battle.

"Do it, Barrin!" Will called. The two of them were defending Barrin from any of the king's troops that made it to the central courtyard. Alexia's magical claws were exposed and glowing and Will's hammer already dripped with blood. Sadly, their Eagle Watch comrade was down; killed by one of the king's guards.

Barrin turned to the Arkenstone and swung the red key in a whistling arc with all his might. He had never attacked stone with steel before, and he didn't quite know what to expect. He half-feared that the sword would bounce off the stone or possibly shatter, but as Mortingas had promised, the red key could cut anything. It sliced right through the Arkenstone as if it were made of butter. The blade slid through, and for a split second nothing happened. Then, with tremendous force, the stone exploded.

The blast was similar to the pots that had held the portal spells, but a hundred times stronger. Fragments of the Arkenstone blew like a blast from a shotgun. Everyone around the pedestal was knocked to the ground, tents were blown flat, and all over the courtyard, the fighting stopped as everyone turned and stared to see what had happened.

Barrin was knocked flat with the others. He had several minor cuts and scratches from the fragments of rock that had peppered him as the stone exploded, and his ears rang from the blast. He staggered to his feet and shook his head to clear it as a howling, amplified cry went up from the balcony.

On the balcony, the king was doubled over in a knot, wrenched in what appeared to be immense pain. As Barrin and the astounded throng in the courtyard watched, the king's back began to swell and grow, his arms and shoulders writhed and lengthened. Great black wings sprouted from behind his shoulders and tore through the cloth, shredding his robes. His neck grew, extending his now enlarging head far above his shoulders as his human face morphed into lizard-like features.

The few guards and noblemen who had stood with the king on the balcony startled with fear. One of them threw himself over the railing and fell two stories to crash awkwardly into an abandoned wagon below him. Most of the others fled through the door and escaped the transforming king.

Ancillon was on the edge of the balcony. He tried to get back through the door, but the rapidly expanding king shut off his escape. He was trapped with the dragon.

The king's tattered clothing fell away as his new shiny, black body became clear. The spiky crown hung jauntily from a horn atop his head. King Arkendor was no more. This was Ishthmar, the Dragon King.

The Arkenstone had been the vessel for a spell that kept the dragon transformed to human form. Till now, none of the friends had considered that the king himself could be the dragon. Like Thallinius, they had assumed that the dragon had enlisted someone to act as a puppet king, but now it all made sense. The dragon himself was King Arkendor.

Like Ancillon, Barrin felt panicky himself. He had come all this way to overthrow the dragon, but now, seeing a real, live dragon in the flesh, he was terrified. He was a high school student, not a knight. What was he doing here? He should be sitting in class reading stories about make-believe dragons, not here in person, fighting for his life against a real flesh and blood one. He looked around frantically. He wanted to run. He could run back to his world – away from dragons, and strange food, and uncomfortable clothes, and no toilet paper.

But then he looked at Tally. She believed in him. So did Will. And Alexia. And the queen of Neferkala, Thallinius, and Mortingas. He thought of Gwyn and Ginny, all the good people of Willet Cliff Falls, the people of Falkshire, Gawan and the Eagle Watch. They deserved a good king; someone who cared about his subjects and used his rule to make their lives better. He thought of the army of Neferkala coming to invade. The people of Saldringal didn't want war, and they had paid enough. His resolve hardened. He would fight for them. If he died trying, then at least he would have tried. Drawing upon all the courage he could muster, Barrindor stood straight and raised his sword in challenge to the dragon.

Ishthmar raised his clawed hands and removed the crown. Ancillon was next to him, sniveling and cowering with fear. As the great dragon turned to toss the crown into the room behind him, the guard captain bolted for the door, but hissing, the wurm snatched him up, and flung him bodily at Barrin far below. Barrin saw the attack coming, and casually stepped aside as the human missile passed him by and crashed through a market stall behind him. The shattered body of Ancillon landed in a mangled heap and ceased to move.

"I warned you, foolish human." Ishthmar growled at Barrin with his still magically-amplified voice. "Now you will pay for your insolence!" As he said the word "insolence," the balcony, which was not built to hold the weight of a full-grown dragon, broke away and fell, dropping Ishthmar. The stones of the balcony crashed onto the wagons, tents and every-thing else below, but the dragon only fell a few feet before he opened his wings and glided to the ground.

With the dragon's entry to the fray, the king's guards and the Eagle Watch resumed their battle throughout the courtyard. The revelation that their king was actually a drag-on raised the guards' fear of failing their leader, and so they struck at the rebels with renewed vigor.

By now, Grum had finished off all the guards around him and he had commandeered a stack of firewood which he began heaving at archers on the walk, and at any other exposed enemies that he spotted. Tally had taken out almost every archer with her bow, but she kept scanning the para-pets for more, in case any reinforcements tried to take up a position.

Landing heavily to the earth, the dragon raised its head back and began to blow fire. Ishthmar was angry, and he wasn't taking much time to aim. Within moments, most of the courtyard was ablaze with guards and Eagle Watch alike scrambling to avoid immolation.

As the dragon blew his flames all about him, he began walking towards Barrin. He narrowed his eyes, and focused his full attention on the boy as he strode purposefully toward his prey.

Suddenly, a huge chunk of firewood slammed into the dragon's head, briefly stunning him. With an angry hiss, he shook his head and then snapped around to glare at Grum, who threw another wooden missile at the wurm. Unfortu-nately, this chunk of wood narrowly missed, and before he could grab another, the dragon took a deep breath and blasted fire back at the giant. It engulfed him with its full im-pact and set the firewood stack next to him ablaze.

Grum already had a couple of arrows embedded into his great body, and a sword wound across his thigh. The terrible damage from the fire was too much for him. Barrin's heart fell as he saw Grum's clothing burst into flames, and watched the grievously wounded giant fall to his knees and collapse.

Fortunately, Tally had seen the dragon's blast coming. As the dragon released his fire, she dove away from her heroic friend in time to avoid the roiling flames. She joined the nearest band of Eagle Watch fighters and renewed her battle with the guards.

This distraction defeated, the dragon turned back to Barrin, who stood staunchly; red key in hand, and ready for battle. Ishthmar glared at the young man and resumed stalking within range of his flameblast.

Although outwardly defiant, inside, Barrin was fighting his rising fear. He was reaching his desperation point. If he was going to have any chance at all, he needed a plan to get past the dragon's flame. He didn't know what to do, and so as the dragon drew nearer, he glanced cautiously at his friends.

Will was fighting with a soldier nearby on Barrin's left. Alexia was off to his right dealing with her own skirmish. The dragon was close enough. It locked eyes on Barrin, drew its head back, and unleashed a huge blast of fire right at him. It was exactly as Barrin had seen before in his dream, and despair gripped him as he knew that this was the end. Just as in his premonition, he saw the flames cascading out of the dragon's mouth, blasting through the superheated air straight towards him. The bright fire burned its way right towards his face. He squeezed his eyes shut, fell to his knees, and then, it all went dark.

But he was alive. Unbelieving, he squinted through his clenched eyes. There was a dark outline of a shield in front of him. Will was there. He had leapt to Barrin's defense and blocked the entire blast at the last second; his magic shield taking the full impact of the fire.

Will groaned, his muscles straining to subdue the power of the dragon's fiery breath. Fortunately, his hard-earned muscles were up to the task, and he was holding fast under the strain of the onslaught. Barrin glanced to his right and saw Alexia drop her soldier and turn towards the dragon.

Ishthmar glimpsed Alexia too, and recognizing her as a threat, he ended his assault on Barrin and swung his head toward the Neferkali, opening his mouth to blast her with his fire. But he was too slow. Alexia screamed something that Barrin didn't understand, and a glorious blue stream of light leapt from her hands and blasted into the dragon's mouth. As the light of her spell waned, Barrin saw that the dragon's entire head was now encased in ice. Shocked by the magical attack, the wurm raised his head to full height and took a step back.

Alexia released her stream of magic ice with a stunned look. "Oh," she squeaked, as she went limp and collapsed, falling face first to the ground; eyes rolling back as she fell.

"No!" Will screamed. Alexia was in danger, and he had to get to her. He sprinted towards her fallen body as the dragon crushed the ice with his jaws and shook his head free from the shattered remnants of the spell. Again Ishthmar tried to blow fire at the downed girl, but the ice had cooled him off. He couldn't generate a flame. With an angry roar, he stepped toward the fallen Neferkali. His fire may have been temporarily extinguished, but his teeth and claws still worked.

The next sequence of events played out for Barrin like they were in slow motion. He saw Alexia fall; he saw Will run towards her. He saw that in his haste to get to Alexia, Will was passing dangerously close to the dragon. And then Barrin was up and moving.

Like Barrin, the dragon saw Will approaching and turned his head, selecting a new victim. Will realized his mistake too late. The savage teeth were already coming for him. He tried to raise his shield to protect himself, but he didn't have time. The fangs were right in his face, and he could smell the dragon's hot breath.Will braced for the bite, and Barrin slipped under the distracted wurm's defense and drove the tip of the red key into Ishthmar's heartstone.

Their past battles with the wraiths had allowed Barrin to recognize the rounded jewel sticking out amongst the scales on the dragon's chest. The lunge strike he used in fencing was second nature to him. He had used it in his matches a thousand times, and he was good at it, so as he neared the dragon, he set up and lunged the red key into his target.

When the red key hit the heartstone, the stone resisted just slightly. The ancient magic at work in the heartstone tried to resist the magic of the dragon-forged blade. The sword tip caught for just a moment, giving Barrin just enough time to experience a flash of panic that his attack was failing, and then the heartstone shattered, cleaved by the unstoppable blade. The key's tip slid through the stone and plunged into the dragon's chest.

Like the cleaving of the Arkenstone, the destruction of the heartstone released an even more massive explosion of magic. For the second time in just a few minutes, Barrin was sent flying by a ground-shaking explosion. This time, the blast knocked everyone down in the entire courtyard and cracked the stone wall that closed off the servants' living area. The force of the blast was so strong that it snuffed out all of the remaining flames in the courtyard.

Everything was still for a few moments. There was no sound but groaning and the occasional cry. Smoke hung in the air, and more was rising from smoldering embers all over the courtyard. Ash drifted down. The dragon's shattered body immolated, leaving a heap of more ash and the shards of his ruined heartstone on the ground.

Talisia was the first one to struggle back to her feet. As she came to her senses, fear gripped her, and she hurried off, searching and calling for Barrin. Her ears were ringing from the blast. She saw others shaking their heads and climbing to their feet around her. The king's guards were dropping their weapons and looking bewildered. She wondered if they had been under a spell to make them serve the dragon; they seemed to not know where they were.

She found Barrin and fell to the ground next to him, holding him tight. She was crying as she pulled his limp body to her. She lay her ear on his chest and felt his heart beating and his breathing on the back of her head. The tears streaming down her cheeks changed from tears of worry to tears of relief. Barrin awoke as she held him. She kissed him, and he kissed her back.

As he rose, she ran to check on Will. The young smith was already sitting up when she got to him. The dragon's teeth had grazed him as Barrin struck and he had several bloody nicks on his head and bad cuts down his shoulder, but he would be okay. She tore a stray piece of clothing from a body nearby, ripped it to pieces, and tied the fabric around his cuts to help stop the bleeding.

Together Will and Tally went to Alexia. Barrin joined them at her side. She was sound asleep, but aside from a few slightly singed spots in her fur, she did not seem to be injured. She had simply overdone her use of magic with the ice blast, and her body needed time to recover.

Poor Grum had not survived the dragon's fire. Neither had his marvelous cloak of intention. Many of the Eagle Watch had fallen in battle as well. The remaining rebels all joined together and formed a protective circle around Barrin in the middle of the courtyard. Everyone else in the courtyard turned to Barrin expectantly.

Barrin felt incredibly awkward. He had been thinking about being king for some time now, but now that he was going to be, he didn't really know what to do. Everyone expected him to say something. He looked to Tally, who stood by him with adoration in her eyes. She smiled and whispered, "Go ahead." All Barrin could think was to start announcing some of the plans he had for the kingdom. He had been forming plans for days; really, since their visit with Mortingas.

"My people," Barrin began. He noticed the pedestal that had held the Arkenstone still stood, so he gingerly climbed up onto it to stand above the crowd.

"My people," he repeated. "I am Barrindor, Son of Pallindor, destroyer of the Arkenstone, and your true king."

There was a lackluster cheer from the assembled crowd. More curious townsfolk were beginning to re-enter through the courtyard gates and join the assembling throng.

"The dragon who was posing as our king has taxed you very unfairly," Barrin said. "He has stolen your wealth, and cheated all the citizens of Saldringal from the life they deserve."

A few in the crowd were saying "yes" and other such agreements as he spoke. Barrin continued, "As your new king, I promise that you will be treated with dignity and respect, and I will begin showing you this new respect today, with my promise to you that we will collect no taxes for the entire next year!" A great cheer went up this time.

"Now, my friends and I will need some time to rest and recover from our battle, but we do want to right whatever damages the dragon has done. I apologize and mourn with all of you who suffered losses today. As your king, I will do my best to see that we never see violence like this again." He paused to catch his breath, then continued.

"If you lost a loved one today, I grieve with you. My friends and I have also lost several great friends in our quest to take down the tyrant. If your livelihood suffered damage from what happened today, we will do what we can to help you get back in business." Again there was a great cheer.

"Now, please give us time to rest and treat our wounds." Barrin stepped down off the pedestal and limped to Talisia's side. Will picked up Alexia, and the four friends entered the keep with their remaining Eagle Watch troops trailing along behind.

· · ·

Three days later, Barrin and Tally were standing on the highest balcony of one of the towers of the keep. They were watching the sunset and enjoying a quiet moment together. Barrin realized that this was the location of the scene in his dream. He suspected, actually hoped, that someday that dream would come true, as had the one about the dragon fire. Tally had her head on Barrin's shoulder, and his arms were around her.

Their last few days had been a whirlwind of activity. When they had entered the keep after their battle with the dragon, what struck them first was how bare it was inside. It was as if every treasure, decoration, and relic had been stripped from the castle.

They found all the missing items, a giant hoard, in the Great Hall. It was a massive mound of gold, silver, gems, artworks, weapons, anything of value really. The king's throne, which was covered in gold and gems, was perched on the mound. Apparently the dragon liked to sit on the pile of wealth.

Much of the hoard had been the dragons' treasure from the lair on Mount Dragon. There were magical items of all kinds mixed in with the treasures of Saldringal. Alexia's gems were there too, still neatly stored in ironbound chests for travel. Barrin decided to return all the gems to Neferkala along with a gift of the gold they needed. He would let Alexia know his plan as soon as she woke up.

Alexia finally awoke on the second morning after the battle. She was thrilled that the gems were recovered. She used her scrying stone, and after several tries, her queen answered, and promised to send a ship and escorts to bring Alexia and the gems back to Neferkala. Alexia respectfully told her that she would not be returning to her homeland. Like her mother, she had fallen in love with a human, and she wanted to remain in Saldringal.

Barrin asked Will to be his personal "Head of Security." Will didn't know what that was, but when Barrin called the position "Captain of the King's Guard," Will happily accepted.

On the afternoon of the second day after the fall of the dragon, a group of nobles from the area brought their families, Barrin invited the townspeople to join in, and they held an official coronation ceremony in the great cathedral to Aeric in Cantigal. Barrin insisted that they use the crown given to him by Mortingas instead of the spiky one that the dragon had used.

On the third day, they had begun hiring staff and filling positions to keep the castle in order. The dragon had chased off, fired, executed, or possibly even eaten, most of the people who had previously worked in the castle.

The guards, and in fact most of the soldiers in general, had foggy recollections of their service to the previous king. The dragon must have used a spell to control them, a spell that was broken when he was.

Now at dusk of the third day, Barrin held Tally as the sunset played out before them.

"You know," he said thoughtfully. "As king, I really need

a queen." With a teasing tone he added, "Should I offer your father a couple of cows, or...?"

She punched him on the arm.

"Hey, hey, hey," he teased. "Assaulting the king. That is beneath a noble ranger like you."

Tally threw her arms around him and they kissed.

"I would love to be your queen," she whispered. She lay her head on his shoulder and turned to face out at the sunset. He felt her jump as she looked off to the distance and startled.

"Look!" she called, releasing him and pointing to the horizon.

Off in the distance, flying toward them, were three tiny black figures. As Barrin's eyes adjusted, he saw what Tally had seen. Outlined against the sunset were three dragons! Jaster had done it. The dragons were back!

Epilogue

A year later, Will and Barrin stood in the ruins of Thallinius's house. They were kicking through the ashes and looking for any artifacts of the old man that may have survived the fire. They didn't have high hopes as the magical fire that destroyed their cabin had burned for six months before it finally went out. Now that the fire was extinguished, Will wanted to see if he could find something that would remind him of Thallinius that he could take home as a keepsake. As they searched, Barrin thought back over all that happened over the previous year.

The cleanup of the courtyard inside the castle had taken a good bit of work. In addition to the fire damage, there was a lot of debris left in the courtyard, but Barrin organized the villagers and tradespeople, much as he had at Willet Cliff Falls, and within a few days, they had the entire place put back together and looking better than before the battle. The market was rebuilt, with permanent stalls instead of tents, with funds provided by the king. The people loved that Barrin got involved personally and helped with the rebuilding. He and his friends didn't sit in the keep and give orders; they got their hands dirty and worked to make Cantigal a better place.

A few days after his coronation, they had held a memorial service and a realm-wide day of mourning for all of the people who died in the fight with the dragon. Barrin also made sure the recognitions at the ceremony included Gawan, who he revealed as Rowan, and the Eagle Watch members who were assassinated the night before the battle. He also remembered the fallen soldiers from the battle at Willet Cliff Falls. They now knew that all the soldiers had been under a spell cast by the dragon. During the ceremony, Barrin revealed a memorial built in honor of the fallen in the center of the courtyard where the Arkenstone once stood.

Barrin had reorganized his military. He split the castle guards off to form their own force called the "King's Guard." This group was led by Will, who was Captain of the King's Guard, and as such, lived in the keep where he could keep an eye on Barrin's safety.

The other portion of the military force was called the "Guards of the Realm." They were divided into three battalions assigned to regions of Saldringal. In each region, they built a fort to be headquarters for the battalion. It was where they trained and drilled, but the troops were not assigned housing in their forts. Instead, they were given a housing stipend and told to find their own place, so that they could live amongst the people of the region and know those whom they were enlisted to defend.

Barrin created a hierarchy of leadership for the military with checks and balances from top to bottom. He didn't want guards going rogue and terrorizing his people like they had done at Willet Cliff Falls. He wanted to build a partnership between the soldiers and the citizens of the realm.

He also created local volunteer militias that would train periodically with the soldiers in their forts. He thought the soldiers would respect the locals more if they trained together, and he paid the militia members for their time, which gave his subjects an additional source of income.

The people of Saldringal were overwhelmingly happy when the next tax time rolled around. At first, they grumbled when they were told that each family had to line up as they had done in the past to pay their taxes, but their anger quickly turned to joy when, instead of being asked to pay, they were each refunded ten silver pieces as an apology for the overtaxation carried out by the dragon.

For handling future taxation, Barrin created a group of tax collectors. They were not part of the military, but were civilians themselves. They had to keep meticulous records, and they were routinely audited. No one would be overtaxed under Barrin's watch. Of course, he had also honored his promise to cease all taxes for a year.

Will and Alexia had married very quickly after Barrin became king. Barrin officiated the wedding himself. It was a quiet, but beautiful service in the newly redecorated Great Hall of the Keep. The happy couple took a week off and went to the port of Bardhaven for a honeymoon. There they met the queen's ship from Neferkala, and returned the gems and Barrin's gift of gold to the queen's designee, who turned out to be Alexia's mother, Bazhena. The Neferkali princess loved Will right away, and she made both of them promise to visit Alexia's homeland as soon as they could.

Will also reconnected with his own mother, and moved her and his siblings into the housing behind the keep. She would not have to raise a garden and work every day to feed her family anymore. Will helped all of his family members find jobs in and around the castle, except his mother, who he believed had earned the right to retire.

Barrin and Talisia had waited two months before their own wedding. They wanted enough time to invite all of their friends and her family from around the realm and to give their friends time to travel to Cantigal for the service.

Talisia was gorgeous on their wedding day. As she walked down the aisle to meet him at the front of the cathedral, Barrin realized with a start that the glimpse of the bride he had seen in his dream was his own Talisia. The dream was the future of his own wedding!

The service was held in the same cathedral as his coronation. It was a beautiful ceremony that ended with the church bells ringing joyously and great cheering from all the attendees.

Gwyn came to the wedding with Ginny and several others from Willet Cliff Falls. Talisia's father, Bergen, was there. He even closed the tavern for the occasion, which was truly a rare occurrence. A company of Woodland Rangers showed up as well, and Tally sheepishly resigned her commission in the Rangers to be their queen. She promised them better support from the crown.

Tally and Barrin honeymooned in Falkshire Hamlet. They stayed in the inn and didn't even argue the price, but they only ate in Prattleton's tavern, the Iron Bell, to the great aggravation of Mayor Grumbleton.

While they were in Falkshire, Barrin and Tally strolled down the hill to see Jaster. The old Falkan was glad to see them and delighted that Barrin was now truly the king. They visited with him and thanked him for helping bring back the dragons. When they left, Jaster asked them to take the gold armlet. He had decided that he had lived long enough; he was tired and ready to move on to the next world. Tally hugged him and promised that they would return the item to the dragons.

Now, ten months after their honeymoon, Talisia and Alexia were both pregnant. Alexia was a little farther along, but they each had a few months left and were due within a month of each other. For this trip, Will and Barrin had left their lovely wives behind at Castle Brackhaven, where the ladies were planning a joint nursery. The four friends wanted their children to grow up together as if they were siblings or cousins, and they planned for them to share the nursery in the keep. Barrin had a feeling that Tally would have a boy. Perhaps a boy who would grow up to be a knight with a black horse.

There were ten dragons now. Once Barrin was able to send the recovered heartstones to the Falkans, their newly trained dragon healers carried out their tradition and planted the heartstones in the existing dragon eggs. It was fortunate that Ishthmar had not destroyed the eggs when he left the dragon lair.

About six moons into Barrin's reign, the dragon king, Ragnussen, flew to Cantigal and met privately with him. He apologized for the tragedy caused by his younger brother, and he swore allegiance to the new king. He promised that the dragons would keep the border safe and also keep a closer eye on each other. Unfortunately, he also brought word that, just two weeks prior, old Jaster had passed peacefully in his sleep.

Barrin returned the dragons' treasure hoard to them, minus an excellent, though not magically enhanced, sword that he accepted as a gift from Ragnussen. He took Mortingas's advice, stored the keys to the kingdom in a safe place, and wore his new sword proudly.

At Thallinius's house, Barrin's mind returned to the present. He kicked around in the ashes, and found the missing heartstone from the captured wraith. It was what he had most hoped to recover. Everything else was gone, consumed in the fire the night Thallinius died.

"How much of what has happened do you think he knew?" Barrin asked. "Did he know we would win? Did he put me with Tally on purpose?"

"I wouldn't put any of it past him," Will replied. "He was always a step ahead."

"I miss him," Barrin said.

"Yeah, me too. Everyday," Will replied.

"Hey!" Barrin pointed to the fireplace. "Look! The secret cache is closed. Didn't we leave it open?" He walked over and counted the stones; eight stones up, and five to the left. He brushed his fingers over the stone to reveal the keyhole and pulling out his necklace, he inserted the key, and opened the cache.

Inside the cache, there was a small jar and a note. Barrin read the note out loud:

"Barrindor, if you find this you must have completed your quest and beaten the dragon. If not, I would assume that you are dead, and that means you won't find this. Ha! This jar is my last spell, and I leave it as a gift for you. If you break it, it will briefly open a portal back to 'your' world. If you want to leave Saldringal, and go back to being Jaxson King, this is your chance. However, you should know that you can't have it both ways. With me gone, the portal will close behind you in just a few moments, and you will be back in your world forever. Choose wisely, my king! With much love, your humble servant, Thallinius"

Barrin smiled at Will. He picked up the jar and smashed it to the floor. A portal opened before him. It looked just like the portal that had brought him to Saldringal. He stared at it, deep in thought. That way led to hoodies, jeans, movies, television, cell phones, internet, pizza, soft drinks, air conditioning, and all the other conveniences he so desperately missed. Comfortable underwear, toilet paper, college, a career, and most of all, driving a car. It was tempting. He waited a few moments, and the portal flickered out and closed.

"C'mon Will," he said. "Let's go home."

Then he shut the cache, and they went home to their wives.

About the Author

J. Douglas Adams is a high school band director in Northwest Georgia. He looks forward to retirement when he plans to move to the coast of Virginia and possibly open a retail store. This is his first novel. He spent twenty years crafting the story after being inspired by a student's note he picked up from the floor of his classroom with the word "obnoxious" misspelled as "obnoc tous."

Adams holds degrees from Eastern Kentucky University, the University of Cincinnati, and Liberty University. He is happily married with four children, and three grandchildren.

He has always had a passion for reading fantasy and science fiction stories. His favorite authors in these categories include: Timothy Zahn, John Scalzi, Phillip Pulman, Lloyd Alexander, Terry Brooks, and (of course), J.R.R. Tolkien.

Author photo by Scott Kuhn Photography LLC

Harringon and Myriad Pro on 50# LSI archival white
Type and design by Karen Paul Stone

www.ingramcontent.com/pod-product-compliance
Lightning Source LLC
Chambersburg PA
CBHW051147030726
47504CB00004B/1079

* 9   7 8 1 9   4   7   5 8 9   5 3   7 *